D1328510

HEARTBREAK BOYS

HEARTBREAK BOYS

SIMON JAMES GREEN

CLARION BOOKS

An Imprint of HarperCollins*Publishers*

Clarion Books is an imprint of HarperCollins Publishers.

Heartbreak Boys
Copyright © 2020 by Simon James Green
All rights reserved. Printed in the United States of America. No part of this book
may be used or reproduced in any manner whatsoever without written permission
except in the case of brief quotations embodied in critical articles and reviews. For
information address HarperCollins Children's Books, a division of HarperCollins
Publishers, 195 Broadway, New York, NY 10007.
www.epicreads.com

ISBN 978-0-35-861725-9

Typography by Catherine San Juan
22 23 24 25 26   PC/LSCC   10 9 8 7 6 5 4 3 2 1

First U.S. Edition, 2022
Originally published by Scholastic UK. This edition published
by arrangement with Scholastic Limited.

*For everyone who is trying to find the courage
to be true to themselves*

ONE

JACK

"Is this a joke?"

OK, it's not the reaction I'd hoped for, but coming from Dylan, it's practically a compliment. I wave my hands up and down my tuxedo in the manner of a game show hostess. "It's Italian tailoring, one hundred percent pure wool, with satin trim details."

He crosses his arms and gives me unimpressed eyes.

"Is it the shoes?" I ask.

"It is *not* the shoes."

"Dolce and Gabbana."

He shakes his head and steps inside like the shoes are *nothing* and closes the front door behind him.

I blow my cheeks out, really giving it some serious thought. "Oh!" I say, feigning suddenly remembering. "Do you mean"—I twirl around on the spot, the rainbow flag cloak that's around my shoulders billowing out like some fabulous gay tornado—"*THIS?!*"

Dylan still isn't smiling, which is *weird* because this has to be the most spectacular thing ever.

"Very funny." He grimaces.

"Thank you, I think, but this is actually my outfit. *So.*"

Dylan glowers at me. I'm pretty sure this is meant to be one of the most romantic nights of my life, the sort you look back on if you're lucky enough to make it to eighty and sigh and remember it all in gorgeous sepia, but my boyfriend literally looks like he's going to murder me—and not with something clever and glamorous like cyanide in champagne (surely the weapon of choice for any homosexual with a shred of self-respect?), but violently. With an axe. "I thought we agreed—"

"I know, but I wanted to—"

"It can't always be about *you*, Jack." He stomps through to the kitchen. "Can I get a glass of water?"

"Sure," I mutter, staying in the hall while he disappears.

So, it's going well.

"You look nice!" I shout through to him. And he does.

He looks fricking *gorgeous*.

The sound of a tap running.

"There's a bottle of Evian in the fridge if you prefer not to drink piss water. I know it's environmentally less friendly but since we're all going to die in the apocalypse anyway, I say *DRINK THE GOOD STUFF, BABY!*"

Silence.

He's pissed off with me, but year eleven prom is, quite frankly, the end of five years of near total *hell* at secondary school and I'm not going to mark its passing quietly. Hell no. This *shitshow* is going out with a bang. And turning up in the same shiny polyester suit that all the other year eleven boys will turn up in is not anywhere close to being "a bang." Screw that. If I'm not going to fit in, if I'm *going* to stand out, then I'm *really* gonna stand out.

Speaking of which, he didn't even *mention* the glittery eye makeup. *Do I need more?* I walk through to the kitchen, where Dylan is finishing off a glass of chocolate milk.

"Sorry," he says, wiping his mouth with the back of his hand. He knows the chocolate milk is mine, and he knows it's precious to me.

"The eye shadow," I begin.

He licks the last of the milk off his lips and looks across at me. "Uh-huh?"

"Do you love it?"

He stares at me, then his face breaks into a smile. "Well, you . . . I mean, you certainly look gay."

"I *am* gay!" I say. "So are you!"

He doesn't deny it, but he ever so slightly flinches, and I know I've said the wrong thing. "Besides," I continue, "you don't win prom king and queen without going to *some* effort."

3

He scratches his tousled dark brown hair. "You really think they're gonna give it to a gay couple? *Really?* Our school?"

He has a point, of course, but he must clock the look of disappointment on my face because he quickly adds, "Hey, but who knows? Maybe things are changing."

I nod at him and smile, although I know he was probably right to begin with.

"I want to have a nice night, so I'm sorry I was a dick about your outfit," he says.

"That's OK."

"I'm a bit tense."

"Why are you tense? Do you need a massage?"

"No. I mean, yes, I do, but—" He gestures to his bow tie. "It's real. I don't know how to do it back up again if I untie it."

I laugh at him. "Were you dressed by your mum?"

"Practically."

I know why he's tense. He prefers me to be "straight acting." He told me that when I turned up to one of his matches in a *Some people are gay. Get over it!* T-shirt. I was just trying to do my bit to challenge homophobia in soccer, but apparently some of the other boys found it distracting and that's why they lost the game. I don't know, it's almost like some people have a poor excuse for everything. I sigh. "Do you want me to lose the rainbow cloak?"

"No."

"I want them all to see it, Dylan. I want everyone who made my life hell for the last three years to see they haven't won. I'm here. And I'm gonna shine so bright I'll blind the fuckers!"

4

"I know."

"Aaaaand I've only gone and bagged the hottest guy in the school. Also worth celebrating."

He flicks his eyes down to the floor, embarrassed, I think.

"You look really good, Jack. You've maybe got a whiff of gay vampire about you, but it works." He smirks at me. "Now make a joke about what gay vampires suck."

I roll my eyes. "I'm classier than that."

He holds his arms out wide. "Come on."

And I go in for a hug.

Dylan.

I one hundred percent truly, madly, deeply, unreservedly, from the bottom of my big gay heart, love this boy. And OK, OK, I *know* what people say. I know how I'm not supposed to really understand the meaning of love because I'm "only sixteen," so how could I possibly get my innocent little head around such a complex thing, but it's not like I see anyone older with their shit together in this regard. In fact, I vividly remember the screaming match Mum and Dad had, before Dad left, when I was ten years old. "I love you!" Dad had pleaded, shielding his head from the onslaught of shoes that Mum was hurling out of the window at him. *"You don't know the meaning of love!"* Mum had snarled back.

So I'm not convinced it's an age thing.

And me, I do know the meaning.

And right now, he is standing in my kitchen, my date for the prom, in a dinner jacket and bow tie, with that dark brown messy hair of his, those goddamn deep brown eyes, and that playful little smile he always has when he knows I'm about to kiss him, and I think, *Yes, this is love,* because if it isn't, then what the hell is it?

OK, maybe right now, it's mainly lust. Let's say seventy percent lust and the rest—I can't even do the math because I'm so horny—is love.

Thirty percent. It's thirty percent love. But normally it's more fifty-fifty.

It's just . . . Christ alive, he scrubs up well. I go in for a kiss.

"You smell gorgeous," I murmur.

"It's actually my dad's," he says. "I just spritzed it on."

"Well, it's certainly a step up from Axe."

"Which there is *nothing* wrong with."

"If you want to smell like the boys' changing rooms after year eight PE."

He chuckles, and his hands snake around my waist and inside my dinner jacket, and he pulls me into him. Him taking the initiative like this is a new thing. Dylan came out at the beginning of year eleven, causing a major stir because he doesn't just *play* soccer, he is—wait for it—*captain* of the goddamn soccer team, *oh, yes, he is!* So basically he was the first person in school to come out who wasn't instantly hated and bullied, because Dylan is *adored* as a sportsman—he's like this *hero* that even the straight boys check out (in fairness, he looks so hot in his soccer uniform, anyone would *lose their shit*), and suddenly gay was cool. Now, obviously that annoys me—anyone should be able to come out and not take crap for it—but on the plus side, it did mean quite a few people found the courage to come out too, so I'm glad for that. And literally, from the LGBTQ+ society having a membership of five, it's now up to fifteen. Next year, I get to be president and plan to double it. Next year is going to be *so* gay. It's totally going to piss off Mrs. Nunn, the evangelical religious education teacher.

But I digress. I was sitting by myself one lunchtime as usual, and Dylan strode right up to me with such a sense of purpose I seriously thought he was going to hit me.

"*What* are you doing?" he said as I cowered behind the bench.

I just stared at him.

He sighed. "I came to apologize." He looked down at the ground, then back up at me. "About the year nine thing. In PE."

The mention of it made my stomach turn to lead. But also the thing happened two years previously, so why was he apologizing now? The story was this: I'd just come out, and some of the boys in my year responded by refusing to get changed with me in PE because I made them feel "uncomfortable." Their ignorant parents got involved too, backing their stupid kids up, like parents of those sorts of kids always do. After a lot of arguing, the school suggested that maybe I'd prefer to get changed in the accessible bathroom, dressing the whole thing up like it was a privilege, my own personal changing room, when really they'd just yielded to the bigots because it was easier.

"It was really shitty," Dylan said.

I shrugged. "You weren't part of it."

"But I didn't stand up for you. Not one of us stood up for you."

"Well, when you're the only gay boy in the year, it goes with the territory."

Then he looked me right in the eye, his bottom lip wobbling slightly. "You're not the only gay boy."

Obviously, I couldn't believe it at first. Dylan Hooper. *Gay.* But over the weeks that followed we started hanging out more and actually enjoying one another's company. Now, it's true there wasn't (isn't!) a wealth of options in terms of gay kids to hang out with. In our year, to start with, it was just me and him. Afterward, thanks to the Dylan Makes Gay OK Factor, there was Theo, who's bi and seeing a girl in the year above, and then Tariq. Tariq's super sweet, super geeky, and has a rich dad who runs an app company, so if any of those appeal, he's your boy. He's now on the LGBTQ+ society committee with me, and next year, he's going to be my deputy. Honestly, he's such a sweet lad, so utterly wholesome, he must be protected at all costs, but I guess he just didn't do it for Dylan. The sixth formers are all in very serious and committed relationships with each other, and apart from a collection of very marvelous girls, that only leaves a couple of lads in year eight and nine and, well, *no.* However, I did eventually shake off the idea that Dylan was only hanging out with me due to a lack of other options and started to entertain the idea that he possibly actually quite *liked* me, and so I took the bull by the horns and asked him if he wanted to come back to mine to start the history homework together. At which he was all,

"Er, um, I guess, yes? OK, then?"

And just as we got to mine, he added,

"You do know I don't study history, don't you?"

And I smirked at him. "I do know that, Dylan, yes." *Bless.*

To start with, whenever we would "do history homework" together it was always me suggesting it. But after a while (at least until GSCE exams got in the way and literally everything was put on hold), it would be him. It's always been behind closed doors, usually his bedroom, which is a monument to dreary masculinity, with its simple, functional decoration and pungent smell of Icy-Hot (a far cry from my own fairy light, scatter cushion, lavender pillow mist kingdom), but he seems a bit more comfortable in his own skin these days. It's nice.

We break away from the kiss. "We should get some pics," I say.

"For Instagram." Dylan does not like Instagram. He reluctantly lets me post pictures of us, but he refuses to be involved—doesn't even have an account. That's the reason I haven't told him that any pictures of him always get significantly more likes than anything I post *without* him. And the comments are something else. But I don't want his head to get big, so blissful ignorance is best.

I take a few selfies of us, a few of him looking all smoldering and James Bond, and then a bit of video of me romping around the garden with my gay cape, before he checks the time on his phone and suggests we make a move, because god knows it would be catastrophic if we got there so late the nonalcoholic punch had run out.

But this is the bit I'm most looking forward to actually. Dylan has a *motorcycle*. Not only that, he has passed his test and is legally allowed to ride it with a passenger—a.k.a. *me*. Which means I am going to roar into the schoolyard for the year eleven prom on the back of a motorcycle driven by a massive hunk, like some glorious moment in an American coming-of-age movie circa 1985. If he also does the *Dirty Dancing* lift with me, like I've made him promise, the prom is going to be so kitsch and camp it will literally explode into confetti.

We walk toward my front door. "Are we technically supposed to be wearing motorcycle leathers for this?" I ask.

"You do know it's a moped, right? Not a motorcycle," Dylan replies.

"I mean, what's the actual difference?"

And then he opens the door, I step outside and I see the thing.

TWO

NATE

I'm pretty sure prom is something you're meant to look forward to, but somehow I've made sure I'm not. Which is me all over. I'm really good at making sure I don't have a good time.

Elements of Dread in Ascending Order of Dreadfulness

1. My outfit. My tux is rented because money is tight and we couldn't afford to buy one that you can get altered. That's no one's fault, but it's classic bad luck that the rental shop didn't have anything left in my

size. So now I look like a year seven kid on the first day of term, all dressed up in an oversized blazer and trousers that are slightly too long.

2. The speech. Oh god, *the speech*. "Someone's got to do it, Nate!" the head merrily told me. "And you're the spokesman for your year!" I mean, I'm really not. I was voted senior prefect, but it wasn't a vote of popularity or respect — it was malicious. The title confers no benefits whatsoever, only loads of horrible responsibilities, like monitoring the lunch queue, putting away chairs after assembly, and giving speeches to people who are just waiting for you to fail, preferably hilariously, so they can upload it somewhere.

3. The BIG THING. You see? And there I go again, already building this one up by calling it "the big thing" in the first place, when I could just call it "the really stupid thing that I've no idea why I'm doing and maybe I won't." Except, of course, thanks to a certain someone, I finally feel like I actually *want* to, so there's that. Yes, I'm going to come out to everyone. And I'm doing it big-gesture style because ~~I'm an idiot~~ (a) it's a special prom surprise for Tariq, and I know it'll make him proud and happy, and what more could I want? And (b) I don't want everyone gossiping about it, I just want to get it out there, all at once, really clear, fresh

start, new page, all that stuff. Plus, it saves me having the same conversation, like, over a hundred times, and the only other effective way of doing it would be to take an ad out in the end-of-term school newsletter: *Nate Harrison would like to proudly announce that he is officially gay—flowers are not necessary, but please send any donations to his PayPal account so his wardrobe becomes befitting of his new status.*

Yeah, I'm not doing that.

But first, I have to deal with THE BIG THING (must stop calling it that) with my parents because if I don't, they'll hear about it anyway from some third party (probably Linda at number fifty-five) and Mum will be upset because she'll think me not telling her first means our parent-child relationship has broken down and that I've got other secrets, like being addicted to meth or keeping a scrapbook under my mattress full of my favorite BTS pics and self-insert fan fiction, with a list of all the boys ranked in order of how cute I think they are, with detailed explanatory notes and appendices. For example.

Anyway, I take a deep breath and enter the lounge, where I know my parents await me and where I've strategically given myself approximately five minutes to get it all out in the open before I really have to go because Mr. Walker says I need to do a "sound check" before everyone arrives in the gym.

"Oh, Nate, look at you!" Mum coos, coming over to tweak my bow tie needlessly.

"Hey."

"Who's a handsome boy?"

I grimace. "Mum, you're doing that thing again!"

"Hmm?" She's only half listening, brushing down the shoulders of my jacket, making me paranoid I've got dandruff.

"Where you're talking to me like I'm a dog," I continue. "Do you want me to start peeing on the carpet?"

She frowns. "You are *not* going to pee on the carpet, Nate."

"No, I know, but that's what dogs . . . Oh, never mind."

"Well?" Mum says, presenting me to my dad.

I stand awkwardly, not really knowing where to put my hands, but eventually just opting to shove them in my trouser pockets, although they turn out to be smaller and higher up than I'm used to, meaning my hands don't really fit properly.

"Hands out of pockets," Mum says, smiling and using her primary school teacher voice—firm, calm, slightly disappointed. "You don't want to look slovenly."

I clear my throat and remove my hands.

Dad is looking impressed.

"If I were thirty years younger—" Dad says.

"If you were thirty years younger, *what*?" I interrupt. Dad looks flummoxed.

"That's not a thing parents say to their kids!" I tell him. "Or to anyone!" I add.

He raises his eyebrows. "No? Doesn't it just mean that you miss the good old days?"

Mum tuts. "No, Mick, it doesn't. It's really inappropriate."

14

I shake my head. "Oh my god, right, listen—"

"Rose? Come and see your handsome brother!" Mum shouts through to the kitchen.

"Mum, *no*—"

But my six-year-old sister has already run through, blond hair, cherubic smile, butter wouldn't melt, and you would never tell she was actually possessed.

"OK, here I am, thank you, please go back to the kitchen," I tell her.

Rose looks me up and down, giving nothing away in terms of whether I look OK or not. "Do a twirl," she demands.

I grit my teeth because denying her will only make this last longer and I really do not have the time. I turn around on the spot. "Ta-da. There we go." I gesture to the door.

Rose sits down on the sofa.

"Oh my god," I mutter. "OK, so—"

"Photo time!" Mum declares, squinting at her phone as she tries to access the camera.

"No, but—"

"I want one of you on your own, one with Dad, one with Rose, we'll need one of you by the front door . . ."

There's a shot of me by the front door for every major, and for that matter *minor*, life event of the last sixteen years. First day of every new school year. Last day of every school year. Joining the Scouts. Opening night of the school play. Grandpa Henry's funeral. *The day Mum decided my voice had started fricking breaking!*

"I'm putting them on Facebook and emailing them to the family—everyone wants to see!" she continues.

"OK, but—"

It's futile. Mum starts shepherding us, adjusting sofa cushions in the background "so the family doesn't think we're messy" and telling Dad to "smile more" so that "no one thinks he's too depressed about losing his job." When she's done, she starts swiping through them and then it's all, "How do you attach a photo to an email again?" and all I want to do is just say the thing I want to say and get out of there.

"You seem tense," Mum says, glancing up from her phone. "Remember to breathe during your important speech, and don't babble. You know how you babble when you get nervous."

Oh my god.

"And who knows," she continues, "maybe a little romance will blossom at this prom?"

My eyes widen.

"Maybe you will lock eyes with a special someone across the crowded dance floor . . ."

"OK," I say. "So, look, about that, what if . . . you know, maybe there already is a someone who is . . . special, you know?"

Mum's eyes light up and then fill with mild panic. "Are you using condoms?"

"Mum! We're not . . . We haven't . . . That's not . . ."

"But you would?"

"I mean, *yes*, but—"

She actually breathes a sigh of relief. "So, tell us, then!"

"Yes, tell us all about him!" Dad says.

"Yes, *him*, that's right, because I'm— Hang on, *what?*"

Everyone's just looking back at me expectantly. This was not as I'd planned it in my head. At least one person should have been crying by now.

"What's his name?" Mum asks.

"OK, so, it's Tariq, but can we just backpedal a little here?" I look at my parents, who are smiling inanely at me. "OK, so, I am"—I pause because *drama*— "*gaaaaay.*"

"Yes," Mum says, with this sort of manic fixed grin on her face.

"I like boys."

"I like boys," Rose adds.

"No, but I *really* like them," I tell her. "I don't like girls, I like boys."

She frowns at me. "*I'm* a girl."

"Right, but—" I glance at Mum for help, but she doesn't seem to clock any problem. "I *like* girls, but I don't *like* like girls, Rose? OK? Makes sense? Good."

"No."

"OK. Mum?" I look at her pleadingly.

"Well, you haven't explained it very well, Nate," she says.

I take a deep breath. "So, like, Cinderella falls in love with the prince, but instead of Cinderella, it's . . . Colin." It was the first name I could think of. It's a shit example. Everyone knows it.

Rose shakes her head. "I'm winding you up, dumb-o. Someone actually *like* likes you? Wow!" And she flounces out.

That girl.

I turn back to my parents. "How are you not surprised? I never told you any of this."

Dad furrows his brow. "I think you did."

Mum nods. "You definitely did."

"I definitely did *not*."

"Yes, because in year nine you went to school with nail polish on that time."

I blink at her. "Mum! Me going to school with nail polish on was not me coming out to you!" I glare at them. Are they actually serious? "What did you think I was doing that evening after school that would require nail polish?"

"Going to Gay Club?" Dad shrugs.

"Gay Club? *Gay Club?*" My voice is squeaking it's so high at this point. "It was the drama department trip to *The Rocky Horror Picture Show*!"

"Oh," Mum says weakly. "Aren't you meant to wear stockings and garters for that?"

"The school wouldn't let us, in case of complaints. I don't know, nail polish was as far as they'd let us go. Maybe a bit of eyeliner." I look at them both and shake my head. I've been fretting about this moment for months, but it seems they knew all along—or they thought they did.

Dad's already grabbed the framed year eleven group photo we had taken on our last day before exam leave from the mantelpiece and is scanning over it. "Which one is Tariq?"

"He's the kid standing next to me."

"On your right?" Mum says.

"Well, the other option is a white girl called Lucy on my other side, so place your bets."

"Ooh, he's handsome! Isn't he handsome, Mick?" Mum says.

"Mmm," Dad replies. "Done well there, Nate."

Not sure how to take that, to be honest. I think he's implying I'm punching above my weight, which, OK, I am, but *to say that. Your own father?*

"Anyway," I say, "I should really—"

"Whoa, hold on a sec there, Nate!" Dad says, standing up and reaching behind the back of the sofa. He pulls out a bottle and twists the cork out with a *pop.*

"It's just prosecco, not champagne," he says, pouring some glasses.

"Why?" I ask.

"Well, because champagne is, like, thirty or forty pounds a—"

"*No,*" I interrupt. "Why are we celebrating with bubbles?"

Dad smiles at me. "End of an era, right? Finished GCSEs, it's your prom, you've got your whole future ahead of you . . ." He thrusts a glass into my hands. I can't drink this, I have to give a speech, but then, maybe it'll help me relax?

"I should get a photo of this to email too," Mum says. "Actually, scrap that, Mum'll think it's irresponsible to give him alcohol at his age." She looks at my dad. "And she already thinks you've got an alcohol problem."

Dad screws his face up, like, *what?*

"Well," Mum says. "You downed all those beers in front of her last Christmas."

"Anyone would, spending three days in her company," Dad replies.

"Mick," Mum warns.

Dad smiles and hands Mum a drink, then pours one for himself. "Life's hard, so enjoy it while you can," Dad says, raising his glass.

Well, that's certainly inspirational, although I don't blame him for saying it. Dad was laid off from the yogurt factory three months ago, and then his best mate was killed while riding his bike. He's had a pretty crappy year so far. "Great!" I say. "Hooray."

Mum just quietly chuckles, looking like she's in her own world. "Well, he's not wrong! I thought I'd have it all when I was younger—now, I'd be happy with curtains that had blackout lining."

We spend about thirty seconds (feels like thirty minutes) sipping the drinks while I wait for any more downers Mum and Dad can come up with.

"Best days of your life, school days," Dad says.

And here we go!

"Life drags you down after about twenty." (Mum.)

"Earn money, pay bills, stress, stress . . ." (Dad.)

"Jo Carter's husband had a stroke he was so stressed!"

". . . on this tax treadmill, like little tax hamsters . . ."

"He's partially paralyzed down the left-hand side now . . ."

I blow my cheeks out. "ANYWAY, yay for life!" I say. "I can't wait for all the things to look forward to."

"Well, there's some good stuff too," Mum mutters, entirely unconvincingly.

There's another awkward silence. "I really need to go," I say, downing the rest of my glass and placing it down on the coffee table.

"Have a great evening, Nate!" Dad says. "Take lots of photos!"

"And don't babble your speech!" Mum says again.

"Mum," I say, "I've done stuff onstage before, I'm OK. Remember the Tin Man in *Wizard of Oz?*"

They both look at me, an expression of concern and mild horror on their faces.

"Oh my god, I'll see you later."

THREE

JACK

So, it's not exactly as I'd hoped. I had been thinking about roaring into the school, sitting astride this powerful, throbbing machinery, skidding to a halt, before my leather-jacket-wearing boyfriend helped me down from the bike and I removed my helmet and shook down my hair in slow motion and soft focus.

The first problematic point being that I don't have long hair to shake down. It's short. And one of my concerns is that the helmet threatens to mess up the product I spent at least twenty minutes very carefully applying.

The other issue is that Dylan doesn't have a leather jacket, but he has got an anorak, which his mum made him bring, "in case it rains." I'm not a vacuous, image-obsessed airhead, but I had to draw the line at the anorak and made him leave it at mine—it's a beautiful summer evening, not a cloud in the sky. *It's not gonna rain.*

Dylan informs me, with a ridiculous amount of pride, that the moped has a top speed of—wait for it—*twenty-eight miles per hour.* But when you're actually on it and you're zipping along, it does feel faster. And the wind is blowing in my face, and it's really quite loud and impressive. My gay cape is billowing behind me, and I'm proud that I'm not in one of those hired limos or the double-decker party bus, because doing my own thing—even though it was forced upon me in year nine—has become something I'm finally happy about. It was survival back then, walking down the corridor to find that almost every kid in my year had arranged to mutter "gay" under their breath at me as I passed by. I responded by embracing it. "Yes, I am!" "No shit?" and, "Here and queer, baby!" I trilled as I bigged it up, head held high, inspired by the loud and proud camp of *Drag Race* but actually dying inside. But now I absolutely want to be that person because why should I hide? And *screw you*, every single one of you who made my life hell. And tonight, Dylan and I will take the prom king and queen crowns and VICTORY SHALL BE OURS!

Also, the pics are going to go down a storm on Instagram—I honestly think it could be our most popular yet. I am so ready for all the brands to start getting in touch.

And I have another little surprise for Dylan that is really going to be the icing on this fabulous gay cake!

FOUR

NATE

People are gathering in the yard outside the main entrance to the school because they're doing group photos as you go in, so everyone's waiting to make sure all their friends are there. I'm standing with Tariq, Alfie, Connie, and Luke—a group I suppose you would call "the kids who survived five years at secondary school by being in the library every lunchtime." The library's the only place there's guaranteed adult supervision during lunch—the rest of the school is pretty much a war zone.

The library is also where I first spoke to Tariq. In the last term of year ten, Mrs. Davidson put this big display up, with a giant rainbow flag, loads of colored bunting, a sign saying "Read with

Pride," and all these books about LGBT stuff. I'd casually walked past it, pretending to be *on my way to do something very different and not connected to the display*, like, three or four times, and I really wanted to pick some of them up but didn't quite dare. So then I did this thing where I pretended I'd dropped my pen, when actually I'd literally just thrown it so it rolled right by the display. I was doing a pretty good job of looking for my pen, all huffing and puffing and like, "Oh, gosh, where could my pen be?" while getting closer to the books and trying to memorize them so I could look them up online later, and suddenly this voice says,

"This one's really good."

I looked up, and it was Tariq, pointing to a book with a big banana on the front.

My cheeks went hot in a flash. "Oh, right, yeah, but I'm not—"

"You don't have to be gay to read a book with gay characters in it," he said. And then he smiled and walked off and I scrambled back to the desk I was sitting at, hot, embarrassed, and ashamed.

I didn't dare even glance at that display again.

The next day, after school, I found a wrapped package in my bag—brown paper, string, no message or anything. I opened it, and it was the banana book with a little card, which said:

I took it out on my account so please return it! Tariq

Points for being thoughtful.

Points for knowing me better than I knew myself.

Points for being concerned about potential library fines.

I think I fell in love with him a bit right then.

And after that, every few weeks or so, a new book would magically appear in my bag. I don't know how he got them in there—I never once saw him—but from me barely acknowledging what he'd done, we progressed to one-word conversations:

"Enjoy it?"

"Yup."

And then longer ones, in quiet corners, where I'd admit how much I shipped the two boys in whatever book it happened to be, and he'd agree with an "I know, right? *Cuuuuuute!*" And I'd smile and blush again and say, "Yeah. Cute."

One afternoon in June, I was sitting next to him in class, the blinds drawn because we were watching some video about coastal landscapes, and he shifted his left leg so it was pressed up against my right. And that's how our legs stayed for the whole lesson. I think it's one of the most excitingly erotic things that has ever happened to me. I couldn't focus on the video. All I could hear was the rhythm of his breathing. All I could feel was the warmth of his leg against mine, and the tingles that touch was sending through my body.

I was careful at school. I was careful not to be seen with him too much. I was careful not to look at him too much. I'd seen exactly what happens when people decide you're not like them, and I couldn't face any of that. A few weeks later, fate put us together to work on an English project, so there was a reason for him to come around to my house after school.

"Are your parents at work?" he said.

"Yes. WOULD YOU LIKE SOME LEMONADE?" I replied, completely failing to play it cool by randomly shouting about lemonade at him.

He nodded. I made some. We drank it. We moved to put our glasses down at the same time and ended up standing really close.

"Sorry!" we both said.

And that was that until two days later, when he needed to come around again for the same project.

"Are your parents in?" he asked.

"No. WOULD YOU LIKE A COOKIE?" I replied.

He nodded. We had cookies. We moved to go upstairs to start the work at the same time and got wedged in the kitchen door.

"Sorry!" we both said.

Two days later, he turned up again.

"But the project is done and my parents are in!" I said.

"Sorry," he muttered.

He turned to go.

"Wait!" I said.

He turned back.

I just stared at him.

"See you at school, then," I said.

He gave me a small smile. "See you at school."

See, I like Tariq because he's an awkward kid like me, but the problem with two awkward kids is that the process of anything actually happening is completely fraught with . . . well, awkwardness. And so, it wasn't until the start of year eleven and a field trip that fate had decreed would see me end up in a hostel bedroom with Tariq when he actually kissed me.

"Oh god, *sorry*," he said straightaway afterward.

"It's fine," I said. "I don't think I'm gay, though. Sorry."

"Oh god, sorry. I'm so sorry."

I nodded. Then kissed him again. And we spent all that night kissing, and the next morning, down at breakfast, I was like, "Behold! I have extra confidence and swagger, because I, Nate Harrison, have now officially kissed another person, I am desirable and desired, I am a stud!" but that was obviously all in my head because no way did I want anyone at school to know what we'd done, and no way did I want anyone to think I might be gay because I wasn't even ready to admit that to myself yet, even if I had just spent all night snogging another boy.

It has taken me a while to get to the point where I'm ready, but I think that's OK. Tariq has been patient — he actually came out shortly after Dylan Hooper, the soccer captain, though he said it was cool if I wasn't ready to yet — but I clocked the look of disappointment on his face when he asked if we were going to turn up to this prom as a couple and I said, several weeks ago, maybe not. It didn't feel right at the time. Plus, it was the middle of GCSEs and there was other stuff to think about. But now I have thought, and it feels right, it feels like something I want to do, and I feel I owe it to Tariq to do it big style. I want him to know that I'm proud. Of him. Of me. *Of us.*

I notice Luke tense as a white limo glides into the yard, and at least three of the boys responsible for the lion's share of all the bullying over the years hop out like they're full-on reality TV stars. Jordan, Mason, Brandon, and Tyler all have skinny-fit suits, worn with no socks and slip-on shoes, and I immediately feel like a full-on knob in my oversized dinner jacket and bow tie.

The Mean Boys help four Mean Girls out of the car, all in what look like hugely expensive prom dresses. Chloe, Megan, Jas, and Amanda—the girls who made fun of my dancing at the year seven dance *so badly* I've never danced since. Funny how both me and Luke remember the things those kids have done to us so clearly, but as they laugh and hug each other and call one another "babe," they don't even acknowledge us. It's like we don't even exist.

They all pose in various combinations in front of the limo.

They're the sort of people that life always seems easy for.

Luckily, before I'm sucked into a vortex of despair, there's this gentle humming noise, the sort of high-pitched buzz you hear when a fly's trapped in a spider's web, and then in pootles Jack Parker on the back of Dylan Hooper's scooter and, honestly, he may as well have just arrived on the back of a sewing machine on wheels. Simultaneously with his arrival, Theo Appleby, who is secretary of the LGBTQ+ society committee, fires up that "St. Elmo's Fire" song on a portable speaker system he's rigged up.

A-mazing.

I can't help but smile. Jack and I may have gone our separate ways in the last few years, but one thing I've always admired about him (not that I'd ever tell him; *not that he'd ever tolerate*

29

a conversation with me anyway) is his dry sense of humor and the way he subverts everything so many times over, you can't quite tell where the genuine ends and the sarcasm begins. No one's looking at the limo kids anymore, which must be really annoying for them when they've spent all that money on renting it and, knowing Jack, arriving just moments after them and stealing their thunder was probably not accidental.

Jack comes to a gentle halt and steps off the scooter, and there's an actual round of applause and cheers from various year elevens who are standing around, waiting to go in. Jack laps it up, does a twirl with this wild gay cape thing he's wearing, and a theatrical bow. I'm well aware that Jack hasn't had an easy ride of it over the last few years, so what does it take to have confidence like that? It's like a switch flipped with him at some point, and he was all, *This is who I am and I don't care what any of you think.* And somehow, because he didn't care, the bullies started caring less too. The thing with Jack is, he's really good-looking — he's five ten, so he's tall, but not *too* tall; he's got a good physique, toned, but not *too* toned; his hair always looks great (textured, blond) and his skin is always clear and radiant. If that weren't enough, he's bright, like one of the top students bright, but he's not geeky. He's witty, he's sharp, he just *sparkles*, and he's completely happy to be himself. He's basically A-list gay. Lucky him, because I feel like that helps. I haven't even come out yet and I already know, with my stunning ability to be awkward in any social situation, complete lack of fashion sense, appalling lack of knowledge about the gay "scene" and even s-e-x, plus low-level anxiety and occasional paranoia, that I'm destined to be the messiest sort of disaster gay. In fact, that will probably be on my gravestone, which everyone will see soon enough because I'll probably die onstage tonight during my speech, metaphorically *and* literally:

NATE HARRISON

2006–2022

GAY DISASTER

Why am I thinking about death? Why can't I just be happy?

Jack catches me looking at him, and he gives me a nod. I nod back, then look away quickly. Part of me does wish we were twelve again, mucking about in my room, before things got weird and we never spoke again. I wonder what he'll think tonight, when I come out.

I watch as Jack gives Dylan a kiss, then they stride off hand in hand toward the entrance. I glance at Tariq, who gives me a small smile. I know Tariq would love it if we kissed and held hands in front of everyone, and sooner than he knows, I guess we will be.

The thought of that suddenly makes me very happy indeed.

FIVE

JACK

I don't want to sound mean, but I was not expecting much. Let's be clear, this is a British secondary school; compared to what happens in the US (if the movies and TV shows are accurate, *which I assume they are!*), our prom was going to be the equivalent of their cheese: *an abomination*.

And yet, hats off to Maddie Maddison (yes, her parents really called her that) and her prom committee because I walk into the school gym and it looks fantastic.

After persuading the school board that Netflix *probably* wouldn't sue for IP infringement, the theme was announced as *Stranger Things*. They've decorated the whole gym like the Upside

Down: white and gray drapes cover the ceilings and walls, there's dry ice fog billowing over the floor, a mirror ball casting specks of light everywhere, and they must have used hundreds of cans of that spray-on cobweb stuff you get at Halloween, which is covering pretty much everything else. The DJ is playing eighties tunes, and Ms. Munroe and Mr. Walker, our heads of year, are dressed up in Scoops Ahoy outfits, serving ice cream. The centerpiece is this huge Demogorgon, about six meters high, which must have taken the committee months to construct. It's impressive, somewhat precarious looking, almost certainly a fire risk, but hey, it's in an enclosed space with a hundred and fifty fifteen- and sixteen-year-olds, half of whom are already hammered on the alcohol they hid around school before we went on exam leave, so what could go wrong?

I pull Dylan over to the photo booth area, where there's a cool red neon sign that reads "Class of 2022" in the *Stranger Things* title font. We put our arms around each other and pose for a couple of "formal" pics, then we do a couple with our mouths wide-open like manic Muppets, and then some where I'm kissing him, and then I jokingly try to dry-hump him, and then he's had enough and pushes me off and the photographer says he's going to delete that last one.

"Kids in America" by the icon that is Kim Wilde starts to play. "Let's dance!" I tell Dylan.

"Let's get a drink," he replies.

"And then dance?"

"We should get some food too."

"And then dance?"

"Maybe," he says.

He slopes off toward where the punch is. He's being way more moody than usual. Dylan is always fairly aloof and moody—obviously, that was one of the main things that attracted me to him—but tonight he's *extra*. I bet it's the gay cape thing. He's still cross with me. Doubtless sensing an opportunity to stick a knife in, Chloe Kendall is suddenly by my side with her meathead boyfriend, Brandon, who spent most of the last five years (until I got together with Dylan) as one of my tormentors. His skinny-fit suit looks several sizes too small, barely containing his ridiculous muscles, the overall effect being reminiscent of the Michelin Man. She's in a full-on ball gown, her bright blond hair cascading over her shoulders, like the sort of Disney princess we're all bored of seeing. "You know he'll cheat on you, right?" she says, glancing over at Dylan by the punch table. "The hot ones always do."

Brandon laughs, then frowns and says, "Not always, babe." I look him up and down. It's amazing how people can look so different from each other at sixteen. If I didn't know any better, I would say he'd had some help along the way. I mean, I'm not saying he's taking steroids, but I did see him in the showers after PE one time, and his balls are the size of peanut M&M's.

Anyway, I'm not going to play Chloe's game. "When are they announcing prom king and queen?"

"About twenty minutes, once everyone's inside. Why?" she asks, crossing her arms. "Fancy your chances?"

"Do you fancy yours?" I ask, even though she's no longer looking at me.

When she's finished waving at a fellow popular kid across the gym, Chloe turns her attention back to me and my unanswered question. "You *could* win, Jack"—she casts her eyes over my cape—"if you get the LGBT sympathy vote."

"And what the hell's that?"

"You know, tick some boxes by voting for the LGBT." She flashes me a cold smile.

"Chloe, first off, it's 'LGBTQ plus' at the very least; secondly, if you're using LGBT as an adjective, it needs a noun after it, LGBT *people* for example; thirdly, if it is a noun, it's *plural*; fourthly, fuck off." I flap my gay cape at her, and she takes a step back.

"God, you people are sensitive. It's hard being straight these days," Chloe announces, totally serious.

I cross my arms and cock my head, ready to listen to the bullshit.

"Yeah, it's *hard*," Brandon repeats.

"I'm sure it is, sweet cheeks. Try thinking about some old politician or math," I suggest, winking.

He squints at me, absolutely not getting it.

But Chloe's still going on. "Like, I thought Straight Pride was a really good idea before everyone freaked out on Twitter."

"Uh-huh?"

"But why shouldn't we celebrate who we are if the LGBT get to? Isn't it supposed to be about inclusivity?"

"OK, so still missing the word 'people' there, Chloe, but sure, sure, let's . . . let's imagine how great that could be." I sweep my hands in front of me, painting the spectacular image for her. "No,

I'm really just seeing a sea of beige and people dancing to 'Mr. Brightside.'"

Brandon moves behind Chloe and wraps his arms around her waist, pulling her into him. "*Ba-be*, why are you talking serious stuff?" he murmurs into her ear. "Let's have some fun."

"Exactly, Chloe." I smile. "Go and have some fun! You don't want to be stuck here chatting to a notorious homosexual who's going to absolutely *whip your ass* in the voting later this evening."

Chloe's about to bite back when Dylan arrives with a couple of cups of punch for us.

"Hey, Dylan!" she says. "You look *great!*"

"Cheers, Chloe. You too." Dylan passes me a cup and nods at Michelin Man. "Brandon."

"Dude."

"Lewis has vodka if you want to top up your punch," Dylan says.

"*Monkeeeeeeey!*" Brandon squeals.

"*Monkeeeeeey!*" Dylan squeals back.

I have no idea what any of this means. It's some entirely separate language that Dylan must have learned before he came out.

The boys start making monkey noises.

And then what sounds like a parakeet.

And finally an elephant, after which they both collapse into laughter.

Christ, it's intolerable.

"Good luck with prom king, dude!" Brandon says to Dylan. "May the best bro win!"

And they bump fists.

When Chloe and Brandon have gone to be straight somewhere else, I turn to Dylan. "Such charming people."

"Yeah," Dylan says. "Oh. Are you being sarcastic?"

I smile at him winningly. "Sarcastique? Moi? Is it time to dance yet?"

"I need another drink," he says, finishing the one in his hand.

"Allow me," I say, giving him a little wink and heading over to the punch table. I get two more cups and surreptitiously slip the little item I've been hiding in my pocket into Dylan's drink. I've seen this in films. It's going to be *so great.*

I hand Dylan his cup. "A toast!" I say.

But he's already downing it. No, no, no, that's not—

Dylan starts choking. "Agh! Argh!" He's smacking his chest with his hand. "Argh!"

"Oh no! Oh lordy!" I squeal. "OK, OK, do you know first aid?"

He makes a frantic pointing gesture to his throat.

OK, no time. How difficult can the Heimlich maneuver be anyway? I scurry behind him, place my fist above his navel with my other hand over it, and push inward and upward, once, twice—

"GAAAAAAHHH!" Dylan splutters, the object flying out on to the floor. "Christ!" He pushes me off him, where the correct response would be some form of gratitude, but I guess he's in shock and not thinking straight.

He bends down and picks up the thing he was choking on.

I'll admit, the moment has *somewhat* been ruined, but it's

happening now, and this is the sort of hilarious story that will be relayed at a later date, during a wedding breakfast, for example.

"What the hell?" he says, with the ring in his hand. Then he turns to me and sees I'm on one knee. "WHAT THE HELL?"

"Dylan!" I say.

"Oh god, Jack, get up! Christ!"

"No, but, Dylan—"

"Everyone's starting to look, get up, stop being a dick!"

"Dylan Hooper—"

"I'm not marrying you."

Well, that stings a bit, but I press on. "I'm not asking you to marry me . . . not yet . . . but what this ring—"

"Ugh!" Dylan says, glaring at me. Is it me he's disgusted with? Is it the ring? The ring is sterling silver. Chosen for a lifetime of durability!

"It's a promise ring!" I tell him.

He stares at me. "What are you promising? To endlessly embarrass me?" He glances around at the small crowd who have gathered around us. "Put the phone away," he mutters to Zoe Cole, who has clearly decided to film this magical moment for a possible cute viral video on social.

"No." I stand up. "*We* are making a *promise* to each other, about our relationship."

He nods. "What about it?" He's not really looking at me, he's still clocking who's watching this and checking their reactions.

"It's a sign of commitment." I look at him hopefully.

He flicks his eyes back to me and sniffs. "Uh-huh. Very nice. I haven't got you anything."

"That's OK. I . . . I brought my own." I take the other ring out of my pocket. "So."

"Right, so what now?"

"Shall we . . . put them on each other?" I suggest. "Here, at this most romantic of proms? A moment to remember and treasure? A story to tell the grandkids—how we gave each other promise rings at prom when we were just sixteen!" I mean, as narratives go, it's a good one; it's Hollywood in its perfection.

Dylan screws his face up. "Grandkids?" He laughs. "You're funny." His eyes dart around the crowd again and he actually nods to a couple of his soccer mates. "Maybe later, yeah? Let's just have some fun for now, yeah? It's prom, chill out! Don't need to get all lovey-dovey until the slow songs at the end. Yeah?"

"Sure." Luckily, I've had a fair bit of practice at masking how I really feel, so I keep my voice light and my face happy, rather than, you know, crushed, disappointed, and embarrassed.

I sigh and glance around the room. Nate Harrison is pacing in the far corner, a manky and wet-looking bit of paper in his hand, gesticulating to himself while he mouths the words to his speech. Cute how it's so important to him. He's always gone full out on things: school projects, hobbies, not speaking to me ever again after I came out. I wonder if he'll get over himself in our final two years of school, or whether we'll just end up leaving this nowhere town and living our lives without ever saying another word to each other.

"OK. If it'll make you happy, I'm good to dance." He sighs and holds out his hand.

I glance back at Nate, wondering if he's clocked what song is playing—"Embers" by Owl City—but he's too deep in his rehearsal, I think.

"Actually, maybe later," I say, flicking my eyes from Nate back to Dylan. "This isn't our song."

* * *

I'm waiting by the side of the stage with the other prom king and queen nominees. Dylan seems way too obviously drunk for an event that isn't meant to have any alcohol. I hope there isn't some clause preventing the prom king from being inebriated, or if there is, I hope Dylan can hold it together long enough for this announcement to be over. His general offish-ness tonight has been totally unnecessary (over a rainbow cape? I mean, c'mon!), but if he screws up the prom and all the Instagram opportunities it presents, I will never, ever forgive him or his perfect abs.

I can tell Nate's unsure about his speech as he delivers it. He keeps saying lines, then glancing at different mates in the audience, looking for affirmation it's going OK. And actually, it is going OK. He opened by saying he was going to "keep it short and sweet so we can all get on with the main event of the night—watching Finn Walker throw up everywhere and claim it's food poisoning again." Finn Walker has dramatically thrown up at every party for the last two years and claimed he wasn't drinking, it was food poisoning; and in a marvelous moment of serendipity,

Finn wasn't even in the room to hear Nate say this, because he was in the boys' toilets . . . throwing up.

I fiddle around with my bow tie and hair as Nate does the obligatory thank-you section to various teachers. Despite my bravado with Chloe, I'm not actually that confident of a win. At least, not from people voting for me. If anything's gonna swing it, it's the Dylan factor. He's loved, so loved, there's a chance the rest of the year might have backed him—and me by default, although I'm well aware that would have been a very reluctant vote for most of them.

Dan and Beth have been dating since year seven, so are like this long-standing beacon of romance and loyalty (so obviously stand no chance because neither of those things are qualities any of this lot admire), but Chloe is a total backstabbing bitch, so is inexplicably incredibly popular and really does stand to take the crown, having been particularly vile for most of the year but going on a huge schmoozing campaign recently, so that people would feel so grateful she was being nice they'd actually vote for her, like some weird Stockholm syndrome type situation.

I turn my attention back to Nate.

"We've been through many ups and downs together. So to every one of us who had to read a passage out in Science that contained the word 'organism' and said it wrong; to every one of us who couldn't contain our laughter when Mr. Higgins explained we'd be having a big discussion in class by saying we'd be having a 'mass debate'; and to every one of us who discovered too late that if you do the high jump while wearing loose-fitting boxer shorts, then there's a high chance you'll end up giving an unexpected anatomy lesson to some innocent bystanders—or maybe that was just me—I salute you. We made it. We're here. So here's to us, the graduating class of 2022."

In fairness to him, there's a lot of applause and a fair bit of cheering and, bless him, just for a second, he looks really proud of himself.

And now it's time.

"Without further ado," Nate begins, using a phrase that people only ever use in speeches, "I'd like to welcome the candidates for this year's prom king and queen!"

More applause and cheering, and we troop onto the stage, forming three couples, all to Nate's right. Dylan's already giggling and I give him a sharp dig in the kidney so he bucks up and takes it seriously. "This is so dumb," he mumbles.

"Just smile," I tell him through gritted teeth.

Nate glances over us all, lingering slightly, but maybe I'm wrong, on me, before turning back to his lectern and microphone.

That's when I notice how much his hands are shaking.

"Um, so," he stutters, "I know the thing about prom king and queen is that it's a vote, and lots of things can influence that, which aren't always about who the most deserving winners are . . . how popular you are, that sort of thing . . ."

I like how he's preempting a win by Chloe by throwing a certain amount of shade her way, but I've no idea where this is going.

"But also, I think prom king and queen is . . . *should be* a celebration of . . . well . . ." He swallows, really hard, like his Adam's apple is stuck in his throat. "Well, it's about being proud, I think. Proud of who you are, proud of your relationship, proud of your friends, of what you've achieved, proud of being you, and I . . . I think that's something maybe we should all aspire to, and so what I think I'm trying to say—"

My eyes widen because I already know exactly how this is going to end (no one says "proud" that much without it meaning *this*), and I'm surprised, shocked, delighted, and I love him all at once, but also a little pang of sadness ripples through my stomach because, despite everything, this feels like something he would have shared with me first, once.

"I'm trying to say, *am saying*, telling you all, that . . . I'm gay."

I turn to Dylan and reach for his hand because this is *so cute*.

"I'm gay and I don't want to hide it from you anymore."

But Dylan is gazing out at someone in the crowd.

"If this is all about being who we are, then, this is me."

I follow Dylan's gaze. He's looking at Tariq. Which is weird, because what's this got to do with Tariq? And then he glances back at me. "Cool," Dylan mutters, rubbing his nose.

Something feels off.

I move my hand back to my side.

"This is me," Nate says again.

There are cheers and applause for Nate. Good for him. I join in, even though there's a prickle of something unpleasant replicating through my veins.

"Something else," Nate says, clearly taken aback, but also buoyed by the show of support in the room. "I am . . . seeing someone. And I really like him, and it's Tariq, so, um . . ."

I glance down at Tariq again. People in his immediate vicinity are hugging him, and there are coos of support, a few "ahhh"s and it feels like now is the moment Tariq needs to leap up onstage and give his brave boyfriend a kiss . . . but he doesn't.

What he does do is shift his eyes, just for a second, to Dylan.

My breath catches.

And in that moment *I know.*

Nate gives Tariq a little wave from behind the podium. It's awkward, heartbreaking in how sweet it is, and clear he wants him to come up and share the moment with him.

Nate swallows again, flushed and hot. "Anyway, that's my super big piece of breaking news—"

A ripple of laughter from the crowd.

I edge a little closer to Dylan. "So," I whisper.

Nate checks his notes. "I guess we should get back to the issue in hand—who will be crowned this year's prom king and queen?!"

"So?" Dylan replies.

"Tariq," I say.

"Yeah," Dylan says. "Who knew? Dark horse, huh?"

"Very sly. How long's it been going on?"

"How should I know? Shut up!" he hisses. "Just be happy for them!"

"Huh." I nod. "Happy. Tariq didn't exactly look happy just now."

"He was surprised!" Dylan whispers.

"Surprised? How do you know he was surprised?"

"'Cause Nate didn't say beforehand he was gonna do this."

I nod, satisfied, and let Dylan think about what he's just said.

"Huh," I say. *And how do you know he didn't tell him?*"

Dylan's eyes widen. "What the hell are you talking about, man?"

He says it too loud. Nate stumbles and is put off his stride. He gives us a nervous glance before carrying on. "The competition was particularly stiff this year . . ."

There's laughter and a "Whoa-hey!" on the word "stiff"—year eleven being as immature and predictable as ever.

"I know what you're implying," Dylan hisses.

"And what's that?"

Dylan licks his lips, swallows. "I dunno."

"Oh, it's just you literally just said you *did* know."

"Stop trying to trip me up," Dylan says, reaching for my hand. "Come here."

I let him hold my hand, keeping some semblance of a smile on my face for the sake of the crowd, because this really isn't the moment for a screaming row. Nate's just come out. Nate's just told everyone about his boyfriend. And apparently Nate's boyfriend is screwing mine. Of that, I am ninety-nine percent certain. I'm in shock, I'm just staring forward, I can feel my whole body shaking, I can't even process the enormity of this yet, I know it'll crush me . . . but I know it'll *kill* Nate.

"Chill, dude," Dylan whispers. "Doesn't matter if we win or not, I'll still love ya anyway!"

I do not reply.

I don't have any words.

Nate's brandishing a golden envelope. "I have the names of the winners from the secret ballot here, and I can tell you it was *close*, but there was a winner!"

Nate does that thing from TV talent shows where he waits *way* too long to announce the result.

"Please just tell us," some girl shouts with literally zero excitement in her voice.

"Sorry," Nate says. He clears his throat, opens the golden envelope, reads it, and takes a deep breath. "The prom king and queen 2022 are . . ."

Total hush falls over the entire room.

"Jack Parker and Dylan Hooper."

The room erupts in cheers.

Dylan throws his hands in the air, basking in it all, then he picks me up, lifts me off the floor, and twirls me around.

I'm like a rag doll, and I just let him.

When I'm back on the floor, Nate is brandishing two golden crowns. "Please step forward so I can crown you," Nate says.

Dylan is right up there, suddenly loving it all. I wander up behind him.

"Who's king and who's queen?" Nate whispers.

"Bit personal!" Dylan laughs.

Nate's face is a picture of innocence, really not getting it.

"I think it's obvious I'm the king," Dylan adds.

"Huh. OK," Nate says. "Please kneel!" he announces.

Dylan makes a big show of kneeling so his face is indecently close to Nate's crotch, which elicits further cheers from the overexcited crowd, and a flurry of photos. "Say that to all the boys now, huh, Nate?" Dylan grins.

Nate just stares at him. "No," he says. He glances nervously at the crowd, and then at Tariq. "I didn't mean *that*."

Whatever poison is multiplying inside me is reaching some kind of critical mass. I don't care if we don't talk anymore. I don't care if he hates me. We used to be best mates and Nate does not deserve any of this.

Nate raises the crown above Dylan's head. "I hereby crown you—"

"WAIT!" I shout.

Everything stops. Everyone's staring. I'm like the person who has barged into the church at the last moment with an objection to the marriage.

Nate's wide-eyed, semi-terrified, frozen in midair with the crown in his hands.

"Do it, crown me!" Dylan tells him.

"Don't!" I say. "Do *not* crown him."

Dylan blows out a breath. "Wow, OK, let's have some drama from Jack so this can all be about him."

There's an "oh my god" from somewhere in the crowd, and the atmosphere switches in that instant. I think, I guess *I hope* it's because no one can quite believe the venom that just came out of

Dylan's mouth, because I certainly can't. Dylan can be prickly, but it's usually good-natured. Now he's spitting poison at me in front of everyone, like I'm actual dirt.

A surge of panic runs through me because there's a chance this is all in my head. There's a chance I'm about to make myself not only look stupid but accuse the most popular boy in the school of cheating on me, and if I'm wrong—or even if I'm right, quite honestly—there's no way back from that. But I know what I saw. I know in my *gut*. Dylan looked at Tariq before Nate even mentioned he was seeing Tariq. And that *look* . . . I know that look. Seen it many times before. A look that speaks of an understanding, a shared history, but something locked away, secret, not for other people.

I try to steady my erratic breathing. "Dylan," I say. "Do you think, hand on heart, you should accept the crown?" He goes to speak but I hold my hand up to stop him. "Do you think, hand on heart, that you embody all the qualities befitting of this accolade?"

"What, being *fit*?" Dylan shrugs. "Um, yeah?"

And in that second all I feel toward him is hate.

But I swallow it down. For now. "No," I say. "The qualities of honesty, loyalty, of—"

"Christ, if you've got something to say, just say it!" Dylan says.

OK, then. "Have you been seeing Tariq?"

Pin. Drop. Silence.

I have way overstepped the mark.

Not a single person knows what to do.

Dylan is staring back at me.

Nate is staring back at me.

I glance down at Tariq.

He's got his head in his hands.

"OK, this is some weird, messed-up shit you've got going on in your head, Jack. And this isn't the time—"

"Answer the question."

"I don't have to answer the question because the question is offensive."

"You're not gonna answer the question?"

"That's right, I'm not."

"Then let's ask Tariq," I say.

And all eyes turn to him, where he's still crouched on the floor, head in his hands. He slowly stands up, and sweeter, kinder, and less able to lie than Dylan, his face says it all.

"Say it, Tariq," I say.

"Just ignore him," Dylan says.

"Tariq?" Nate mutters. "What's . . ." He makes a little gasp that's half a nervous chuckle.

Tariq's face is stony. He knows he's screwed up. "Nate, maybe we should—"

"Just say it's not true!" Nate says, voice wobbling. "That's all you have to say. If it isn't true, if it's just Jack talking crap, you just have to say it!" He looks pleadingly at Tariq. *"Please,"* he mutters.

But Tariq gazes at Nate with this huge sadness in his eyes, like the game is well and truly up.

"Fucking hell," Dylan mutters.

Nate's shaking now. "No . . ."

Tariq is speechless.

I catch Chloe Kendall's eye and she has this smug look on her face of "I told you so!" It kills me how she managed to be right about this.

"No," Nate says. "Please. No." He starts crying, tears streaming down his cheeks. All the years we haven't spoken don't matter in that moment. I move toward him—he needs someone, and no one else is gonna do it.

"Get off me!" he screams as I reach for his shoulder.

There's this second where he just stares out at the shocked crowd, his face a red, blotchy, wet mess.

And then he runs, jumps off the front of the stage, trips on his trousers, which are way too long, staggers forward, and collides directly with the Demogorgon, ramming it with his shoulder so the whole thing wobbles. Nate turns, trying to push his way through the crowd, and then there are screams as the Demogorgon falls, straight down onto Nate, who collapses under its open petal-like head.

It's chaos.

More screaming.

Nate scrambling out from underneath the thing. I see him charge for the exit.

He doesn't look back.

SIX

NATE

- Come out to whole year.
- Discover boyfriend has been cheating you, live onstage.
- Get attacked by Demogorgon.

Seriously. FML.

I shouldn't have come out.

I shouldn't have told everyone.

I shouldn't have been all "look at me" like I had anything to be proud of.

This is my comeuppance for being a little bit happy.

Of course this was how it was going to end.

* * *

It's been twenty-four hours. I'm lying on my bed, staring up at the ceiling, wearing the same gray jogging shorts and white T-shirt I collapsed into after I got home last night. My eyes are tired and sore from no sleep and too much crying, and my hair's sticking up in random tufts. If I were capable of growing facial hair, I would definitely have stubble. I mean, I look like absolute crap, but I don't even care.

There were no clues. No signs. Or if there were, I didn't spot them. I don't understand how long things had been going on between Tariq and Dylan. I don't understand how it first happened, who contacted who, who made the first move. I don't understand why he didn't tell me, why he acted like he wanted me and him to be a visible couple around school if he was getting with Dylan anyway. I don't understand how someone as nice as Tariq could do this to me.

I don't understand how I didn't realize I wasn't good enough for him.

I'm so empty. So humiliated. When I got in last night, I threw my phone on the kitchen table and left it there. I don't want to face anyone. I don't want their questions or their sympathy. How could I feel something was so right yet get it so wrong?

"Nate?" It's my dad, from the other side of my bedroom door. "What are you doing in there?"

"Shutting myself off from the whole of humanity."

"Your phone's downstairs."

"I know."

"It's bleeping a lot."

I take a deep breath. "I'm sure."

"Can I come in?"

I stay silent and hope he takes the hint.

Of course, he doesn't. "So, your mum heard on the grapevine that something happened last night?" he shouts through the closed door.

"What grapevine's that?"

"Linda at number fifty-five."

Who else?

"Apparently you and Tariq had some cross words?"

I have to laugh because that's beyond an understatement.

"These things happen sometimes," Dad prattles on. "Misunderstandings and so on, maybe you two can—"

I'm over at the door in a flash and fling it open. "He's been cheating on me, Dad! He's seeing some other boy!" I scream in his surprised face. "I really liked him, I thought he liked me, and all along he's been—all along he was, he—" And I can't go on because I'm crying again. "Just go," I manage to mutter.

Instead, Dad wraps his arms around me, I bury my face in his shoulder, and he holds me tight while I sob for what feels like hours.

Eventually, he helps me back over to my bed, and we both sit down.

"Sorry," I say.

"I'm sorry too," he replies. "I know it probably doesn't feel like it right now, but you'll be OK. Reminds me of a similar thing that happened to me at your age. Me and Debs McClintock." He sighs wistfully. "Ruined me, that girl did."

"Life has shat on me big-time," I say.

"Well, I know what that feels like."

I glance at him, and his eyes say it all. His job. His best mate. Of course he knows how it feels, and I know he's had it worse than I have, even though, right now, I feel like I'm going through absolute hell. "I know, Dad. It's just . . . how do you carry on? When you feel this empty and stupid and . . . how do you do it?"

He shrugs. "One minute at a time. You take it minute by minute. And then hour by hour. And you try to spend time with people who love you." He clears his throat. "If you feel like it, get a change of scene. A vacation, perhaps . . ."

I was buying it, but now it feels like this is heading somewhere. "Right." I sniff and wipe my eyes with my hands. "Well, I'm not going on vacation, so."

"Or you *are.*"

I look at him. "No."

"OK, so you remember my mate Clint?"

"The hippy?"

"He just doesn't have the internet, Nate. That doesn't make him a hippy."

I shake my head. *"He doesn't have the internet."*

"Anyway, he's got this old VW bus, and he said I can borrow it over the summer."

"Great. What are you planning on doing with it?" Because no, I'm absolutely not doing this. Being in a car with my family for the summer was not in the plan. The plan was, I don't know, skipping through meadows with Tariq, laughing, rolling in the hay, and kissing. I won't be doing that now, so maybe I'll just paint my bedroom black and devote my summer to worshipping Satan instead.

"I'm just thinking, let's keep it free and easy. Go some places, see some things, we'll take tents to camp, maybe do a bit of Airbnb some nights, the odd hotel if we can afford it." He lowers his voice to a whisper. "I mean, your mum is adamant there should be some structure to this—you know, she's a teacher, *she likes plans*—so a trip to London's on the list, plus some Outward Bound center—"

"Well, that sounds horrible."

"I know, mate, but it's exercise, isn't it? You do PE."

"I really don't, Dad. But sure." I sniff again. "I'll think about it." The soft rejection. I can't deal with this right now.

He squeezes my knee. "You do that. Might be just what you need to take your mind off things. Now, that big, gaping void you feel like you have inside of you?"

I let out a long sigh. "Yeah, I know. Say something about there being more fish in the sea. Dismiss my pain as teenage drama. Go ahead."

"Yeah, I'm not gonna do that, but it's also caused by *not eating anything all day*."

"Ohhhh, *funny*, you are *funny*, Dad."

"Deliveroo are bringing Japanese food in approximately T-minus twenty minutes."

"Kat—"

"Katsu curry, yes, for you." He smirks at me. "You smiled. Good." He stands and walks to the door, then stops and turns back. "When did you last have a shower?"

"Oh, sorry, do I stink?"

Dad cocks his head and grins at me. "I'll sort it out."

He nods and closes my bedroom door.

And then I spot the red rose that I was going to give Tariq after my announcement last night, and I start crying all over again.

* * *

When I finally feel ready to appear downstairs, I'm greeted by the sight of Mum hurriedly doing her makeup in the hall mirror.

I'm assuming this isn't for the benefit of the Deliveroo guy. "What's going on?" I ask her.

"How *dare* this Tariq boy treat you like this!" she says, aggressively applying lipstick.

So Dad has told her everything. I shrug. "Yeah, well."

"Yeah, well, *unacceptable!*" Mum replies. "I'm going 'round to see his parents—see what they have to say for themselves and their badly behaved child!"

My eyes widen. "You don't know where they live!"

"Fifteen Willow Crescent. Linda at number fifty-five told me."

I fling myself across the front door. "Mum! No!"

She throws the lipstick in her bag and turns to me. "I'm going to give that boy a piece of my mind!"

"No, no, no, you're not."

56

"Yes, *I am*," Mum insists. "Who does he think he is? Cheating on you!"

"Mum, we're sixteen, this is isn't the sort of —"

"No one's got any class nowadays. Know who I blame? *The Kardashians.*" She advances toward the front door and my flimsy teen boy barricade. "Shift."

I brace myself against the edges of the doorframe. "Mum, I beg you, just leave it, *please.*"

"I'm really angry, Nate!"

"I know, I know you are, so am I. We're all angry, but this will only make things a thousand times worse for me. I can't have my mum turning up at boys' houses every time one upsets me. Besides, if you did, that would literally be your full-time job."

She looks me in the eye and sighs. "You're so much better than that little toad."

"Thanks."

She takes a deep breath, glances over her shoulder, then lowers her voice. "Nate? It's totally fine, there's no shame, and we can even go to one in another town, but do you think it might be an idea to visit the STI clinic? Just in case?"

I stare at her, eyes wide.

"We can't be sure how many other boys he's —"

I shake my head vigorously, trying to make some words come out. "We haven't! I told you that last night! No. It's fine. Really. There's literally no chance."

Mum nods. "So there's nothing —"

I say it quickly because it's the best way to get it over with. "We never did anything that would risk me catching an STI. We literally only kissed and held hands, OK, god, I just want to die."

"OK," Mum says to her wholesome, pure, virgin son.

"So can we just leave it? Just stay here. I don't want you talking to Tariq or his parents."

Mum nods, smoothing a bit of my hair down. "Your phone's been bleeping a lot."

"Yeah."

"It's on the kitchen table."

"I know."

"And Rose wants to see you in the garden."

"Why? What's she doing?"

"Burying Tariq in a shallow grave."

"Huh," I say, shaking my head as I walk through to the kitchen. I pick my phone up and scroll through the barrage of messages. There are various ones of increasing concern and hysteria from Alfie, Connie, and Luke, so I fire back a few quick texts saying I'm OK (which is a lie) and that I'll "message them properly later" (which is probably also a lie). There's a message from Jack too.

Hey. I'm sorry about everything. Hope you're OK. Here if you want to talk. J x

I nearly laugh at the very idea he thinks he's someone I want to talk to right now. No surprises that Jack is at the epicenter of this

58

massive scandal. I've also got ten missed calls from him. I bet he's lapping up all the drama.

And then there's Tariq:

I'm so sorry, Nate.

I didn't mean for this to happen.

I didn't mean to hurt you. Really want to talk.

Nate?

I really messed up. I'm sorry. Understand if you don't want to see or talk to me again. But hope you might give me a chance to explain.

I feel myself start to well up again, because however angry I am, however much I hate Tariq, the gentleness in his messages is why I loved him so much to start with. And what's all this about wanting to "explain"? That sounds like it's not straightforward, but why? Was Tariq somehow seduced by Dylan? Did something happen that he immediately regretted? Maybe Tariq made a mistake and was trying to find a way to break it off with Dylan and then come clean to me, but the whole thing . . . Uh. Not now. I can't do this now. I put my phone back on the table, facedown, and head out of the back door to see what Rose wants.

Rose has dug a small hole in one of the flower beds that doesn't have any flowers in it because this is the *back* garden, and most of the neighbors only ever see the front, which, literally, rivals

Kew Gardens. There's an Action Man figure on the lawn, which I assume is meant to be Tariq. Not accurate, he's not that toned, but anyway. It's kind of sweet of Rose, if you discount the weird voodoo doll element to this, and the fact her first thought was to *kill* Tariq—you know, she's looking out for me, she's loyal . . . but then she raises the huge spade she's been using (which she's only a little bit taller than) and brings it crashing down on Tariq's—I mean, Action Man's—torso, slicing him clean in half.

And now all I can see is me on one of those tacky documentaries in a few years' time called *When Cute Kids Go Bad.*

And as she kicks the two halves into the hole, haphazardly shovels on some soil, and sings, "Goodbye, Tariq!" I don't know whether to laugh, cry, or scream.

And then I remember what day it is tomorrow and I'm very nearly sick right there and then.

SEVEN

JACK

"Jack?" my mother shouts up the stairs. "You'd better be up and dressed!"

I do not reply.

I'm boiling over with rage.

Dylan the Judas has set up his own Instagram account. That would be the same Dylan who *hates* social media. Or at least, that's what he's always told me, but since everything about him is apparently a lie, maybe that was too.

And the abominable twink hasn't just posted some predictable pic of a cappuccino on a wooden table—oh, no. He's posted a picture of him and Tariq, holding hands but looking mournful. The caption is so appalling I want to exterminate him:

We know we didn't handle things right. We know we've hurt people we cared about, and for that we're sorry. But life is about making mistakes and learning. It's also about loving, and with each other's love we both hope to grow.

I can't even look at the hashtags because the caption is bad enough. Anything else is going to make me smash my phone to bits.

It has already been liked by *one hundred people*. He already has *five hundred* followers.

How has he managed to make this all about him when *I'm* the one who has been shafted?

I am not going to let him play this game. He is not going to come out of this looking good. I take a selfie. Not one of my usual ones where I look fabulous, well groomed, with flattering lighting. My hair's a mess, my eyes are red. I look *wrecked*.

It's perfect.

No witty caption. No hashtags. Just plain and simple:

Gave everything. Wasn't enough.

It's maybe a little OTT, but I need it to really capture the sense of what Dylan has done. I'm not as upset as the post implies. I haven't gotten to that stage yet. I'm still blinded by white-hot anger toward both of them—partly at their disgusting duplicity, partly because Dylan hasn't even bothered to so much as message to express a modicum of regret about what has happened, and partly because they have completely humiliated me in front of the whole year. Should I have seen it coming? I think I'd put Dylan's coldness down to exam stress or something. Everyone went weird around GCSEs—even me! I'm normally pretty Zen, but even I had a meltdown in a bookshop when they'd sold out of a review guide I was looking for. My point is, you have to give people some slack around exam time. I assumed Dylan was under pressure and all would be well afterward and we'd have a great summer Instagramming our love. It didn't cross my trusting mind that he was "Netflix and chilling" with Tariq. I tried messaging Nate. Would have been good to talk to someone who understood. He didn't reply. Which is not a surprise.

Mum slams in through my bedroom door, all dressed up in her office outfit. "You're supposed to be there at nine."

"I can't go. I'm sick."

"You're going. It's compulsory if you want to do A levels at the same school next year."

"Mum, I am literally sick. If you just call the school, they'll understand and waive the compulsory thing."

Mum smiles at me. "No time, I'm already late. Up to you, Jack, you're a big boy now. You can take responsibility for your own actions. Call Mrs. Carpenter yourself."

"No, she scares me, she always makes you feel like you're not sick, just lying."

63

"That'll probably be because you *are*."

"OK, just, you need to remember these words when you get the call from the hospital saying they're sorry but there was nothing they could do to save me."

"I'll go one better and get them engraved on your headstone."

She eyeballs me until I can't take it and have to look away.

"Why do we even need a Sixth Form Orientation Day when I've already been at the school for five years? I couldn't be more orientated if I tried. There is no part of that school I couldn't orientate myself to."

"I don't think that's what they mean. Get out of bed." She turns to go, then comes back. "Are you getting a summer job?"

I stare at her. "Oh my god. Just send me down the mines, why don't you?"

"I was thinking you could do some work experience at my place."

"Helping criminals get off scot-free?"

"I don't do that sort of law. It's commercial and corporate."

"Oiling the wheels of the capitalist machine so that rich guys can carry on wrecking the world? Mm, I'd love that, Mum, thanks."

"OK, you're a dick."

"Thanks, Mum, love you, bye!"

She shakes her head and leaves.

I turn back to Instagram and check my post. Three likes. *Three.* Oh my god. Worse, two comments:

Is this the bit where I'm meant to write "You OK hun?"

They're both clearly sorry, get over it.

If I'd been hoping I might get through this with support from anyone in my year, I was obviously wrong. Clearly, the only thing stopping people from openly hating me these last few months was Dylan. Dylan—the acceptable face of gay because he's not *too* gay. He plays soccer. He's one of the lads. They *tolerated* me because they *loved* him. With him gone, it's open season, and the school is full of people who cannot wait to see me fall. A very familiar dread creeps back into my stomach. I don't even know if I've got the energy to put on the front anymore.

I don't expect people to love me.

I just wish they didn't hate me quite so much.

*   *   *

Since we're classed as sixth formers in potentia now, we don't have to wear our uniforms for this utterly pointless orientation. But that brings myriad complications. I could opt to really dress up, look really good, as a way of showing that Dylan has not gotten to me, that I'm strong and powerful and I don't need a man, especially not a CHEATING one who still hasn't messaged to express even the tiniest bit of remorse. Or I could dress down, so it doesn't look like I'm trying too hard and also to be more in keeping with the Instagram post I stupidly made so, you know, that doesn't come across as entirely fake.

I eventually opt for a light pink hoodie with some balloon-fit, light blue jeans and sneakers, but owing to the seven complete changes of outfit, it's five to nine by the time I'm slurping some chocolate milk in the kitchen and Mum calls to see if I'm out of the door yet.

"I'm *literally* moments from the school gates," I lie, putting my glass in the dishwasher.

"I can *literally* hear you putting something in the dishwasher. *Get your arse to school!*"

Since I can't get away with it any longer, I head out of the door, and I don't let the knowing smirks from some kids in the year below break the confident bounce in my step. It's all for show because I'm crumbling inside, and it's a relief when I spot Theo by the entrance to the school, dressed like an estate agent in smart chinos and a slim-fit shirt, like he's actually taken on board the guidance that sixth formers should dress "business casual."

"I've been messaging you," he says.

"I've needed some space."

Theo nods. "Pretty brutal, how it all happened."

I sigh. "Yeah."

"I'm sure . . ." Theo hesitates for a second. "I know Dylan can be a prick sometimes, but I'm sure he never meant for you to find out like that."

"OK, I get it, everyone loves Dylan. Dylan can do no wrong."

Theo goes to say something but clearly thinks better of it and presses his lips tightly together.

"He cheated on me, Theo. There's no planet on which that is acceptable."

"He didn't mean it to happen like it did," Theo says.

"But it *did*, and—" I stop and stare at him. "Have you been speaking to him about this? Did you *know* about this?"

Theo flicks his eyes to the ground.

"Oh my god," I say. "You *knew*."

"Jack, before you go off on me—"

"Go off on you? You *knew* and you didn't tell me? We're friends! Aren't we?"

"Dylan and Tariq are my friends too! They asked me not to say anything!"

I nod, my blood turning ice-cold. "Oh my god. OK, you made a choice, and you chose them."

"That's not what—"

"Well, thanks a lot."

"Jack, it was up to them to tell you, not me."

"You knew, and you made an active decision not to tell me. I think that sucks, Theo."

Theo sighs and glances up at me. But there is *no fucking apology.*

I shake my head. "Go. Go inside, you'll be late."

"Aren't you coming?"

"Not with you."

Theo gives me an understanding nod, goes to say something, doesn't, then turns and walks off instead.

So, great. I wonder who else knew? I wonder if everyone has just been laughing about me for, what? Days? Weeks? How long has this even been going on for? And what hurts more, in this very second, is that no one seemed to have my back. Theo was happy to look out for Dylan and Tariq but couldn't do the same for me.

I cannot walk into that school. I can't do it.

Maybe I can enroll somewhere else instead, do my A levels there. A fresh start where nobody knows me.

I turn around, and there's Nate, head down, shuffling along the pavement, wearing skinny black jeans and an oversized sweater, like some tragic rom-com character, and he's the only person in the world I want to speak to right now.

"Hey," I say.

He stops and looks up at me. His eyes are full of pain and full of hate. "Hey."

I don't understand why he's so cold toward me, why he didn't even reply to my message or any of my calls since last night. I can feel my throat getting tighter; my chest hurts. I don't know why every single person hates me so much. "Are you going in?" I mutter.

"Got to, if I want to study here next year."

I nod. "Can we go in together?"

He looks up at me sharply. "Why did you do it onstage?"

"What?"

"Had to make it into a spectacle, didn't you? Had to be this big thing, make it all about you, and people like me are just the collateral damage."

I shake my head. "Nate, no! That's not what—I promise you, I literally only realized what was going on as I was standing up there. It was Dylan and Tariq—the way they looked at each other—"

"OK, whatever, I'm not interested," Nate says. "Even if that's true, you could have waited until after. Now it's legend, isn't it? It'll go down in history as the biggest prom embarrassment of all time. Cheers for that."

"Nate—"

"No, piss off."

And he pushes past me, toward the entrance of the school.

But then I hear him come to an abrupt stop and this little gasp of breath, like he's been shot or something.

I turn, and he's looking at Dylan and Tariq. They're up ahead on the steps that lead to the main door, arms around each other, heads nestled into one another's shoulders. And it hits me too. Before, Dylan and Tariq being together was just a concept. I hadn't allowed myself to properly think about what that actually meant—I couldn't, I was too angry. But now I see it. And it's tender, and strangely beautiful, and even though I'm meters away, I can tell they feel something for each other that is so much *more* than anything Dylan and I had. I can't help it, a tear escapes. And then I'm annoyed at myself for feeling like that, and I'm furious at *them* for making me feel like that. I'm burning up with so many conflicting emotions I could honestly scream.

"I can't do it," Nate mutters. He urgently wipes at his eyes. "Shit. Oh god. But if we want to come back for sixth form— Can you please stop crying?"

"*You're* crying!" I splutter.

"Well, we both need to stop and figure out what the hell to do. This is such a frigging *mess*!"

I nod. "I think I have a plan. I can get us out of having to do this, but we need the most sympathetic member of staff. Who would that be?"

"Mrs. Davidson," Nate says.

"The librarian? OK, take me to your leader," I say. "And let me do the talking."

* * *

There are thirty year sevens sitting in pin-drop silence in the library, having some sort of supervised reading lesson, which is less than ideal. Mrs. Davidson is behind the counter, with some kid on an office wheelie chair who's in charge of the computer for issuing books. She glances up as we approach. "The orientation day is in the main hall," she says.

Thirty pairs of year seven eyes look up at me and Nate.

"We"—I keep my voice hushed and low to try to convey the gravity of the situation—"have a small issue."

"Right?" she says at normal volume.

"So, for various reasons, we're unable to attend the orientation session, but we really need a member of staff to sign us off."

"What reasons?" she says.

"Various reasons," I tell her. She is not the pushover Nate led me to expect.

She laughs. She actually *laughs*. "I'm going to need a bit more than that—attendance is compulsory if you want to come back next year."

Nate goes to open his mouth, but I bat him away. "Yes, no, *absolutely*, and we wouldn't ask, except it's an emergency."

She frowns. "Emergency?"

"Emergency."

"What sort of emergency?"

I lick my lips and briefly glance at more than a couple of year seven kids who are blatantly listening but are pretending not to. I lower my voice to the merest hiss. "It's a . . . it's a *gay* emergency." Throwing in the gay thing is usually enough. She won't ask any more. If she does, that's homophobic. Probably.

"It's a what?" she says.

"A gay . . . a gay emergency!"

"Well, what's that?"

"It's gay!"

"And—"

"It's *gay* and it's an *emergency!*"

"But what is it?"

"Private! Very private!" I hiss. "Please, miss! It's a private, terrible, *gay* emergency that means we really *cannot* be at the important thing, and we need your help."

"The thing is—" she begins.

"Please!"

"I really can't—"

"We just need your help!"

"Without you being more—"

"We're not comfortable talking to anyone—"

"LICE!" Nate suddenly says really loudly, and then, just in case anyone at the back of the library didn't hear, he repeats it. "It's *lice*. We need help. Medical help."

Mrs. Davidson stares at him in shock.

The kid on the wheelie chair slowly pushes himself away from us.

I close my eyes because, *what the actual hell, Nate?*

And that boy is not done yet.

"We didn't know who else we could trust to tell," Nate explains. He glances around the library, and at all the year sevens who are now openly staring at us. "We didn't want anyone else to find out."

Mrs. Davidson nods. "OK, boys. It's good you've sought help. I think the first thing is to see the school nurse, she can advise you, and then—"

"No, we just need you to sign us off and we can go to the clap clinic," I say. I can't *believe* I'm saying it, but here we are.

"Why are you talking about the clap clinic?" Nate hisses. He points to his hair. "*Head* lice, I meant!"

I glare at him. "And since when did head lice constitute an emergency, Nate?"

"Well, don't just jump in with the clap clinic when I didn't mean that!" Nate mutters.

"How am I meant to know what's happening in your brain?

Hm? Do I look like a mind reader?" I take a deep breath and shake my head.

"OK, I'm not sure exactly what's happening here," interrupts Mrs. Davidson, "but I'm going to ring for the nurse. It's important you get the support you need, for whatever this actually is." She's picking up the phone. "We have a duty of care toward you, after all."

"Wait!" I say. "It's OK, we understand that. Since you're so busy here, we'll just go and see the nurse ourselves, it's . . . really no problem." I give her what must be a really fake smile, despite my best efforts. "Thank you so much." I glance around the library. "Yay, books!"

Thirty disgusted faces look back at me, and I'm pretty sure one kid is already messaging under the desk.

EIGHT

NATE

It just came out. I'd always assumed head lice was a big thing, you know, a school wouldn't want it to spread, and we'd need to be quarantined or something, so Mrs. Davidson would agree to whatever we wanted and be all understanding. I hadn't accounted for the fact that Jack would assume I meant *pubic* lice, and of course the staff at school like to be all up in your business these days because otherwise it's neglect.

We should have just both agreed we had the flu, put on the coughing and the croaky voice, and it would probably have been fine. Except, it probably wouldn't because that's an age-old trick, so maybe I did right.

"You are *such a dick*," Jack mutters.

Or I possibly didn't.

"Why the hell would you say *that*?" he continues. "Of all things! *Lice!* You had to pick the grossest thing."

"It's not gross," I tell him. "Head lice, or any sort of lice, are nothing to be ashamed of."

"Anything you can use in a sentence with the word 'infestation' is something to be embarrassed about," Jack tells me.

"Are we going to see the school nurse?" I ask.

He turns to me sharply. "No, Nate, we are *not*."

"What if Mrs. Davidson asks about it later?"

"Tell her you got yourself fumigated and it's all fine!" Jack hisses. He stomps off up the corridor.

"Where are you going?" I ask.

"Orientation session," he says, not looking back.

I watch him go, mulling my options but realizing that this is school and I basically don't have any. I sigh and follow Jack, eventually finding him hovering outside the double doors that lead to the main hall, where the workshop is happening. I guess he doesn't want to go in either. Seeing Tariq with Dylan on the steps earlier cut me up. But going in there, seeing them again, being all together and apparently in love, I don't think I can take it. And then there's the fact Jack made the whole situation a billion times worse by announcing it in front of the whole school. Maybe to him it's not a big deal. He loves the limelight, he's confident. He might be upset, but he can deal with it better than I can. I know life hasn't always been easy for Jack, but he comes out of it sparkling, whereas I always feel like it crushes me.

I hover with him for a few moments. We stare at the double doors, the frosted glass panels masking the horrors lurking on the other side.

"What are we waiting for?" I ask eventually.

"For everyone inside that room to die so I don't have to face them."

I nod. "That could easily be eighty years."

He doesn't reply.

"Just do your Jack thing," I continue.

He grimaces. "And what, pray, is that exactly?"

"You know," I say. "Ta-da!"

He frowns at me. "What was that thing you did?"

"What thing?"

"Was that some sort of shimmy when you said, 'Ta-da!'?"

"I guess."

"OK, because it looked like you were having some sort of fit. If you're going to shimmy, hold the whole body still and alternate your shoulders back and forth. That's the move. It's not hard."

"I wish I hadn't bothered."

"So do I."

He stares at the door, breathing hard.

"Anyway," I say. "*You* don't have to face them. *We* do."

He glances, just quickly, at me. "What a beautiful thing to say, Nate. How very touching."

"Piss off."

"We can walk in there together, the jilted exes—"

"I think, considering your boyfriend probably seduced mine—"

"What?" Jack screams. "So, I have no idea who started what first, but how is that my fault? I don't control Dylan, Nate, I'm not responsible for him! I didn't realize what was going on until we were onstage with you!"

"And you had to make a big show of it when you did find out!"

"Oh, this again? So, what, I should just have smiled and not caused a scene because we're British and all too polite? I should have let Dylan take the crown for being prom king because he's such a great guy? I mean, what a load of crap!"

"All I'm saying—"

"Well, don't 'say,' Nate. Don't say anything. You've said enough." He glares at me. "Congratulations on coming out by the way."

"Thanks," I mutter.

"Welcome to being gay."

I look down at the floor.

"As you can see," he continues, "*it's hell.*" He gives me a sarcastic smile and pushes both swing doors open with a huge flourish, bounding forward into the hall. "TA-DA!" he says to the whole room, doing a shimmy, which looks a lot more technically accurate than mine.

The doors flap back and hit me in the face, whacking my nose, so my eyes immediately start to water. I wince in agony as the doors flap open again, and Jack's hand grabs my sweater and pulls me into the hall. And there I am, standing next to Jack, the rest of year eleven looking at me, while I'm apparently in tears.

Jack glances at me in dismay. "Why are you crying?" he whispers.

"I'm not," I whimper.

"Jesus, Nate, don't let them see weakness. They'll eat you alive."

Mrs. Taylor, head of sixth form, studies us both with the tired resignation of someone who has spent too much time with sixteen-year-olds. "You're late, boys."

"Sorry, Mrs. Taylor," Jack says, giving her a smile. "Unfortunately we were disorientated. Thank god we're here now, though, right? I suppose that's a fundamental flaw with this whole thing— how do you find your way to a session before you've actually *had* the session about how to find your way?"

"Amusing," Mrs. Taylor says.

"It's a riddle!" Jack grins.

I'm well aware that Jack's being a bit of a knob, but right now I'm just grateful he's pulling the focus to *him*, so fewer people are looking at *me*.

Mrs. Taylor ignores him. "You can form your own group since everyone else is already in one—there are some paper and markers over there."

"Due north." Jack nods. "I'm getting the hang of this."

Jack bounces over to the far corner, where there's a huge sheet of blank paper on the floor, about three meters long and two meters wide, as well as a load of markers. I keep my head down and shuffle after him, feeling the heat of everyone's eyes. I'm deliberately trying not to see where Tariq or Dylan are, and I'm not sure if it's the stress from everyone looking or the panic that Tariq and Dylan might be right next to where our spot is or if it's connected to the door hitting me, or maybe it's all of the above, but a tiny bit of blood trickles out of my nose.

"MISS!" Jack gasps, seeing me. "Nate's bleeding!"

"I'm fine," I mutter.

"Miss, he's hemorrhaging blood! I'll take him to the nurse!" He's gripping my arm and pulling me back the way we came. "It's OK, we can catch up —"

But Mrs. Taylor is having none of it. She's a secondary school teacher: she knows the difference between a genuine emergency and teenage histrionics. "Just sit down, I'm sure it'll stop."

"But, miss —"

"*Jack*," Mrs. Taylor warns.

Jack sighs and goes back toward our piece of paper, while I dab at my nose with a tissue. I got through five years at this school by keeping my head down and being as invisible as possible. Now, in the space of forty-eight hours, it feels like I've become a circus act and my whole body is just filled with *dread*. I flop down on the floor and keep my head bowed, trying to shut everyone out, not daring to glance up in case the first eyes I meet are those of Tariq or Dylan.

"First task," Mrs. Taylor announces to the whole group, "is to create the perfect sixth former! One of you lies on the sheet of paper and your partner will draw around you. Then, together, I want you to fill in the body shape with the words and phrases you feel embody the perfect sixth form student—for example, you might pick 'hardworking' as one quality. As many as you can, twenty minutes—off you go!"

There's an immediate hum of activity as everyone starts to get on with it, although by the sounds of the suggestions already being made by the groups nearest us ("Fit!" "Sexy!" "Goes to second base on a first date!"), I'm not sure everyone quite understands the point of the exercise.

"Lie down, then," Jack tells me.

"You lie down."

"I can't risk you getting marker on this hoodie," Jack says. "It's vintage, and I'm not being funny, but you're literally dressed all in black, like some sort of angel of death, so even if I did get some marker on you, which I won't because I've got a really steady hand—literally, I could be an actual surgeon if I was taking the right A levels—it won't show up anyway."

I briefly wonder where Alfie, Connie, and Luke are, and whether I could work with them, but I simultaneously don't want to look (in case I accidentally see Tariq and Dylan) and can't be bothered with the hassle from Jack if I go and work with someone else. "Fine." I lie down on the sheet of paper.

Jack selects a pink marker, because of course he does, and sets to work, starting at my head and working around my left side, carefully moving the marker around the fingers of my left hand, then back up my arm, down my side, right down my left leg, around the left foot, then up again, until . . .

"How do you want me to deal with your crotch area?" Jack asks.

"I don't want you to 'deal' with it at all, thanks."

"So do you want some approximation of genitals, or shall I go full eunuch?"

"Just be vague," I hiss.

He maneuvers the marker up my left thigh and I close my eyes because I really cannot deal with this right now. At least the giggles emanating from the other groups suggest I'm not alone in this hideousness. Jack must have nearly finished drawing when I hear a *"We need to talk!"*

I open my eyes and Dylan is looming over Jack, deadly serious, while Jack is still on his knees with the marker. "There's a rumor that you've got lice?" Dylan says. "So were you going to say anything? I mean, that would be the adult thing to do."

I can practically see the steam coming out of Jack's ears. *"Adult?"* he says. "Oh my god. First of all, *how dare you*? Second of all —"

"So where d'ya get lice from? 'Cause it wasn't from me."

"Well, how can we be sure? It's not as if our relationship was monogamous as far as you were concerned." He glares at Dylan. "Also, I don't have lice. I probably should have said that bit first because it doesn't sound convincing as an afterthought."

"OK, well, I heard you did and you were asking to see the school nurse, so that seems weird."

"OK, well, maybe you should try not getting your information from twelve-year-olds."

"If you've given me lice, I will actually kill you. Not metaphorically, *actually*, literally kill you."

"Just give me fair warning so I can make sure there's something glamorous I can die on nearby—a chaise longue or sweeping staircase perhaps."

"Screw you."

"Again?" Jack retorts.

Dylan gives him the finger and stomps off.

"Just to confirm, I don't have lice!" Jack repeats, loud enough for half the room to hear.

All I want is for this to be over. And by "this," I mean life. Maybe if I just keep staring up at the ceiling, it'll be fine.

Jack looks down at me again. "Let's write some phrases to describe the perfect sixth former," he says. "I'm going to start with 'not a twat.'"

"Are we allowed to use inappropriate language?"

"Who cares?" Jack says. "Shift off the paper, else I'll write it on your forehead."

I roll off and heave myself to a sitting position, watching as Jack finishes "not a twat" and then adds "truthful" and "loyal."

"Add something!" Jack tells me.

I take a cap off a marker and write "kind to animals."

Jack narrows his eyes at me, then crosses out "animals" and replaces it with "their boyfriend." "I think that's what you meant," Jack says.

Twenty minutes later, the exercise is complete, and I can't speak for Jack, but part of me feels a tiny bit better for scrawling down certain home truths about Dylan and Tariq. And you know what? They are all completely relevant because the perfect sixth former is not someone who goes around lying and cheating, so this all feels pretty justified. Anyway, I'm hoping we can now move on to the next activity and then ideally go home, when Mrs. Taylor says,

"Right! Let's have some of you up here to discuss what you've written — Lottie and Beth, Dylan and Tariq . . ."

There's a collective held breath as everyone waits and prays — in my case, that this doesn't head the way we all know it will, and in everyone else's case, that it absolutely does.

"And, yes, since you were late, Jack and Nate!" Mrs. Taylor says triumphantly.

A prickle of anticipation ripples through the room.

I glance at Jack. "Huh," he says, chewing his lip.

"No, no, no," I whimper. My main thought is whether running straight out of the exit is a viable plan, and if I could plead a breakdown or something. Or a stomach bug. I *feel* sick. I think it could be a legit excuse.

"Chop chop, boys!" Mrs. Taylor says, clapping her hands. "Up you get — has your nose stopped bleeding, Nate? Yes? Good. Let's have a nice line of you along the front here, one of you hold your sheet of paper up, so we can all see."

Jack's on his feet first, and he offers me his hand to pull me up, which I ignore because if we hadn't been late, this wouldn't be happening, and who made us late? Whose ridiculous plan to get us out of this workshop backfired? *Jack's.* He is such a dick. And thanks to him, the hotly anticipated next episode of this Big Gay Soap Opera is about to continue — which is probably what he was hoping for all along.

My feet and legs barely cooperate as I haul myself toward the front of the hall. It's like they *know* this is a mistake. And then, just as I'm shuffling behind Jack, picking our way through the audience to the front, I glance up and there he is—Tariq. He smiles at me. *He frigging smiles.* A gentle, sweet, apologetic, hope-you're-OK kind of smile. And I *know* that's what sort of smile it is, because I *know* him and he was my boyfriend (and technically still *is*, since he hasn't formally broken up with me with words that unequivocally say that).

I try to smile back but instead I nearly start crying, and then he's no longer looking so it doesn't matter anyway. So we're standing in our pairs in front of everyone, Dylan and Tariq on the far right, Lottie and Beth in the middle, and then me and Jack.

"So what we'll do is have one word or phrase from each group and go along the line, until we've done them all, so just shout them out!" Mrs. Taylor says.

"Hardworking," Dylan says.

"That was Mrs. Taylor's example to start with!" Jack immediately complains.

"So?" says Dylan.

"It's fine," Mrs. Taylor interrupts. "It's a perfectly good start. Lottie and Beth?"

"Organized," Lottie says.

"Excellent! Hardworking, organized . . ." Mrs. Taylor looks at us. "Jack and Nate?"

"Not a twat," Jack replies, flicking his eyes to Dylan as he says it.

There's laughter, which Mrs. Taylor immediately quells. "All right! All right! Let's keep it clean and sensible, shall we, Jack? You're going to be a sixth former now after all."

Dylan rolls his eyes. "Exactly."

I glance down the line to Tariq. He's not smiling anymore.

"Back to Tariq and Dylan!" Mrs. Taylor says brightly.

"Committed," Tariq says.

I find myself nodding in agreement, just because it's Tariq.

"Good!" Mrs. Taylor beams, as Jack pipes up with, "Committed to *what?*"

"We're just going through the words for now, Jack," Mrs. Taylor says.

"OK, but committed to *what?* Like, committed to bettering themselves? To world peace? I think it's good to clarify, or else you might mistakenly think they were referring to, oh, I don't know" —he blows out a breath— "*committed to backstabbing and cheating on your partner,* for example."

"Shut up, Jack!" Dylan says.

Jack shrugs. "That's just an example."

"Shut up, Jack!" I hiss.

Jack glares at me like *I've* just stabbed *him* in the back.

"Lottie and Beth!" Mrs. Taylor says, moving quickly on. "Enthusiastic!"

"About *what*?" Jack asks Beth. "Enthusiastic about your subjects or about *backstabbing and cheating on your partner*, for example?"

"Argh!" Dylan screams.

I take an unsteady breath, then lock eyes with Tariq down the line. He looks awkward and embarrassed and there's a small shred of comfort to be had in the fact we're both clearly feeling the same right now.

"Truthful!" Jack continues, pointing to our paper, like a TV weather person. "Which I happen to know at least two people in this room not so far away from me would definitely struggle with, so maybe they shouldn't be allowed to study here, I don't know."

"*Mature*," Dylan growls.

"Sorry, is that an item on your list or something you just wish you were?" Jack asks, peering down the line toward Dylan.

"Forgiving when people make mistakes," Dylan replies.

"HA! Oh, the LOLs!" Jack replies. His face turns from mirth to deadly serious. "Not a lying BITCH."

"Not your turn, and no offensive language," Mrs. Taylor jumps in.

"Responsible," Lottie says. Lottie and Beth are so not involved in this at this point, but they're carrying on either valiantly or obliviously.

"Able to take criticism," Tariq says.

"Here's some criticism!" Jack announces. "Tell the truth! Don't lead people on!" He points to our paper. "Be kind to YOUR BOY-FRIEND!"

"That says 'animals,'" Lottie says.

"I think both count," Dylan says.

Jack snaps his fingers. "Exactly!" he says triumphantly.

"Exactly," Dylan echoes. "They're basically the same thing—my ex-boyfriend is behaving like an absolute *pig* right now."

"Such an obvious choice of animal!" Jack hurls back. "And also, THIS IS YOUR FAULT, NOT MINE!"

"OK! OK, that's absolutely enough!" Mrs. Taylor says. "Whatever is going on here, I don't want to hear any more about it. OK? We need to learn to leave our personal lives outside the sixth form. OK? OK, Jack?"

"OK."

"OK, Dylan?"

"OK."

Mrs. Taylor looks between me and Tariq. We both nod.

"OK, then," Mrs. Taylor says. "One more example each, please."

"A team player," Jack mutters.

"Able to manage workloads," Beth adds.

Dylan's eyes have a dangerous twinkle in them. "Doesn't. Have. PUBIC *LICE*!"

It's at that point that Jack launches himself at Dylan, and they both topple to the floor in a mess of squeals and flailing limbs, none of which look like actual punches but more like a very homoerotic wrestling match. Various classmates have their phones out, filming. Once again, Jack's made this whole thing into The Jack Show. Suddenly I'm so completely furious I have to stop myself jumping into the scrum and wringing his stupid neck.

Mrs. Taylor is on her walkie-talkie right away. "Office? I need some backup in the main hall please."

NINE

JACK

Nate is so super furious, I mean, honestly, talk about overreaction. Personally, it felt good to air my considerable grievances, plus, don't Dylan and Tariq deserve to be embarrassed in public for what they've done? Also, thanks to the element of surprise, I basically won a wrestling match with the soccer captain, so that's another humiliation for Dylan.

Nate clearly does not feel the same though. I can barely keep up with him as he charges down the street, all red-faced and breathing heavily.

"Nate! It's not like it even matters!"

He doesn't look at me. "I have *never* been thrown out of a class in my life!"

"OK, (a) it *wasn't* a class. Not a proper one. It was a—"

"Seriously, you should shut up."

"OK, but also, (b) we're not officially *at* school. We're technically—"

"Jack, shut up."

"OK, but finally, (c) the school gets money for each sixth former they recruit, so all this 'compulsory orientation session' thing is just them pretending they've actually got power over us because they'll want us regardless. Like, whatever we've done wrong, they will still want us in September because otherwise we'll just probably go somewhere else that'll get the money for us instead. Literally, we could have committed a heinous atrocity, nuked an entire continent, millions dead and they'd be like, 'Yeah, OK, you can still study A level English here.'"

He stops dead and turns right into me, so we're almost nose to nose. "I just want you to leave me alone."

I can tell it's more than that. I can tell he actually wants to wring my neck. His left eye is twitching, which always used to happen when he was stressed. It's kind of sweet. "Maybe talking about it will help," I suggest.

"What's there to talk about, Jack? How I've been humiliated? How I just want to crawl under a rock right now? How you're making everything a billion times worse by being so . . ."

I raise an eyebrow at him. "Fabulous in the face of adversity?" I suggest.

90

He scowls at me. "I don't want to talk."

And off he goes again, charging down the street. Trouble is, I *do* want to talk. I'd *love* to. Between us, maybe we could piece this whole thing together, get some answers. And there isn't anyone else I *can* talk to about this. It's not like I have anyone I would call a best friend. I mean, Nate *was* my best friend once, so I guess he's the closest thing, even if he does now hate me. "Nate!"

He doesn't look back.

"Don't make me wrestle you, Nate!"

But he doesn't seem to care.

I try to catch him up, until I'm literally doing a light jog next to him as he strides along. "This is ridiculous," I tell him.

He gives me nothing.

"Our boyfriends both cheated on us. Don't you think we have something in common to talk about?"

"No."

"Talking helps!"

"No."

He arrives at his house, where his mum and dad are both in the driveway, packing things into a VW bus.

"Hey, Nate!" his dad chirps. "We're just—"

Nate barges past, doesn't even acknowledge either of them, heads in through the front door and slams it shut behind him.

His parents glance at one another, and then at me. "Jack!" his mum says.

"Hey," I say, smiling. Nate's mum hasn't changed a bit—she's dressed practically (but not unstylishly) in jeans and a floral blouse, and her whole vibe still exudes "mum," if you get me? It's like, you can tell she's caring, she'd protect you from bad guys and would always have a tissue handy, but you'd better not swear in front of her. His dad, who always was a little rough around the edges, is slightly rougher these days (he totally wouldn't care if you swore in front of him), although it's nothing a trip to the barber, a shave—and possibly a spa day—wouldn't solve.

"We haven't seen you since you were—" Nate's mum illustrates my height as a thirteen-year-old with her hand. "Look at you! All handsome and grown-up!"

"It's true, very grown-up—I actually had to shave two weeks ago. Sort of."

"You and Nate used to hang out all the time," Nate's dad says, putting down a box that has *cooking stuff* written on it in marker.

"Yes, well, that was before your son turned against me because he turned out to be a massive prick" *is what I want to say.* Instead, I give a shy smile and go with, "We kind of started doing our own thing."

His parents nod.

"I miss him," I add, and as soon as I say it, I realize just how much I really do. Until we were thirteen, I had a wingman. I had someone to laugh with about everything, someone who was there for me and who I never needed to be anything other than *me* with. Nate was my best friend, and we were unstoppable, until we . . . weren't.

His dad gestures toward the house. "So, um, what's going on with him?"

I shake my head. "He's in the foulest of moods."

"Is it Tariq related?"

"I think, yes, it is." I am not going to elaborate.

His mum sighs and shakes her head. "That terrible boy. Nate wouldn't really say much about it—just that he was secretly seeing some other shameful individual."

"Otherwise known as my boyfriend," I say.

"Oh," she says, flushing in the cheeks.

"Well, *ex*-boyfriend now."

She nods. "Sorry, I didn't realize he . . . So you didn't know—"

"Correct. I found out at the prom too. It was a great night. One to remember."

"That's terrible," his mum says. "You poor boys." She steps closer to me. "And how are you holding up?"

I open my mouth, but no words come out.

"Came as a shock, I imagine?" she continues.

My throat tightens, and I nod, panic shooting through my veins because I can feel myself about to lose it.

"It's OK, you don't have to talk about it."

"It's not that I mind talking. It's just that Nate *won't*," I say.

"That's Nate all over," his dad says.

I glance at the bus and the boxes over the drive, keen to talk about something else. "Are you going somewhere?"

"Kind of a freewheeling road trip," Nate's dad says.

His mum clears her throat. "Can you stop telling everyone that, Mick? Most of the neighbors already think this is part of a midlife crisis."

"A road trip with a *bit* of structure," his dad concedes.

"Well, with *quite a lot* of structure because it's ultimately a perfectly ordinary planned family vacation that normal people would have, and, yes, we could have gone to the stunning South of France like Jean from reception, but we simply chose not to, probably out of concern for the environment." She gives Nate's dad a tight smile. "Right, dear?"

"Right, *dear*," he replies. He turns to me. "Getting a head start on the packing because we're off in a couple of days. Well, *we* are. Nate's still saying he's not coming, last we heard."

I break into a wide smile. "Nate being unenthusiastic? How unusual!"

They both laugh.

Then Nate's dad turns to his mum and sort of cocks his head toward me, at which she raises her eyebrows, and then nods.

"Jack," his dad says, rubbing his hands together. "Got a little proposal for you."

TEN

NATE

I'm so angry. I'm angry with Tariq for doing this to me. I'm angry with Jack for making it worse. And I'm angry with myself for being so utterly stupid in the first place. Guys like me are better off just keeping our heads down and getting through life as best we can, maybe occasionally being thrown a scrap of something that isn't completely horrible, awkward, or unfortunate. Romance? Actually dating someone? Big announcements in front of classmates? What was I thinking?

Meanwhile, everyone can just go to hell. Especially Jack.

I slam my bedroom door, whip my curtains closed, whack

my headphones on, crash on my bed, squeeze my eyes tight shut, and blast "Total Eclipse of the Heart" at an obscene, eardrum-shattering volume.

Do not judge me on my song choice.

I think about Tariq, forensically analyzing his every facial expression and body language from this morning. Is there a part of him that's regretting this whole thing? Does he still like me? Before I can think better of it, I do it. I message him:

Hey.

And after thirty seconds that feels like thirty hours, he replies:

Hey.
Nate: I'm sorry about Jack earlier.
Tariq: No worries.
Nate: So I guess I'm not your boyfriend anymore?
I just wondered what I did wrong.
Tariq: You did nothing wrong, Nate. It was all me, and I'm sorry. I'm so sorry. But, I guess . . . We were always kind of hiding. And that's cool, I know you weren't ready to tell people, but I wanted to get out there and live life. I didn't mean for it to happen like this, but Dylan just made me feel like I could. I hope we can still be friends.
Nate: That's OK.

Wow. I put my phone on airplane mode and crank the music volume up. After the original song, there are five remix versions, which gives me ample time to dwell on the fact that, once again, I find myself watching everyone else doing their thing and getting on, while I sit quietly on the sidelines, wishing, so hard and so much, that I could do the same. Nate Harrison: a masterclass on missing out on life. Maybe this whole thing was my fault? I feel like I don't ever want to open my eyes again, just lie here and shut it all out, but I eventually let my eyes drift open and there's Jack standing at the foot of my bed, grinning demonically.

"ARGH! Get out!" I scream, flinging my headphones off and sitting bolt upright. "How did you get in?"

Why the hell can't he leave me alone? Why is he intent on making everything a million times worse? I would have quite happily skulked at the back at the orientation today. It would have been shit, but at least everyone would soon have forgotten about me. But no! He has to make it all about him. It's all about Jack! Jack, Jack, bloody Jack!

"'Total Eclipse of the Heart'?" Jack says. "I'd know that bass line anywhere."

"*Get. Out.* Why are you here?"

"I've been talking with your folks."

I glare at him.

"We have a proposal."

I open my mouth to give it to him, but—

"Please do *not* reply with something along the lines of 'Well, *I propose* you get out of my room,'" Jack says.

"Well, I do propose that!"

"I'll be downstairs," he replies, smiling and heading out of the door.

I'm boiling over with so much fury and indignation I honestly don't know what to do with myself, so I kick my wastepaper basket across my room.

"Nate!" Mum's voice calls up from downstairs. "What are you doing up there?"

I want to scream. I *do* scream.

"NATE!" Mum again. "Don't make me come upstairs!"

I silently jump about on the spot, arms flailing, while I mouth, *Fuuuuuuuuuck oooooooofffffff!* I make a huge, exaggerated jerking off gesture at the door. Then Mum walks in. I freeze. She just looks at me, slowly blinks, and says, "Whatever you're doing, stop it and come downstairs."

She turns, leaves, and I bow my head and follow her out.

My dad and Jack (legs crossed, all serene) are in the lounge, waiting. "Sit down," Mum says.

I plonk myself on the end of the sofa. Jack's at the opposite end examining his fingernails. I flick my eyes to Dad.

"So!" Dad begins. "An idea for you! You're not keen on this road trip id—"

"Road trip *with structure*," Mum interrupts.

"Road trip *with structure* idea of ours, so we have a thought for you."

Finally. Hopefully they're about to suggest I can stay here and do my own thing for the summer.

"After all, you're sixteen, and of course you don't want to spend all your time with your loving family," Dad continues.

"Dad, it's not that—"

"You want to spend time with people your own age," Dad says.

I release a breath. Thank god, they're just going to leave me alone. "OK. Thank you," I say.

"That's fine, you're welcome," Dad replies. "So that's why we've asked Jack if he wants to come along on the trip too."

My eyes widen as the blood drains from my face.

"It'll be nice for you to have a boy your own age around!" Mum chirps.

I open my mouth, trying to form words.

No.

God, *NO!* I don't want this trip at all! What's wrong with just being sad and on your own? And even if I did want to go, being on the trip *with* Jack? I could go on tour with a circus clown belting show tunes through a PA system and it would be less embarrassing and more chill than spending weeks in close proximity to Jack. *Oh god!* Everything is wrong. *Everything.*

I start shaking my head. "I, no, I don't want a boy my own age, I've just been left heartbroken by a boy my own age, I hate boys my own age, they're the absolute worst."

"It'll be nice for you to have a friend, Nate!" Mum says, smiling like there's no problem here. "Someone to talk to, *someone who knows exactly what you've been through—*"

"Oh, please, god, no," I mutter.

"Jack could be a bit like a therapist!" Mum declares.

I look at her in disbelief. "He's not a therapist! He's a . . . self-centered egotist!"

"Harsh and hurtful," Jack says.

"Apologize," Mum tells me.

"No."

"Say you're sorry. That was mean," Mum insists.

I clamp my mouth shut.

Dad grins. "Well, you know who *loves* boys who are rude?"

I inhale sharply. "Dad, *no*." I turn quickly to Jack. "Sorry, Jack."

"Do we know who loves boys who are rude?"

Jack is all ears. "Who? Who loves them?"

"Nate?" Dad grins, flexing his fingers.

"OK! I'm being nice! I've apologized to Jack! I'm . . . please, can you just—" I indicate Jack. "*No*."

"Tickle Monster!" Dad declares, launching himself at me, waggling his fingers.

I scream and try to dart out of his grasp, but he's too quick, he's got me, and my humiliation is utterly complete as he starts to actually tickle me like a small kid. Worse, I am super ticklish, so it looks like I'm probably enjoying this.

When he's done, I'm gasping on the floor, exhausted and spent.

"Have a chat with Jack—offer's there," Dad says.

He and Mum leave.

Jack runs his tongue over his lips. "So, that was tremendous."

I scramble back up to the sofa.

"If you don't want me to come, I won't," he says.

"How did this even come up?"

"I don't know, your parents suggested it."

"And you agreed! Why would you do that? Why would you want to come on their stupid trip anyway?"

He shrugs. "I know it would have been a pretty crappy summer. It's just it would have been a little less crappy than staying in town, constantly bumping into Dylan and Tariq being love's young dream. But it's fine, forget it, I won't come."

"Good."

"Sure. You, your folks, and your little sister in a bus. It'll be just like *Priscilla, Queen of the Desert*, minus the drag queens and all the fun."

I close my eyes because, as God is my witness, I am not spending the summer in a VW bus with my family. And why Jack even considered it might be a good idea is beyond me. We've barely spoken for three years. We've only been brought back together by some treachery of the highest order—that's not a basis for restarting a friendship, especially when we blatantly do nothing except irritate the hell out of each other.

"Jack, I'm not going anywhere in a bus with anyone. Not gonna happen. You know, and maybe this thing with Tariq and Dylan will blow over and he'll . . . well, whatever."

Jack squints at me. "I'm sorry, *what?* You're expecting Tariq to come back to you?"

I shrug. I don't really know if I think that or not. Maybe, with me coming out at prom, Tariq can see I'm changing. Maybe he'll start to see we could be "out there" and "living life" after all. But whatever. I have no intention of discussing any of this with Jack of all people.

"Oh, OK. You're serious. Amazing."

"Whatever. I'm just going to have a quiet summer here, doing my thing."

"Oh please! Doing what?" Jack laughs. "You'll just spend your entire summer masturbating. It's horribly inevitable."

I close my eyes and take a breath. "That's simply not true."

ELEVEN

JACK

So I walk out of Nate's house, and that's that. He's not up for it, *whatever.*

And, like, the very next day, I see him at the pharmacy, and he's literally holding a bottle of hand lotion and a box of Kleenex, and I don't need to say anything. I just raise my eyebrow, and he knows. *He knows.*

TWELVE

NATE

Jack's face at the pharmacy says it all. I know *exactly* what he's thinking and, just so we're clear, I'm buying Sudocrem because I have this patch of eczema on my forearm that comes up when I get stressed.

Also, tissues are tissues, there's nothing going on there, not that I have to explain myself to anyone. Jack can go to hell with his suggestive eyebrow raising and knowing smirks.

Anyway, the next day, I'm applying the aforementioned healing cream and wiping my greasy fingers on a tissue when Jack appears in my bedroom again, my parents clearly just treating him like a member of the family and letting him come and go as he pleases.

The fact he doesn't immediately crack a joke about the scene he has walked into puts me on edge.

He doesn't speak. He just hands me his phone, which is displaying the most recent post on Dylan's Instagram account: him and Tariq in the first pic, a couple of plane tickets in the second pic, Dylan kissing Tariq on the cheek in the third pic, and the pair of them clinking cocktail glasses together, laughing, in the final pic. And it begins to occur to me that Tariq seems to quite like Dylan. You know, there's a lot of smiling and happiness going on in the pics, a lot of love, and the dull ache that's been in my stomach for days suddenly becomes a stabbing pain, and I feel a bit sick, and cold, and, and, huh, I think the odds of me getting Tariq back just got a whole lot worse.

THIRTEEN

JACK

I needed him to see this. I don't deny part of it is selfish: I wanted someone to be indignant with. But also, Nate needs to stop being in denial—Tariq ain't coming back anytime soon, and hard as it is, the sooner Nate can accept that, the better.

He's pacing the room, rubbing the back of his neck, chewing his lip, and staring at the screen. "'Summer with this one'?" he mutters, reading the caption. "*This one?* God, I hate that phrase. Why can't you just use his name? 'This one' is second only to 'the boy' in the league of top phrases used by douchebags!" He clears his throat and glances at me. I nod my agreement. Other than grown adults who count down to a significant event by telling you how many "sleeps" remain, it's the absolute worst.

"Loads of stuff planned, and just booked for Ibiza later in August, flying Club Europe?" Nate scoffs. "Ha! Courtesy of Tariq's minted dad, that is! 'Summer of *frigging* love'? I mean, that sounds . . . corny?"

He looks at me again. I nod again.

"How is this even a thing? How has it got so many likes?" He scratches at his forearm. "Hashtag living our best frickin' life? Hashtag gay? Hashtag Instagay? Hashtag gay boys? Hashtag gay couple? I dunno, do you think they're possibly *gay* or something?" He throws the phone on his bed. "AAAAARGGHHH!" he screams. "They're such DOUCHEBAGS! Such utter DICKS! Fuck me, I HATE THEM BOTH!"

"Good, Nate, goooood," I purr. "Let the hate flow through you!"

"SHUT UP!" he barks. "What's in the comments?"

"Don't read them," I tell him.

"Let me see."

He grabs the phone again and scrolls down, his breathing erratic. And then he collapses on his bed.

"Please don't cry," I tell him.

But he's consumed with tears. I probably shouldn't have shown him, though at least it looks like he's running the full gamut of all the stages of grief, so I guess that's good?

"Why did they have to do this?" he sobs. "Why is everyone so happy for them? Why does no one else see that they've completely screwed us over and now they're acting like everything's fine? I don't get it. I don't get any of it."

"Well," I say. "That's probably more to do with me than anything."

"Why, what have you done now?"

He's staring at me, and I can't take it, so I drop my eyes to the floor. "I haven't *done* anything, Nate. It's just me, isn't it? People don't like me." I fiddle with the bracelet around my wrist. "The bullying only stopped when I got together with Dylan, and now I'm not, the knives are out." I feel a thickness in my throat, but then I remember it's Nate I'm talking to, so it doesn't matter. He won't use it against me.

"It's not everyone. You've got friends."

I look back up at him, and it's his turn to look away. For a moment I wish it was like it used to be, when he'd put an arm around my shoulders and tell me to ignore the haters. He starts scratching at his arm again.

"You'll make it worse," I tell him.

He stops scratching, grabs the phone, and starts going through the rest of Dylan's pictures, sniffling, probably barely able to see the screen through the blur of tears. He's a mess. I'm a mess too, but right now, I'm less of a mess than him, and this has got to stop. Dylan and Tariq have already ruined prom, and they're about to ruin our summer. And one thing I'm sure of—I don't think you should allow other people to dictate your happiness.

"Nate?" I say gently. "We need to turn this around."

He doesn't reply, just laughs contemptuously.

"Only we have the power to do that."

"What the hell are you talking about?" he mutters, wiping his eyes with the palms of his hands.

I turn an idea around in my head. "They're not the only ones who can have a good summer."

He laughs again. "Oh, sure, I mean if they could see us now!"

"They don't have to win—"

"They've already won! Don't you see? They've won! They're kissing and drinking cocktails and booked to fly Club Europe, and I'm—"

"Sitting on your bed, surrounded by jerk-off tissues, crying at Instagram."

He looks up at me and takes a deep, unsteady breath. "Sudocrem!" he barks at me. "I have a patch of eczema!"

"Right, well, as fabulous as all that sounds, I think we can do one better."

He looks at me with dead eyes.

"We'll have an amazing summer too."

"Bullshit. How?"

"OK," I say. "So this has literally just occurred to me—"

"We're not doing the thing with my parents."

"And I think doing the thing with your parents is the perfect opportunity."

"Brilliant." He looks like he's about to cry again.

But I reckon this is possibly my best idea ever. A way to wipe the smug smile off Dylan's face, to show the world I've moved on . . . and hey, maybe even to gain enough followers to finally launch myself as an influencer and have some brands want me to review their new cosmetics or herbal teabags. I'm going to get over this thing, and if I'm getting over it, I'm bringing Nate with me, kicking and screaming if I have to. It might have been three years since we were properly friends, but I'm not going to leave him behind, wallowing in his grief, unhappy and unloved. Nate deserves better than that.

"Hear me out," I tell him. "Social media is a lie. We all know it, but we all buy into it anyway. Instagram is only ever the highlights reel, right? Famous for it. It's the best bits, carefully curated to make the world think you're happy, successful, or whatever. And believe me, you can dress up pretty much anything to look fabulous. Things can look fabulous when really they're . . ." I swallow and glance away briefly.

"They're not?" Nate offers.

"Huh? Exactly!" I give him a huge smile. "Highlights reel, baby! This has every chance of being the worst summer road trip ever, with your parents, of all things. But we could make it look amazing . . . if we fake it! Me and you, on the road together! How do our followers know that road is really the A46 to the arse-end of nowhere? Having the time of our lives! If I say we are, then it must be true, right? What better way to show Dylan and Tariq—"

Nate groans and throws himself back on his bed, staring up at the ceiling.

"What better way to show *everyone* that Jack and Nate are happier than ever before? Happier, out there, living life!"

Nate carries on staring at the ceiling, chewing his lip. "Happier, out there, living life?"

"Right!" I say.

Nate sits up again, a look of determination on his face. My eyes widen in anticipation.

"No," he mutters finally.

I sigh. I feel my whole body deflate.

"Not just a highlights reel. If we're gonna do it, it's got to be the best, the most *epic* highlights reel ever."

* * *

Mum is characteristically unconcerned about the fact I've packed a load of bags and am clearly leaving the house.

"I'm going on a summer road trip," I tell her.

She doesn't look up from the piles of papers she's sifting through on the dining table. "Sounds lovely."

"Uh-huh."

I wait to see if there's any more—I don't know, some parental objection, some questions—but there isn't.

"So, yes," I continue, "I'm basically just going with these two middle-aged blokes I met hanging around the children's playground?"

"Mmm . . ."

"One of them isn't actually allowed to drive after he lost his license, but the other one is fine to, as long as he's had a few drinks to stop his hands shaking at the wheel."

"Yup . . ."

"They've asked me to take as many packets of Sudafed as I

can lay my hands on, but I guess they're just worried about nasal congestion, right?"

Mum looks up at me. "Nate's mum called me last night, but very amusing, Jack."

"Huh."

"Sounds like a nice idea. I didn't realize you and Nate were still friends."

"Well, we're . . . we're *not*, really. I mean, I don't think. Not like we used to be."

Mum nods. "Sounds dreary. I've put some money in your account."

"Amazing. Thank you."

She taps her pen up and down on the table. "If by any chance you're passing near Norwich, why don't you message your cousin and see if he's about?"

"Elliot? Pourquoi?"

Mum shrugs, which is a super-suspicious reaction from her. "He's your *cousin*, and you haven't seen him for a couple of years."

"Uh-huh."

"Be nice for you all to hang out, maybe. Do whatever it is teenage boys get up to."

"OK, you made that sound a lot more gross than was necessary," I say.

Mum flicks her eyes to mine. "All I'm saying is I spoke to Jane last night and I think Elliot might appreciate spending a little time with you."

The cogs in my head turn. "*Ohhhhhh. Is he a gay boy now?*"

"Well," Mum says, hesitating just enough that I know it's true.

"Elliot's come out?"

"You know, that's not completely what Jane said, but reading between the lines . . ."

"What lines? What's he done?"

"Taken up the ukulele and joined an LGBT youth group."

"OK, only one of those things is indicative of him definitely being gay, Mum—he might have gone to the youth group simply to support a friend."

"Anyway," Mum says. "If you're passing."

"Sure." I check the time on my phone. "OK, they'll be here in a minute. I love you, I'll be careful, I won't drink, I won't do drugs, I won't have sex."

Mum rolls her eyes and gets up to give me a hug. "Have fun."

"OK."

"Call me."

"OK, but also we're Instagramming the whole thing."

Mum frowns. "Seriously, just text me occasionally to confirm you're not dead—you don't need to add me to some account you'd probably rather keep private."

"No, this account is public. Very much so. That's kinda the point. It's not the secret one that I use to share deeply inappropriate content with strangers." I grin at her. "@TheHeartbreakBoys because, you know, overcoming hurt, angst, and torment is what the people want. Living our best lives to get revenge on our exes." I do a sad face.

New start, new account. My other public account has been

shedding followers faster than Mr. Fowler (geography teacher) sheds dandruff. Plus, my old account was full of pics of *Dylan*. I set up this new one last night after Nate finally agreed to everything, and it already has a good handful of followers, even though we haven't posted anything yet.

When Dylan and Tariq discover it—which they will because as soon as we've got our first pic, I'll follow them both, so they'll get a notification—they'll start to get a taste of their own medicine. They started this thing, and while they might, possibly, have won round one, that's where it'll end. I'm not going to return to school in September as the loser. Nope. Dylan or no Dylan, I'll be back happier, more fulfilled, and more successful than ever. Even if I have to fake it. Gonna have a good summer, are they? Well, we're gonna have a *spectacular* one.

FOURTEEN

NATE

Happy. Out there. Living life. If that's what Tariq sees when he scrolls through our pics, maybe he'll feel differently about us. Am I deluded? But Tariq was *my* boyfriend before he went off with Dylan, so why can't I win him back? I want him back. Despite everything, that's what I want. As soon as I agreed to the idea, my parents and Jack immediately swung into action, and before I knew it, everything was packed, everything was happening. And now here I am, rammed in the back of the bus among all the bags, already way too hot because there's no air-conditioning and it's nearly ninety degrees outside, with Rose asking a series of questions that are going to be awkward if she carries on after we've picked up Jack:

"Who is Jack, exactly?"

"He's a . . . *friend.*"

"*Boy*friend?"

"Just friend. You remember him."

"No, I don't." Pause. "Do you *love* him?"

"Definitely not."

"Will you marry him?"

"Why would I marry him?"

"Boys can marry boys."

"Rose, I know they can, and that's great, but just because we're both boys doesn't automatically mean we're going to marry each other."

And that was all before we'd even backed out of our driveway.

But I have to do this thing. I want Tariq to *see* happy, fun-loving Nate. All smiles and . . . and whatever else happy people are when they're busy living their lives. Sunshine and rainbows, I don't know.

We pull up outside Jack's, where he's already waiting with a collection of Louis Vuitton suitcases of varying sizes, one of those bags you carry suits in, a smaller holdall thing (also Louis Vuitton), and sitting on top of it all, a pack of six cartons of chocolate milk.

"Jacky-boy!" my dad says, like they're already best mates.

"Mr. Nate!" Jack replies. Then he nods at my mum. "Morning, Mrs. Nate."

Jack always used to call my parents Mrs. Nate and Mr. Nate, because that's what he did when he first met them, when he was five, and it stuck because everyone deemed it hilarious.

"Traveling light, I see," Mum says.

Jack nods gravely. "I know. I think I'll be able to get by, but I have had to make a lot of sacrifices."

Mum gives him a tight-lipped smile.

Dad starts loading Jack's stuff into the bus, while I remain in my seat, staring into the middle distance, wondering what Tariq and Dylan are up to right now, until Jack starts tapping at the window to my right. I turn to him. *What?* I mouth through the glass.

"Get out!" he tells me. "We should Instagram this!"

"Instagram *what*, exactly?"

"The start of the trip! Get out!"

I shake my head in disbelief. I'm on board with giving this a go, faking an amazing summer or whatever, but I'm not sure a picture of me and Jack outside his house (expensive and nice as it is, thanks to having a lawyer mum) is going to achieve that.

"Nate!" Jack shouts. "Come on!"

I sigh and scramble out of the bus and around to the front, where Jack is brandishing his phone, experimenting with potential angles for our first photo. "So, what? Just a selfie or something next to the bush?"

Jack squints at me. *"A selfie next to the bush?"*

"Seems like a . . . nice bush? Nice flowers on it."

"Next to the bush?"

I sigh. I'm so crap at social media—that's why I usually don't bother with it. And I realize now that fact puts me entirely at the mercy of Jack and his whims, but this scheme is happening, I agreed to it, so I guess I have no choice but to go along with whatever he suggests. "OK, so what, then?"

Jack looks around, pulling his mouth in various directions as he contemplates options. "On top of the bus," he finally says.

"Really?" That seems like a lot of effort.

"First pic, Nate! It's gotta be a good one! Both of us, sitting atop this fine, majestic beast!" He gives the bus a firm slap, and a large piece of rust falls off. "The sun's in the sky and the boys are on the road! Actually, that's a *great* caption for it, remember that; god, I'm good at words."

I shake my head. "Fine—"

"Up you get!" Jack says. He laces his hands together in front of him. "Here, I'll give you a step up."

I place my left foot on his hands.

"One, two, THREE!"

And he thrusts upward so I smash, splat, into the side of the bus, nowhere near the roof.

"Pull yourself up! Swing your leg!" Jack tells me.

I laugh to myself at the very idea. *Pull myself up? With these arms?*

"Nate, what *are* you doing?" I hear Mum ask.

"He wants to get a photo," Jack tells her, which is really irritating, because obviously this was all his idea. "He wants to sit on top of the bus!"

"Ooh, good idea!" I hear Mum say. "I can send it to Auntie Karen—she's always bombarding us with photos of her kids being happy and successful!"

I can feel myself slipping off. Physically *and* mentally.

"Do you want us to push your arse?" Jack asks. "Give you an arse boost?"

"No!"

But they do anyway, and then I've got Jack, Mum, and then Dad all "arse-boosting" me up as I scramble and pull myself onto the roof. "Jesus," I gasp.

Jack's looking up at me. "I forgot there's a step stool in the garage. I'll just get it."

I glare at him as he nips off to get the stool, returns, ascends the steps, and hops onto the roof next to me. "That would be an easier method," he tells me.

"No shit."

"OK, Mrs. Nate?" Jack calls down. "Are you good with a camera?"

"I won a photography competition in secondary school," Mum replies. You would think this was the proudest moment of her life, the amount she goes on about it. I think a big part is that her sister, Karen, came second, and this is Mum's one major achievement over her. She gets her phone out and starts tapping at the screen, trying to find the camera function—a process that could potentially take five hours.

Jack turns to me. "What is that artifact in your mother's hands?"

"It's a Nokia." Jack's eyes widen.

"Mrs. Nate!" Jack hands his iPhone to my mum. "Use mine. It'll be easier for me to upload after. It's ready to go, you just have to press the button." Jack turns back to me. "Happy, big smiles, Nate! And we'll stretch our arms out wide, like, *Hello, world, here we come!'* type of thing."

I shake my head. "Is that a thing?"

"Ready, Mrs. Nate?"

"I think your phone's gone off . . ."

"Passcode is 6969," Jack tells her.

"Jesus," I mutter.

"What?"

"6969?" I say. I have no problem with Jack's lewd and attention-seeking passcode. I might normally even crack a smile, *if he wasn't chatting to my mum!* But embarrassing me in front of my folks is something Jack always used to love doing (example: the time, age twelve, he "innocently" asked my mother what "boner" meant), and one of the many reasons why him coming on this trip still fills me with dread.

Jack squints at me. "My mum's birthday? June 9, 1969?"

"Oh."

"OK, ready?!" Mum says, aiming the phone like it's a piece of alien technology.

"Plus, mutual oral sex!" Jack grins, flinging his arms out, his left one smack into my chest, knocking me off balance.

"Argh!" I squeal as I fall back, then slide off the roof, topple over the edge, crash down, but snag the leg of my shorts on the side mirror, so I'm sort of hanging off the bus, upside down, head on the ground, legs in the air, my balls all caught up somewhere in this complicated side-mirror-in-my-shorts nightmare.

"Oh, that's a brilliant shot!" Mum says, looking at the screen.

"I got the exact moment you hit Nate with your arm, and there's this look of surprise on his face, and one of joy on yours, and he's falling back, so there's this real energy about it—"

"Mum? Dad? Anyone?" I mutter.

"So *vibrant*!" Mum continues. "And so *funny*!"

Jack has hopped off the roof and is looking too. "Oh, yeah, that's the one. That's the shot! I can see why you won that contest, Mrs. Nate!"

"Still got it!" Mum says.

"Still here!" I shout out.

Mum, Dad, Jack, and Rose gather around me.

"I'll help you down," Jack says.

"Are you Nate's BOYFRIEND?" Rose asks.

"Ha!" Jack laughs. "Just friend."

"Do you love him?"

I close my eyes because, *really*?

"Rose, I *adore* him. What's not to love about a boy so awkward he's literally hanging off a VW bus by his gym shorts."

"They're not gym shorts," I mutter. "What do you think I am?"

"Whatever you are, we can remedy it," Jack replies.

"I'm sorry, I didn't realize I was meant to dress up for a five-hour drive on the highways of England."

"Dress to impress!" Rose announces.

"A girl after my own heart," Jack says.

Rose smiles, a demonic twinkle in her eyes. "I think you should marry my brother."

"WILL SOMEONE PLEASE HELP ME DOWN, FOR THE LOVE OF SWEET JESUS?!"

"He's very grumpy," Rose says to Jack in the voice that six-year-olds think is a whisper but is actually like a foghorn.

"Well, that's puberty for you," Mum says. I groan.

Jack laughs. "Come on, you grumpy pubescent mess, let's get you down from there." He grabs me around the waist, lifts me up to detangle the legs of my shorts, and helps me to my feet. I brush myself down, stomp back around to the other side of the bus, and plonk myself back in the seat.

"And uploaded!" Jack trills from outside, looking up from his phone. "The games have commenced!"

FIFTEEN

JACK

I offer this information entirely without comment, but we pull up at what I can only describe as a "checkpoint" at the entrance to the campsite (complete with barrier and guard booth) at the exact moment a stricken figure is being loaded into an ambulance and a rabid woman is being carted off by two police officers into a van screaming, "That's what yer get for bein' a cheatin' bastard! Wendy said I should never 'ave married yer!"

Actually, I *will* comment: this place is very clearly hell on earth. I'm pretty sure Mr. Nate described our first stop as "wild camping"—getting back to nature, spending the night under the stars. It sounded very enriching and incredibly Instagrammable. And this is not.

The guard hands Mr. Nate some paperwork. "Sector D5," the guard says, like this is some sort of dystopian thriller. "Right next to the toilet block."

I turn to Nate. "Bliss!"

He just looks at me and doesn't respond. I think he might have become brain-dead during the five-hour journey here.

"The canteen does food between five fifteen p.m. and six . . ."

"An oddly specific and narrow window," I mutter.

"Here's a voucher for a free plastic cup of wine, beer, or soda at the bar. Children must be supervised at all times . . ."

I glance across as two feral twelve-year-old boys who look like bulldogs in tank tops kick the shit out of each other on the yellowing grass.

". . . and please take your own toilet paper if you use the toilets—it's not provided. Have a nice stay."

"Thanks, mate!" Nate's dad says. He seems happy. I don't understand.

We chug around the site, eventually locating Sector D5 next to the picturesque toilet block, which boasts a sign that reads: *Warning! Asbestos!*

Our small patch of heaven is littered with cigarette butts, a manky chicken takeout box complete with gnawed thigh bones, and, more alarmingly, a discarded pair of women's underwear.

"This is what it's all about!" Mr. Nate says, hopping out of the bus, stretching his arms in the air, and taking a deep breath.

I turn to Nate again. "Is your dad OK?"

"He's had a pretty rough year," Nate mutters. "Happiness is relative, I guess?"

"It's only a couple of nights, right? Then we move on," I reply, as brightly as I can. I mean, I'm aware this is terrible, but we have to somehow make it work. "How bad can it be?"

Barely thirty minutes later, and I see just how bad it can be.

So, I've quickly established that we absolutely can't take any wide shots—there are just too many appalling things that we'd get in the background. What we can do is some nice close-ups, and I convince Nate that we'll get one of me and him, just sitting around a simple gas burner with a camp kettle on top of it, and we can do one of those stripped-back, enjoying-the-simple-life type of posts that is all about freeing yourself of the unnecessary clutter of modern life (e.g., bad boyfriends) and getting back to the basic things while holding a blue-and-white tin mug. Me and Nate will be in our hoodies, and I've told him we need to aim for a look of "natural chill" on our faces—so nothing that looks posed, just something that captures a moment.

The first issue is that expression is really hard for Nate to pull off, and in every photo he looks bored.

"That's just my face," Nate says.

"Well, can you try to do something else with it?"

125

"You said natural!"

"*Looks* natural, I said."

Nate tuts. "Do you have to sit so close to me?"

"It's a *selfie*! How am I supposed to get us both in *and* the camping stove?" I wait for some sort of response but get none. "Also, we're sharing a tent, Nate, so you might as well get used to me being in close proximity to you. *Wow.*"

"I like my own space. It's nothing personal."

"Well, it sounded pretty personal."

"Well, it wasn't."

"OK, well, it sounded it."

"So I *sound* personal, but I don't *look* natural? Fuck this," Nate says, heaving himself up.

"Stop! Where are you going? We haven't gotten the photo yet!" I get up and grab him by the sleeve of his hoodie.

He takes a deep breath but doesn't turn to look at me. "Fine, then get someone else to take the photo, and then we can go and get some food."

OK, he's hungry. That's probably why he's grumpy. I glance around to see if there's anyone nearby who looks like they won't steal my phone if I ask them to take a pic. The options are:

- Bald, middle-aged white man, beer belly, St. George's flag tattoo, who has just called his dog a "bender" for trying to sniff another dog's bottom.

- The two twelve-year-old boys who look
  like bulldogs in tank tops.

On balance, I feel my chances are higher with the boys. "Lads?"
I call over to them. I obviously hate using the word "lads," but I
want this over as soon as possible and with no incident.

The boys look over to me, seemingly sniff the air like feral
wolves, glance at each other, then start to approach.

"All right, lads, yeah," I continue, adopting the tone of the
common man, "can you take a quick photo of me and my mate?"

"Gis your phone, then," one of them says, holding a grubby
hand out.

"OK, so . . ."

He snatches my phone from me. "Nice phone. You rich?"

"We're here, aren't we?"

They stare at me.

"I saved for it."

The boy turns my phone over in his hand.

"Just take the photo," Nate says.

"Oi! Little bit of respect for the photographer!" the second boy
says.

Nate's eyes widen and he starts scratching at his forearm.

I clear my throat and look at the boys. Time to bring them
onside before they batter us. I know they're twelve, but they're
scary and fearless and probably have "blades" or whatever the
youth call them these days. "See the match today?"

"What match?" the first boy says.

"The . . . soccer match."

The boy squints at me. "Which one?"

I don't know why this is so hard. I literally hear straight guys say that line all the time, and the other straight guy always seems to know what is being referred to.

"Let's just take the photo," Nate says.

"You gonna cuddle up, then?" the second boy says.

"Ha ha ha ha!" I say. "We're just gonna sit around this camping stove. Try to get us looking relaxed and natural, ideally with a bit of the flame from the stove in the bottom of the shot. We'll just pose with these simple metal camping mugs—make sure they're in shot too."

"Righto," the first boy says, kneeling down to get his angle, which I must admit impresses me.

Nate sighs as I pass him one of the mugs, and I sit down next to him. "Yes, so, I've always enjoyed laughing in a relaxed way!" I say, laughing in a relaxed way.

"What the hell are you saying?" Nate asks.

"I'm talking, so the picture can capture us in mid relaxed conversation!" I explain. "Jesus, Nate, surely that's obvious?"

"I'm still shooting!" the boy says.

"Just laugh, Nate. All you have to do is laugh. And if you can't do that, just talk to me."

"Saying what?"

"Improvise. Impro-fucking-vise." I cannot believe how hard Nate is making this. I *get* that he's sad about Tariq, I *know* that this campsite is a long way from ideal, but unless I can somehow get him to smile and enjoy himself, he's not that great an actor that he's going to be able to fake the whole "time of our lives" thing, and this whole project will have been pointless.

Nate grits his teeth. "I hate you, I hate this, I wish I wasn't here."

"Ha ha ha ha ha!" I reply, entirely for the camera's benefit.

"Yeah, I think I got some good 'uns," the boy says, standing again and handing me back my phone.

I swipe through the photos. "Oh, these are good. Nice light." I show him.

"Huh, yeah, not bad." He smiles.

"Thanks," I say.

The boy nods.

"So, are you two . . . just friends?" the second boy asks.

"YES!" Nate says.

I roll my eyes. "We *are*," I confirm. "In the sense that we barely tolerate one another."

The second boy nods. "I'm Callum. This is my boyfriend, Parker."

I do my absolute best not to even skip a beat. "Well, that's awesome—welcome to Gaysville!"

"Huh?" Callum says.

"I mean, I'm gay too," I clarify.

Callum shrugs. "Yeah, I kinda thought, maybe." He glances at the Pride flag pin I forgot I had on my hoodie.

"The old gaydar!" I grin.

Callum makes little antennae on his head with his fingers. *"Beep, beep, beep, beep, beep!"*

I laugh. I love this. It's great that two twelve-year-olds can be this open to basically complete strangers.

"We're not out at school or anything yet," Parker says. "Just to Callum's parents and my mum."

The boys look over to where Nate is still sitting on the ground, but he doesn't look up, just continues to draw a circle in the dirt with his finger.

"Anyway, cool to meet you," Callum says.

"Yeah, have a nice stay," Parker adds.

And off they go, Parker giving Callum a playful push, Callum pushing him back, then they chase each other in a circle before Callum leaps on Parker's back and Parker runs off with him on piggyback.

And I never thought I'd feel jealous of a twelve-year-old in a campsite like this, but here we are.

"Huh," I say, sitting down next to Nate. "Well, there's a lesson. I've come here, I've made a whole load of terrible assumptions, I've *judged* this place and all the people in it, and actually, those lads, who I assumed were trouble, are the nicest gay kids."

"Too soon," Nate says.

"Too soon for what?"

"For you to have some epiphany about your flawed character on the first day of the road trip."

I let out a long, deep breath. "*Cynic.* I'm going to see the good in people from now on." I pat Nate on the leg. "Come on, let's go and get some lovely food from the canteen, make some friends, and have a nice evening."

* * *

The canteen food doesn't look amazing—the options are limp fish fingers, gray fatty burgers, or a tragic slice of pizza, with sides of chips, fries, or mashed potatoes—but maybe it will *taste* amazing. After all, you shouldn't judge on appearances! Nate is sitting miserably by himself at one of the far tables, unenthusiastically picking the tomato off his margherita pizza while I wait for the very nice man in front of me to finish loading his plate with burgers. Buoyed by my experience with the friendly lads, I need an icebreaker with this dude, and what better form of icebreaker than an ironic cliché?

"Come here often?" I quip.

The man freezes and turns his head toward me.

"Are the burgers good?" I continue.

He stares at me. "Are you having a laugh?"

His tone is . . . somewhat aggressive. I swallow and try to smile. "What? No. I just . . ."

"Do I *come here often?*" he snarls.

"That was a joke," I say.

"So you *were* havin' a laugh."

"Well, it was an ironic cliché, not really a joke—"

He stares at me, then glances at the Pride flag pin that's still on my hoodie. "Say that if you're chatting someone up."

"Well, not unless you're really bad at it. Ha!" He isn't laughing. "Ha ha ha." He still isn't laughing. "Ha."

He looks like he wants to smash my face in.

"I should smash your face in," he tells me.

"Yes," I say.

He's right up close to me. His breath is acrid with cheap beer.

"If you so much as look at me again, mark my words, *I will end you.*"

SIXTEEN

NATE

It's very hard to make sense of what Jack is saying because it's basically just a stream of words.

"I didn't even say anything bad I was just making funny small talk but he completely took it the wrong way why are people so angry like literally he went from normal to violent in three seconds flat what is wrong with everyone here I can't stand it it's awful and now he's said that if I even just look at him again he's going to end me he's going to *end me* Nate I mean what the actual hell and I think he's serious!"

I push the limp pizza slice to the edge of my plate. "Well, don't look at him then."

"But now he's said that, all I want to do is look!"

I shake my head. "Where's your food?"

"It's fine, I think I saw your dad has some Werther's Originals in the glove compartment. I'll just have a couple of them."

"Jack, much as I really don't care, you have to eat."

"I think we should go."

I shrug. "Fine." I think we should go too. Back home, preferably. I'd convinced myself that if I showed Tariq how I was happy and winning at life, he'd start to have second thoughts about being with Dylan. But now all I can think about is maybe those aren't the only reasons Tariq doesn't want to be with me anymore. Dylan is fantastically good-looking. He's got actual muscles. I reckon he has to shave too. You know, he's basically a *man*. And I'm not. I'm pretty much one hundred percent *boy*. So even if I can fake the summer of a lifetime, I can't fake the actual *me*, in which case, none of this stuff matters. I'm wasting my time.

"Fuuuuuuuuck," Jack whimpers.

I glance up and see he's locked eyes with a man I assume to be The Man Who Will End Him, who appears to be on his way back from getting a bottle of ketchup. Jack's just staring, unable to break his gaze, a deer in the headlights. The Man Who Will End Him makes a throat-slitting motion.

Jack gasps. "Get me out of here," he mutters. "I'm too young to die. At least at the hands of that oaf. I'd mind less if it was a yachting accident or a private jet crash."

"Come on," I say, pushing my chair back and standing up. The last thing I need right now is Jack causing yet another scene. All

I want is some peace and the chance to wallow in misery about Tariq, and maybe start reading some Camus and embrace my existential crisis. I don't have the energy for all this drama.

He keeps his head bowed, shuffling along, looking at the floor, and we make it to the entrance of the cafeteria and there's these little kids sprawled all over the floor, playing with toy cars, and Jack steps one way to avoid them, and then another, and then he just says, "Excuse me, please."

In a flash, a hard-faced woman with scraped-back hair and leggings is in front of us. "Why you speaking to my kids for?" she demands.

Jack takes an unsteady breath. "I just needed to get by."

"So why you speaking to them like you're more important?"

"I didn't!" Jack protests.

"Got as much right to be here as you 'ave!" the woman continues.

At which point Jack loses it. "They're playing in the bloody doorway! Does it really hurt your little brain that much to see they're in the way?"

"OH MY GOD!" the woman screams. "I'm fuming! Darren? DARREN?"

"Jack, come on," I say, trying to pull him away.

"Maybe," Jack says, "if you could parent your kids properly and make them understand this cafeteria is not a playground, we wouldn't have a problem."

Darren arrives on the scene, and of course, it's the same man who was going to "end" Jack. At which point I just grab Jack, who literally looks like he's on the brink of tears, pull him out of the canteen, and bundle him across the campsite as quickly as I possibly can.

"What the hell, Jack?" I say, as we hotfoot it toward our tent. "Why couldn't you just leave it?"

"*She* had a go at *me!*"

"Ugh!" I say. "Always drama!"

Jack stops dead.

"Now what?" I ask.

"What do you mean by that? Always drama? What's that about?"

I sigh. "Nothing. Come on."

"Oh, no, no, no. No. What did you mean?"

I meet his eyes. "I dunno, just that not everything has to be a big deal all the time."

"All the time?"

I break his stare and glance down at the ground. "Can we just chill out and go back to the tent?"

"Better just to take other people's shit, huh?" Jack says. "Better just to shrink away, say nothing, not stand up for yourself?"

I flick my eyes back to him. Maybe it's my paranoia or guilt, but does he mean what I think he means? Is this about year nine? "I don't want to talk about this."

"No change there, then."

We stare at each other for a few moments. I can see the hurt in his eyes and he's challenging me, seeing if I'm going to go there and admit it. Then, over his shoulder, way back at the entrance to the cafeteria, I see The Man Who is Going to End Jack struggle out, held back by three other blokes, shouting, "I'm gonna find that *fucker*!"

"We need to go. *Now*," I tell Jack.

"*Shit,*" he says, glancing back. "This chat continues later."

And we zip off in the general direction of our tent, but taking a detour in case we're being followed (Jack's idea), and all the while I'm thinking about what Jack's just said. How, for all this time, he's believed our friendship broke down because I'm a coward who didn't want to stick up for him against the bullies, who probably agreed with some of the teachers that Jack brought a lot of the trouble on himself by being so loud and proud. And, look, in some ways, that's true. I am a coward, I know I am—although in year nine, it wasn't for the reasons Jack clearly thinks. Not everyone has his confidence, so it's not that simple. It's not that simple, Jack! And just because something might be easy for you, doesn't mean it's easy for someone else. I know I owe him an explanation, but I barely understand it myself, so what do I even say?

* * *

I'm dreaming about Tariq. I'll spare you the exact details, but let's just say it's a nice sort of dream. He's lying next to me, so close I can feel his breath on my face, gently stroking my arm as he gazes longingly into my eyes . . . stroking my arm . . . pressing my arm . . . *jabbing* at my arm . . .

"OW!"

I'm awake. Eyes open. Jack blinking at me through the darkness, eyes wide. "He's outside," Jack whispers, voice wobbling.

"Who?"

"The bad man."

I sigh. "What time is it?"

"Three."

I wince. "Three a.m.? Just go to sleep, Jack."

"Can't," he says. "I've been awake all night. In case he comes." He leans closer in to me. "He's going to slash the tent with his knives."

"No, he isn't. Go to sleep."

"Someone's outside. I heard footsteps."

I take a deep breath and sit up in my sleeping bag. "Jack, we're at a campsite with a lot of other people. Maybe someone went to the toilet."

"Slow footsteps," Jack continues. "Footsteps like you might hear in a horror film. Like, step . . . step . . . step . . ."

"OK, I get the picture."

"And then . . . AH! AH! AH! AH! AH!" Jack screams, making a knifing action with his hand.

"Shut up!" I hiss.

Jack sighs and flops back down on his back. "So I did some research—"

"Tell me in the morning."

"OK, but I looked it up, because I overheard some other couple talking about these luxury cabins? Near here, apparently? So I googled it, and it's true, and you can get an actual luxury cabin in the woods, like the real deal, and they have one free tomorrow, so I booked it."

"*What?*"

"It's peak season, we were lucky," he explains.

"We're here with my parents!" I tell him. "I mean, I guess anything's better than here, but my folks are all about this being a family thing. I don't think it's in the cards for me and you to just go off to some shed in the forest."

"*Cabin.*"

"They'll never agree. Especially Mum."

"Well, it's booked now, so. I can't stay here. I'm persona non grata. Leave your folks to me—it's only one night, I'll talk them 'round. Plus, you'll love it. Plus, we'll definitely get some better pictures. And we need them, because guess who's started following our account?"

I flick my eyes to his.

"*Exactly,*" Jack says. "Judas and Iago. And they've recently posted a picture of—"

"Don't tell me. Just don't tell me."

Jack nods. "Were you dreaming about him?"

I close my eyes.

"You were saying some stuff. In your sleep."

"No, I wasn't."

"OK then."

We lie in silence for a bit.

I can't stand it. "What was I saying?"

"You were saying 'Boo Boo' a lot. Is that what you called him?"

I flinch at this private, slightly sickly thing now being public.

"Aww!" Jack adds. "That's cute."

It's because that's what Tariq used to say when he'd come and find me in the library—"Boo!" I sigh at the memory. God, I loved it when he did that. I would look forward to it through every morning class and then wait in hope at lunchtime, in case today would be the day Tariq would step out from behind a bookshelf or creep up behind me at a desk: "Boo!"

I miss him so much. I want to put my arms around him, but now someone else is doing that. It's unbearable, and I can't help it, a tear escapes and I wipe it away angrily.

"Do you want a hug?" Jack asks softly.

"I'm good, thanks," I tell him, even though I do, because you're right, Jack, I am a coward.

* * *

"Morning, sleepyhead!"

Jack's dressed in shorts, a T-shirt, flip-flops, and sunglasses, grinning at me from where he's standing beside Mum, who's cooking bacon and eggs on the camping stove. I blink at them through sleep-crusted eyes. "What time is it?"

"Seven!" Jack chirps, lifting his sunglasses up onto his head.

"*Shit,*" I mutter, starting to edge backward into the tent. Seven is not morning time. It's still night as far as I'm concerned.

"Don't you dare, Nate!" Mum says, brandishing her spatula, like she might use it to spank my arse. "You should take a leaf out of Jack's book—he's been up since six!"

"I've been up since six!" Jack confirms. "Best part of the day— the morning—right, Mrs. Nate?"

"Exactly!" Mum says.

I narrow my eyes at Jack. Sometimes I wonder if he's a real teenage boy, because a real boy wouldn't be as happy as he is to be up at such an ungodly hour. There's even science now that *proves* kids my age need sleep, so why the hell doesn't Jack?

"Coffee's ready!" Jack trills. "Coffee, sleepyhead?"

I groan at him.

"I shall take that as a yes — luckily I speak Grumpy Teen Boy!" He grins at my mum, who laughs at his joke. God, he is such a kiss arse.

He hands me a tin camping mug of coffee. "Two sugars, don't worry."

"How did you —"

"Know? I know everything." Jack smiles. "I'm very observant and caring."

I sip the coffee.

"So your parents are cool with *Le Plan*," Jack continues.

"What?" I mutter.

"Lovely idea!" Mum says, flipping the bacon. "Truth be told, it's the sort of place I implied to Linda at number fifty-five we'd be staying, so you can get the lowdown in case she asks — we don't want to be caught out." And then in a sentence that has more wrong with it than I can possibly get my head around, she adds, "And it'll be nice to have a bit of Boy Time with your best mate!"

I groan because I know this will just encourage Jack, and what do you know . . .

"Boy Time!" Jack agrees. "I love Boy Time, just the boys, being boyish!" He grins at my mum again and then winks at me.

* * *

So we're trudging along this ramshackle sidewalk (because it's "only the next village along"), Jack still in his pink shorts and flip-flops, pulling a Louis Vuitton case on wheels, and me in *not* my gym shorts and a red checkered shirt. "Look at you, a vision in gingham!" Jack said when I emerged from the tent. I didn't reply.

It's hot. And Google Maps is being worryingly vague about where exactly we are, currently positioning us in the middle of a patch of green, nowhere near a road.

"Aha!" says Jack, as we arrive at a bus stop. "I mean, we could walk, or we could just hop on the bus to the village."

"Jack, my parents would have given us a lift. Why did you claim you wanted to walk?"

"Nate, Nate, Nate," Jack coos. "I just think, if they see where we're staying, you know, all luxurious, fluffy towels, robes, and so on, it's just a bit awkward, right? Knowing they'll be staying in a literal shithole."

I mull it over for a second, then nod. "Yeah, I guess."

"But obviously I don't want to walk. We've already been on the road for nearly ten minutes and I'm practically in a coma. So. Yay for public transportation!" He consults the timetable.

"Fine," I say. I glance over the timetable too, then turn to Jack, who looks equally confused.

"The bus times are missing," Jack says.

142

"Right," I say.

"Because this just says the bus comes every Wednesday, and it's Friday today, which would mean the bus will come in five days' time, which is ridiculous. This is England in the twenty-first century."

I notice a sign with a phone number that purports to be a "Travel Hotline" but Jack's already on his cell. "The number's dead," he says. "Let's see what Google has to say."

He taps away at his phone, his brow becoming increasingly more furrowed. "Huh," he says. "Well, the timetable does not lie. There won't be a bus for five days."

"What if Google's wrong?"

Jack raises his eyebrows. "Google is never wrong. And do you want to live in a world where it is?"

I shake my head. I wish I could google: *Why did Tariq cheat on me?* and get a definitive answer. I wish I could google: *How can I get Tariq back?* I wish I could google: *How can I stop thinking about Tariq?* because, honestly, I'm doing my own head in.

"We'll just have to walk," Jack says. He narrows his eyes at the bus stop. "This bus stop is so homophobic."

After we round the bend in the lane, the sidewalk ends and Jack comes to an abrupt halt. "Where's the sidewalk?" he asks.

"I think we just walk in the road now."

Jack scowls at the sidewalk. "This sidewalk is so homophobic," he says.

It's about half a kilometer on when we see a signpost that

reads: *Public Footpath to Newton Ottery*, pointing over a stile in a fence and along a dirt track, through a wood. We both agree it'll likely be a more scenic, and hopefully quicker, route to where we need to be, so we hop over the stile and head on up the path.

And shortly after that, the killing starts.

SEVENTEEN

JACK

There's a fork in the path. The right-hand path leads deeper into the woods—and presumably to certain death, because that's how these things work. The left-hand path opens out into bright, light countryside—freedom, safety, and happiness.

So it's an obvious choice.

Well, it is for me. Nate wants to take the right fork because the village is in a north-easterly direction and he's convinced himself with some half-remembered mariners' sayings that because of where the sun is, we need to go right. But I don't like these woods—not because they're scary (they're not) but the ground is covered in pine needles and other spiky things, and they're getting all over my flip-flops.

"Where are you going?" Nate asks, as I skip off toward the left fork.

"Toward the village," I reply.

"It's *this* way," he says. "We need to go *right*."

"Well, I'm down this path now and I'm not walking all the way back."

"Jack, you're three paces away from me."

"I'm exhausted, Nate. I need to rest my lallies."

"You can rest your 'lallies' when we get to the barn, can't you?"

"*Not* a barn. *Cabin*." I lean weakly against a tree. "I'm fading fast."

"I'm not taking the left fork," Nate insists.

"Hmm," I say. "How shall we resolve this impasse?"

"Shall we toss for it?"

"Ooh! Isn't he bold?" I squeal.

I'm hoping all my campery will cheer Nate up, so he's nicely Instagrammable by the time we reach the cabin, but he just makes a frustrated growling noise. "Shut up, Jack. OK, fine, we'll take the left!" And he barges past me.

That boy is a tough nut to crack. But he'll thank me. This is definitely the right path and we'll be at the cabin in no time.

We emerge, blinking, into the glorious daylight, and it's a magnificent vista. It's open moorland, stretching for as far as you can see, just space and air and not a soul in sight. It's breathtaking. It's beautiful. It's going straight on Instagram.

The shot is simple enough even for Nate to get right. I'm standing in the center of the frame, arms outstretched, embracing the open space (and a possible promotional deal for a meditation app), and Nate takes the pic from behind me, so you just see my back, my outstretched arms and a huge expanse of countryside. We'll hashtag it up afterward, something about getting back to nature, breathing, mindfulness, that type of shiz. Dylan and Tariq are all about the capitalism with their plane tickets and cocktails. We're stripped back and real. I mean, I'd follow us.

So I'm standing there, eyes closed, the wind blowing gently on my face from across the moor, arms stretched out, doing my best to live in the moment to lend authenticity to this photo, and—

"Jack!"

"Have you taken it?"

"Jack!"

"Is that a yes?"

"Jack!"

"Jesus, Nate, all you—"

I open my eyes and freeze. Off to my right, in the distance, two men are running toward us WITH GUNS. Actual, literal guns. And before I can even think, let alone scream, there's a huge explosion and smoke starts billowing from down in a ditch to my left.

And then I hear the shots.

I am in pink shorts and *flip-flops*. I could run for my life, but what's the point? It'd be like Bambi trying to escape the Terminator.

"GET DOWN!"

It's Nate. He tackles me to the ground and throws himself on top of me, just as there's another explosion, more smoke, and another rattle of gunfire.

If this is it, if this is the end, I'm surprised to realize that my one wish is that I had been wearing better boxer shorts—just thinking of the staff at the morgue. And I don't know what's more alarming—the fact I'm in the middle of a war zone, or the fact I'm more concerned about my underwear. I guess extreme stress does weird things to people.

Just so you know, they're *Ralph Lauren*. I suppose not the end of the world, right?

There's the sound of heavy footsteps running toward us, a crackle of radios. "Hold fire! Hold fire!" I mean, Jesus Christ, what have we stumbled into?

"Lads? You OK?"

I can't look up because Nate is still firmly planted on top of me, but I can see a pair of heavy-duty army boots.

"What are you doing here?" the voice continues. "You lost?"

"Yes, lost!" Nate wails.

"We come in peace!" I add, because that's definitely a thing people say in these situations.

"This is an army reserves training exercise—this whole area is cordoned off to civilians," Boots says. "How did you get yourselves here?"

"We took the fork!" I mutter.

"I told you we should have taken the one further into the woods!" Nate says.

"The one into the woods leads to the village," Boots says.

Nate jabs me in my side with his elbow. "See!"

It's at this point, possibly with the realization we don't seem to be in any imminent danger, that my brain clocks the fact Nate basically protected me from the gunmen, and I wonder if that means, despite all outward indications to the contrary, that deep in his subconscious, some part of him still likes me.

"Should have been some cordon tape though, so you couldn't get down here," Boots continues.

"Tape?" I say. "Shouldn't it really be a fence? I dunno, call me Generation Snowflake, but explosions and bullets maybe warrant a little more than—" Nate forces my head into the ground, presumably to shut me up, but I manage a muffled, "Tape!"

Army Boots laughs. "It's not live ammo. They're just blanks. And they're smoke pellets to reduce visibility. There's actually no risk to anyone. Honestly, you two are *hilarious*."

Nate giggles. He actually *giggles*, which makes me super suspicious, so I wriggle and squirm out from underneath him, sit myself up, and, yep, just as I thought, Army Boots is hot. He must only be a few years older than us, nineteen tops, and apart from his buzz cut, he's a dead ringer for KJ Apa.

"Ugh," I groan, "so we go back the way we came, then?"

"Uh-huh," Army KJ Apa says. "I've got a map if you want to check your route."

We scamper after Army KJ Apa and "check the map" and I may, or may not, act more confused than I really am about how maps work so that he has to explain a few times and I giggle and bat my eyelashes and say, "Oh, you are clever!" but after we've done that, and after he tells me off for hiking in "inappropriate footwear" and I say I'm totally down for whatever punishment the army doles out for such footwear transgression (which he rolls his eyes at!) and after Nate says he's "thirsty" and he gives us both a drink of water (even though I'm pretty sure Nate didn't mean *that* type of thirsty), we're on our way again.

"Do we need to discuss how you tried to save my life?" I ask Nate, as we clamber over a fence, back into the woods.

"No."

"How you thought there were actual bullets and how you threw yourself on top of me?"

"No."

"OK, but that's what you did, so."

Nate sniffs. "I threw myself down. You just happened to be there."

I laugh. "Riiiight."

"Right. Why would I save your life and sacrifice mine?"

I shrug. "No idea."

Nate shakes his head and picks up the pace so he's walking in front of me. He's acting like he doesn't care, but as we trudge on, every so often he slightly glances back over his shoulder to check I'm still there, and I can't help but smile. And I'm thinking, you know what? If the only outcome of this trip turns out to be that Nate and I start talking again, then I reckon that would be good enough for me.

* * *

You see, it shouldn't be as hard as this, because on the map it seemed like a straight line, but somehow we must have gone wrong again, because it's several hours later and we don't seem to have found Raven Farm, which is where the cabin is meant to be. He hasn't said it explicitly, but it's clear Nate is blaming me. About an hour ago, he stopped the glancing-over-his-shoulder business and just stomped onward regardless. Literally, I could have fallen down an old well and he wouldn't have known. He also ate a Tic Tac about twenty minutes ago but didn't offer me one, which makes his feelings *very* clear.

In worse news, clouds have been gathering for some time, the light is fading, there's a light drizzle and, honestly, I think this might be the part where we die of exposure and it's actually The End. The idea of phoning for help did cross my mind, of course, and despite what usually happens in thrillers set in rural locations, there are four bars of full-fat 4G on my phone . . . or at least there were until my battery died. Meanwhile, Nate doesn't have any credit and is adamant we can't call the police because it's not an emergency, even though *I'm* adamant that my not having had access to iced coffee for four hours very much *does* constitute an emergency. Anyway, we're crossing yet another field, because Nate is convinced he saw a lane up ahead, and suddenly,

MOOOOOOO!

I mean, this *cry*, this *guttural wail*, honestly, it's terrifying. I slowly turn my head and see this vast beast standing behind us. It's huge. Surely cows are not this big? Surely this is the product of some genetic mutation that's escaped from a lab?

MOOOOOOOOO!

I jump, because it's so loud it vibrates through me. "What does it want?" I whisper to Nate.

"It's probably just saying hello."

"Like that?" It seems unlikely. The beast takes a few heavy steps toward us as we back into the hedge. "Offer yourself to it," I tell Nate, pushing him in front of me.

"Chill, it's just a cow."

"It has *horns*, Nate!"

"Some types of cows do have horns."

"Uh-huh?" I say. "What, the *bull* type, you mean?"

MOOOOOOOOO!

"It wants something." I look around. "What does it seek?" I gasp. "Milk?"

Nate screws his face up. "What?"

"It must want milk!"

"Why would it want milk?"

"It's a cow! That's what it drinks!"

"Jack, cows do not drink milk!" he snaps.

MOOOOOOOOOOO!

I scream. "Wahhhh! Ohhh! Nate! You've angered it!"

The cow gets closer, flaring its nostrils and licking its chops.

"There's some chocolate milk in my case," I whimper.

"You think feeding it the stolen mammary gland secretions of its friends is going to help, do you?"

"Then what, Nate? What? Oh, sweet Jesus, it's going to gore

us on its horns! And my shorts are pink! What if it mistakes them for red?"

But then, up ahead, joy of joys, a battered old Land Rover is coming toward us, so with the *chonky boi* just meters away, I risk waving my arms about and flag it down. The driver is an old guy, with a weather-beaten face, flat cap, and a permanent scowl, probably from a great many years of working the land in extreme weather or toiling in the cotton mill, I don't know.

"We've been cornered by this *absolute unit*," I shout as the guy gets out of the Land Rover.

He shakes his head and pats the cow on its rump. "Off you go, girl! Go on! *Hup! Hup!*"

The cow makes a few huffing noises, turns, shits everywhere, I'm talking buckets of the stuff pouring out of its arse, then meanders off. I just stare in utter horror at the ground. Why would anyone want to live like this?

"Can I help you, lads?' the man says.

"Please, sir," I say, for some reason adopting the tone of a Dickensian orphan. "We're looking for Raven Farm?"

The old guy frowns. "Old Man Cooper's place? What business have you there?"

OK, so I immediately don't like the sound of this "Old Man Cooper," his "place," and the idea that it wouldn't be obvious what "business" we had there when it's meant to be the location of a luxury cabin that's featured on various reputable vacation websites. But anyway. "We're meant to be staying there," I tell the guy.

There is a low rumble of thunder.

"Raven Farm's over yonder," he says, pointing toward a gate at the end of the field.

"*Yonder?*" I repeat. Why is it suddenly, like, 1836?

"'Bout a mile up the lane, then left at the old oak, along the dirt track 'bout another half mile. Entrance is opposite the abandoned mine."

Nate flicks his eyes to mine. "Abandoned mine?"

"Since the accident," the old guy says, shaking his head. "Terrible business."

"Well!" I say brightly. "This all sounds *perfect*, thank you for your kind help, and I'm *loving* the fact there are no road names in the country, only vague landmarks. We'll be on our way."

I turn and start to head off.

"Lads!" the old guy calls after me. "If you see any roadkill on your way, take it—there's usually a dead rabbit or a pheasant on the lane somewhere. If he's still got that old dog, the only thing that placates Daisy is the flesh of the fallen."

I nod my thanks and head off with Nate. "OK, gross, we're not doing that."

Nate is notably silent.

"I'm sure it sounds worse than it is," I say.

"What website did you find this place on?"

"Oh my god, literally Booking.com, I'm a hundred and ten percent confident it'll be fine!"

"You can't get a hundred and—"

"I know, but everyone says it anyway!"

There's another rumble of thunder.

We plow on.

Now it's really getting dark.

I can't tell you how much I wish I wasn't wearing flip-flops.

I'm not going to cry.

Eventually, we come to a big tree, which, since it's next to a dirt track, we assume is the "Old Oak," although there is literally no way of telling.

"Look," says Nate, pointing to a dead rabbit at the side of the lane.

"Yes?"

"Should we take it? For Daisy?"

I'm about to tell him *no, don't be ridiculous*, when we hear, in the distance, the most savage and ferocious barking that sounds more like a demonic wolf than it does a dog.

Nate swallows and looks at me. "If Daisy gets to us before Old Man Cooper, we might be in trouble."

"I'm not even considering this," I say, "but, hypothetically, how would we carry it?"

Nate pulls a plastic bag out of his backpack and glances at me, with a look in his eye of someone who is about to do something unutterably gross. Nate is unbelievable. You just know he'd be the first to tuck in to his fellow passengers in the event of a plane crash on a remote mountain.

"It's my dirty clothes bag," Nate explains. "Mum always makes us carry one, because it's easier to separate what's clean and what needs washing."

I shake my head. "Great. I love information about how other people handle laundry logistics." I cock my head at the dead rabbit. "Pick it up, then."

Nate chews his lip, then pokes round the side of the path, eventually finding a big stick, which he tries to wedge under the rabbit. But every time he manages to lift it up, the rabbit wobbles off and falls back to the ground.

This goes on for about five minutes, Nate repeatedly trying to pick the rabbit up with the stick, and the rabbit falling back down, until I find him another stick, so now he can—I'm sorry, this is obviously disgusting—skewer it with a pincer movement, and I close my eyes and hold Nate's dirty laundry bag open, and he drops the rabbit in.

And then it starts to rain.

We hurry up the dirt track, thunder echoing around us, as the rain gets harder and heavier, until we come to a ramshackle wooden sign, onto which the letters *Raven Farm* have been stuck.

But Nate isn't looking at that. He's looking at the other side of the road.

"Is it fine that there's a big stick with some sort of animal skull on top of it stuck in the ground?" he says.

I glance at it. Admittedly, it's not the sort of welcome I would expect of a "luxury" establishment.

At this point there is an actual crack of lightning, and suddenly a fearsome, craggy face is illuminated, right in front of us.

I can't help it, I scream again.

The man stares at me, death and murder in his eyes. "Jack

156

Parker?" he says. "Hope you didn't have trouble finding the place. I just need you to sign some paperwork, then we can get you settled in — have you brought a car?"

I shake my head. "We can't drive yet."

"No problem, son," he says. "Need any help with your—" He glances down at Nate's carrier. "What have you got there?"

"Rabbit," Nate mutters.

The man frowns.

"For Daisy?"

The man crosses his arms. "Daisy? Who's that, then?"

"Your . . . dog?" Nate says.

The man shakes his head. "Someone's been feeding you boys a pack of porkies! Ain't no dog by that name lives here. Who you been talking to, then?"

Nate's eyes are wide. "The man! He helped us . . . He said we had to be careful of the dog at Old Man Cooper's place — and the abandoned mine."

"OK, lads, that's Trevor Hardingham, absolute *dickwad* of a bloke, thinks he's funny, but all that is nonsense, OK? There's no mine here. No dog. And no one calls me 'Old Man Cooper,' OK? Leslie will do. Come on, I'll show you to the cabin." He heads off, muttering, "Why would you bring a dead rabbit for a dog anyway?"

"*Yes*, why, Nate?"

Nate glares at me.

We stumble our way across a yard, around the back of some abandoned farm buildings, across another lane, and into another wood, eventually coming to a beaten-up cabin.

"Here she is!" Leslie says. "Enjoy your stay!"

"Do we need a key card?" I ask.

"No keys," Leslie says. "Perfectly safe here, never any trouble, we just leave it unlocked."

I want to ask, *Really? Never any murders?* but Leslie already thinks we're ridiculous.

"W-what shall I do with the rabbit?" Nate asks.

Leslie rolls his eyes. "Give it here, I'll sort it." He takes the bag from Nate and ambles away into the night.

I push the cabin door open. "Home sweet home!" I say, flicking the light switch.

EIGHTEEN

NATE

The cabin is pretty rustic, by which I mean it's *basic*, hardly "luxury," unless the complimentary toiletries and bathrobes count as that. I don't actually care. I'm just relieved we're finally here, and it's way better than being at that campsite with my family. Jack doesn't seem to mind either, and no sooner are we through the door, and he's plugged his phone in to charge, than he starts prattling on about getting some photos and talking about how we need to use words like "decompress" and would I like to sit by the wood-burning stove with my knees drawn up to my chest, cradling a mug of coffee and looking content?

"Jack, I've never looked content in my life, never cradled a cup of coffee like that, and should we really be lighting a wood-burning stove because, you know, *the environment*?" I say. It's not that I'm not up for this Instagram thing, but Tariq's gonna spot the deception a mile off if he sees pics of me doing things I'd never normally do.

Jack accuses me of pissing on his bonfire. But he's not done yet.

Another idea: Would I like a candid photo of me just by the fire in my "loungewear"?

"Do you mean my pajamas?"

"Yes," Jack says. *"Loungewear."*

God, I hate the world and all the stupid words and phrases.

"OK," I say.

I can tell Jack's surprised by my sudden enthusiasm, but his delight soon fades when I reappear in the pajamas — Detective Pikachu branded, a joke from my (hilarious) dad last Christmas, which I packed purely for comedic value.

"OK, so that's *funny*." Jack scowls.

"No good?"

"I was anticipating a gray marl jersey short or some open-hem joggers."

I look at him blankly.

"Maybe with your top off . . . ?" Jack continues.

"Not happening," I tell him.

"It's not very *hygge*."

"Is it not, no?"

"I don't think you're taking this seriously," Jack tells me. He grabs his phone off the charger, swipes, and offers it to me. It's

Dylan and Tariq's latest post. They're both at the edge of an open-air infinity pool, apparently on the roof of some tall building, arms around each other's shoulders as they gaze out over what looks like London. They're so fucking serene and loved up I want to commit a homicide.

"Just tell me what to do," I tell Jack.

Jack smiles. "Amazing. OK, you'll be snuggled up in the armchair, fire in the background, and we'll have a candle, a blanket, and a book in the shot, you can't get more freaking *hygge* than that!"

I give him a nod, and he scurries around the cabin, trying to find the props. There's a candle on the shelf at the side of the main room, and then he heads into a bedroom to find a blanket and a book. But when he comes back, he looks ashen.

"Nate," he whispers.

"Yeah?"

He comes up to me and tugs at my shirt, so I follow him into the bedroom, and we're both peering down at this corn dolly thing that's sitting on top of a chest of drawers.

"What?" I say.

"It's like a weird voodoo doll thing."

"It's a corn dolly."

"It's like from a horror film. It's *cursed.*"

"Jack, it's a corn dolly. It's a harvest custom thing in the country. It's fine."

"There's one on the shelf in the main room too."

"So?"

"And don't you think it's weird that Old Man Cooper—"

"*Leslie.*"

"—said there was paperwork to do, and yet where is the paperwork? There wasn't any!"

"We're not starting this again. I'm going to go and chill in the other room." And I walk back out, just as Jack shouts, "Oh my god, *there's another one in the en suite!*"

I'm tired of his relentless paranoia at this point, so that's why I do it. If he's determined to be scared, I'll play ball. I flick the lights off in the main room, then stand like a statue in the corner, facing the wall, like what happens in that film *The Blair Witch Project.*

And then I play the waiting game.

"So, there's actually *two* in the bathroom, and—Nate?"

I keep perfectly still and quiet.

"Oh my god," Jack whispers to himself. "Nate? Nate, where are you?"

He's already bricking it. This is hilarious. "Nate?" His voice is quivering now. "N-Nate?"

Then he flicks the main light on, and I hear him gasp as he sees me, standing in the corner. I'm expecting him to say, *Ha bloody ha, very funny,* or something maybe more cutting, because this is Jack. What I get is:

"AAAAAAARRRRRGHHHHHHH! AHHHHHHHHHH-HHH!"

And he is literally TOTALLY FREAKING OUT, running around all over the place, crashing into a floor lamp, which falls over, TOTAL PANIC. He is SCREAMING. I've never seen such unmitigated HYSTERIA and nothing I can do will calm him down, and he's still,

"AAAAAARGGGHHHHH! AHHHHHH! AAAAHHH-HHH!"

So I wrestle him to the floor and try to put my hand over his mouth, but he's fighting me off like he thinks I'm possessed and—

"Um, hi, guys?"

And we both stop and look up, and there are three girls about our age standing in the doorway.

NINETEEN

JACK

So it turns out that Abi, Beth, and Josie are an absolute *riot*. They're actually staying in the cabin next to ours because, funny story, I didn't book a remote cabin the woods, but a cabin that's near quite a few other cabins, because this is actually a *holiday park*, and now we're all in the hot tub together, we're drinking prosecco (will look like champagne in the pictures), and we're actually having a really nice time, like, *finally*.

"And you were screaming because?" Beth asks.

"It was just a bit of banter," I assure her.

"And you were wearing those pajamas because?"

"Again, banter," Nate says. "Just a joke."

Beth doesn't look entirely convinced, but we've already established she and her friends are actually a year older than us, so they probably see us as jokes anyway—although luckily I flipped Nate's shirt over from where he'd dropped it at the side of the hot tub, so the name tag his mum sewed in there wasn't being proudly displayed for our new sophisticated friends to see.

Abi takes a long sip of her drink. "So what's the deal with you two, then?" She's pretending to be interested in her drink, making it sound like an off-the-cuff question.

I sense Nate tense.

"No deal," I say. "We're friends."

"You're gay though, right?" Abi says to me.

"Right."

She shifts slightly toward Nate, who she's sitting next to. "What about you?"

He doesn't look at me. He doesn't look at anyone. "Well"—he shrugs—"it's the twenty-first century, isn't it?"

My eyes widen because what the hell is *that* supposed to mean? Like, seriously, what does he mean? Because what it sounds like is some "let's not label it, it's the twenty-first century, we're so edgy and futuristic, we've moved beyond all that" thing—coming from the boy who literally just told everyone at prom he was gay.

Whatever, it seems to satisfy Abi. "Ha ha! Right, babe."

Nate laughs too, sips his drink.

OK, fine, of course it's up to him. He came out as gay at the prom, but if he's changed his mind or it's different now, then that's his business. I guess he caught me off guard. Maybe I need to be more open to things. I mean, it's the twenty-first century, isn't it?

"Top up, Jack?" Beth pours the fizz in anyway.

"Why not?" I say. "It's the twenty-first century!"

Beth laughs. I glance up and Nate is giving me daggers.

"Ahhhh!" Abi squeals, suddenly excited. "You know what we should play? Never Have I Ever!"

"Really?" Josie says. Josie is wearing a vintage-style one-piece swimsuit—she's clearly controlled and together and I suspect never loses this game.

"Yes!" Abi says. "No one is anywhere near drunk enough!"

So that's decided. Beth refills all our drinks, and Josie has the first question. "Never have I ever . . . said 'I love you' without feeling it," she says.

Abi drinks.

Beth drinks.

I think about Dylan. I told him I loved him—but did I? At the time, I felt I did. But if I *really* did, why am I not more cut up? Why am I not more like Nate is about Tariq? I drink anyway, because YOLO, and no one's gonna ask (or care) about reasons.

Josie and Nate do not drink.

"Aw, you're really cute, Nate," Abi says, smiling at him, all doe-eyed.

Nate takes a big gulp of his drink. "Huh? Am I? OK. Thank you," he says.

"My turn!" Beth says. "Never have I ever . . . watched porn."

Here we go. Beth takes a drink, I drink, Abi drinks, Josie does *not* drink but just sits there smiling sweetly like she's really trying not to look disapproving about this, and finally Nate drinks.

"*So!*" says Abi. "What sort of porn do you watch, Nate?"

Nate chews his lip a bit. "Oh, er . . . you know, just . . . like, nothing too . . . not hardcore stuff, obviously." (I mean, this is all sounding like lies, but OK.) "Maybe just like . . . hand stuff?" he continues.

Abi screws her face up. "*Hand stuff?*"

Nate's eyes widen. "Like, um . . ."

And he comes *this close* to making a jerking-off gesture with his fist, I mean, *that boy*, I just have to stop him.

"Nate!" I say. "Button it! Seriously, you're ridiculous."

"You're ridiculous!" he hits back.

"Never said I wasn't," I mutter. "My turn. Never have I ever kissed someone of the same sex."

I down the rest of my drink, just to be absolutely clear that I've done a fair bit of that and I'm damn proud of it too.

Abi doesn't drink.

Beth takes a small sip. Not sure what that means.

Josie takes a huge gulp, which delights me. I always end up loving girls in vintage wear.

Nate just stares into the bubbles of the hot tub. *Oh boy*. But fine, OK.

It's Abi's turn. "Never have I ever . . . forgotten my first love."

There's some appreciative and nostalgic-sounding awwws and

ahhhhs from the girls and not one of us drinks.

"Who was your first love, Jack?" Rosie asks.

I flick my eyes from Nate to her. "Um . . . SpongeBob," I say, smiling.

"Nate?" Abi says.

Nate shakes his head. "Nah, it's . . . Let's just leave it."

"Still hurts?" Abi says.

Nate won't look at anyone. "A bit. It's fine."

"They say you never quite get over the first," Beth muses, looking into the middle distance.

"I think it's really special," Josie agrees. "I mean, they're *the first.*"

Nate's still just staring into the water. "Well, anyway—" I begin, knowing we have to move away from this.

Abi ignores me. "His name was Archie, my first. I mean, we were young, but I was *so* in love with him. You know? And when we split up, I was sure I would never get over him."

Nate glances up, his eyes a bit puffy. "And did you? Get over him?"

"Kind of," Abi says. "But also, kind of not. It's funny. In a weird way, no one since has ever lived up to the . . . I don't know, the *magic* of him. But maybe that was just because he was the first. Maybe that's the thing."

I watch as Nate exhales unsteadily. He's in so much pain, he's literally seconds away from losing it, sobbing uncontrollably, I can tell, and I can't let this carry on. I crash down to my left, water splashing everywhere. "Oh! Ahhh!" I shout. "Oh my god, sorry—dizzy!"

"Are you OK?" Josie says.

"Should we call someone?" Abi asks.

"No," I say. "It comes and goes sometimes, I'm not sure what it . . . I just need Nate—I'm sorry—sorry to put a downer on all this . . ."

Nate looks utterly confused as I lean weakly on him, and he helps me out of the tub, puts a towel around my shoulders, and we both hobble back toward our cabin.

"I'm so sorry, ladies!" I call back to them. "I'm OK, I'll be fine, just need . . ." We're by the door to our cabin. "I just need to rest, and then . . . oh!"

Nate bundles me inside and once the door is closed, I straighten up and slide the bolt.

He just stares at me.

"I just thought you needed to get out of there," I tell him.

His face darkens. "I can look after myself."

"I know, but—"

"Don't need your help," he mutters.

"OK. Sorry!" My stomach knots as I realize I've somehow done the wrong thing again and upset him. I swallow and gesture to the door. "Go back if you like."

He stares at me, mouth clamped tightly shut.

And then he walks into his bedroom and slams the door.

TWENTY

NATE

We're back in the VW bus, heading nowhere fast because of constant traffic jams, and I haven't said a word to Jack since last night.

Sure, I didn't want *that* conversation with the girls, but I don't need Jack assuming he has to get me out of there, like he knows me so well, when actually he doesn't. Just like he assumes he knows the reason we stopped talking in year nine when actually he doesn't. Like he assumes I'd wanted to be outed in front of the girls with his stupid "kissed someone of the same sex" question when all I want is to go back to my quiet life, keep myself to myself, because honestly, that's the best way. That's safest.

If it weren't for something else, I'd be calling this whole thing off.

I messaged Tariq last night. I know, I know.

But I was feeling angry with Jack; we were both just shut in our rooms, not talking, and I was generally confused and upset and just wanted to see how he was.

The WhatsApp message is showing two blue ticks.

He's seen it.

He has not replied.

I mean, in the circumstances, that's a big "fuck you." That's a "hey, look, I'm with someone else now and you are no longer a priority in terms of responding to messages." So I don't know where that leaves me, except I'm going to double down on this whole Instagram thing because what else have I got and also . . . how dare he? How dare he rub it in with his pics of infinity pools and not return my message? Did I really mean that little to him?

Jack's just acting like everything's cool, but he must have noticed I'm barely talking to him. "So the hot tub pic went down *a storm*," he says to me. "It's an absolutely *mint* photo—looks really glamorous—laughter, bubbles, hot teens in a hot tub!"

"Good." At least that's something. I hope Tariq's seen it. I hope I was laughing in the picture. It's unlikely, but I hope it.

"Just one problem," Jack continues.

"Uh-huh?"

"Someone reported it as being in violation of community guidelines."

"What?" I squeal. "Why?"

Jack shrugs. "Literally. No idea. I mean, sure, you're shirtless in it, but I hardly think your underage nipples would be considered 'inappropriate content.'"

"There's nothing inappropriate about my nipples," I mutter. "What's the betting it's Dylan's doing?"

"Or Tariq's?" Jack suggests.

"Either way, you should report their shot in the infinity pool."

Jack nods. "One step ahead of you. Did it while you were in the shower. I'm pretty sure if you squint, you can see a highly suspect bulge in Dylan's swimming shorts."

I manage the smallest of smiles.

He's still staring at me like there's more.

I grit my teeth. *"What now?"*

"Dylan and Tariq went to a huge concert last night— Wembley, no less. Looks like a VIP box too."

I sniff. "Good for them."

"Apparently they're 'living their best lives' and are 'blessed.'"

Well, of course they are, because they've got money and freedom and, more importantly, *each other.* I keep going over in my head where I went wrong. What did I do, or not do, that made Tariq want to get with Dylan? I know Dylan's better looking than me, and I know he's charismatic and confident, but I thought, I really thought, that Tariq liked me for *me* and that maybe not being those things didn't matter to him.

"Nate?" Jack says softly. "Are you OK?"

"I thought I was," I reply.

The traffic gets no better, we're hours away from where we're meant to be, so by early evening, somewhere south of Manchester, Mum and Dad have given in and booked rooms in a Travel Inn motel for the night—them and Rose in one room, me and Jack in another.

"We need two single beds," I tell the lady at reception.

She shakes her head. "We only do doubles, but some of the rooms have sofa beds you can sleep on too." She taps at her computer. "They've all been taken now, sorry."

I look at my parents. "There are no beds."

"There's a perfectly good double!" Dad replies.

"They're actually king size, so plenty of space!" The lady at reception smiles. "Plus, it's fun!"

I stare at her. "What's 'fun'?!"

"Bunking up with your friend for the night!" She smiles again, like we're the Famous Five. "Sleepover style!"

I can't stop staring. What the hell is she taking about? "Sleepover style"?

"Be fun, Nate," Mum adds. "You shared a tent."

"A *tent*. Not a *sleeping bag*." I turn back to the reception lady. "We're not together. We're just friends."

She gives me an unimpressed look. "OK."

I look at everyone else, and everyone else, including the old couple who are waiting in line behind us, seems equally unimpressed. "What?" I say.

"Jack would make a *great* husband!" Rose says.

"Didn't ask anything, why are you speaking?"

"You said 'what?' so I'm answering!" Rose replies.

"Anyway, get over it, Nate," Mum says. "Sleep in the parking lot if you're that bothered."

"I mean, it's the twenty-first century after all," Jack says with a grin.

I absolutely give him one of my death stares; it's like that boy just cannot help but mess with me all the time. Does he not understand I said that because I was being deliberately evasive? I didn't want to come out to the girls, but I also didn't want to totally lie. Why is that such a problem?

"Here's your key card," Reception Lady says, handing it over. "Breakfast from seven, check out by eleven. Enjoy your stay — I've put you in the honeymoon suite!"

My eyes widen.

Her face falls. "That's a joke. We're a motel — we don't have a honeymoon suite."

TWENTY-ONE

JACK

Absolutely sick . . .

. . . of Nate's shit.

Literally, I'm over him. I have a really high tolerance for fuckery, but Nate's just smashed right through it.

We both stomp to the bedroom in silence, and the moment the door closes behind us, I throw my case down and I'm so ready to give Nate a piece of my mind that—

"What's your problem?" Nate barks at me.

"Oh my actual god, what's *your* problem?"

"Dig, dig, dig! All the time! I can't take it! If I annoy you so much, why did you come on this thing?"

"Well, if I annoy *you* so much, why did you invite me?"

He's right up in my face. "I. Didn't!"

He's sort of right, which is deeply annoying. But none of that is the actual point here. "Nate, you've been grumpy—well, OK, you've been grumpy since forever, but you've been *especially* grumpy on this trip, and I get it, *Tariq*, but you're just letting them win by being like this."

"Well, they have won, so."

"And, like, what exactly did I do wrong last night?" I ask.

Nate stares at me, unblinking.

"I was trying to look out for you," I add. *"Because I understand how raw this all is for you."*

He's still just staring.

"Or maybe it's not raw?" I say. "Maybe you're actually cool with it, don't care, have moved on, and you're looking for someone new? After all, *it's the twenty-first century.*"

Now I get a reaction. "What's that supposed to mean?" he says.

"It's cool, you don't want people to know you're gay."

"That's not the case . . ."

"Well, except you did the same thing with the motel receptionist just now—made a big old song and dance about how we weren't together and could we have separate beds—"

"Oh my god, Jack, so what if I don't want to be all gay and in everyone's face about it?"

I snap my fingers. "And there's the crux of it! You hate the fact that I am! Don't you? You can't stand it. Is that why you didn't speak to me after year nine when I came out?"

Nate's face goes stony. "That's not—"

"That why you stayed quiet when those lads made a fuss about changing with me?"

He looks down at the floor.

"Deserved it, I suppose, did I? Like Mrs. Nunn said, I bring it on myself because I don't try to hide it!"

He looks up. "Why are you bringing all this up?"

I actually laugh, his question is so ridiculous. I mean, where would I start? How hurt I was when we stopped hanging out? How I know it's because he didn't like me being so overtly gay? How, aside from Instagram, this trip could have been a chance to repair things a bit, except Nate's still Nate and he clearly still has a problem if I'm not straight-acting? Exactly the same as Dylan did?

"How shall I be more straight for you, Nate? Maybe I could start walking slowly along sidewalks, with no purpose—would that be more straight? Wear a nice button-down on a night out in town? I could stop asking for oat milk in my lattes, just go for good old cishet full-fat dairy!"

"Shut up, Jack."

I nod. "Yeah, because that's exactly what everyone wants, isn't it? Fine to be gay as long as you're not *too* gay. As long as you can be slotted into some nice little inoffensive category that doesn't make anyone uncomfortable. Not like it affects you anyway, but god forbid I should celebrate any scrap of happiness in who I am!"

"I'm sleeping in the bathroom," he says, going in and slamming the door, like I might not even need to pee or floss or anything.

"*Fine.* Sleep in the bathroom."

* * *

Thirty minutes later and Nate is out of the bathroom and standing by the side of the bed.

"I don't want to argue with you," he says in a small voice.

"Or is it just that you don't want to sleep in the bath?" I ask.

He shrugs. "The shower's dripping."

"Right. Well." I flip the page of my novel.

"I'm sorry," Nate says.

"OK."

"Can I get in the bed?"

I sigh, put my book down on the little bedside table, and turn to look at him. I do it all really slowly though, to give the moment the gravitas it deserves. "Yes," I say eventually.

He gives me a little smile, walks around to the other side, and hops in, lying straight down on his back.

"Shall I turn the light out?" I ask.

"Yeah."

I flick it off, then lie down on my back too. For a moment, there's just the sound of our breathing, until Nate shuffles over so he's lying on his side, facing me. "Jack?"

I don't turn to look at him. "Uh-huh?"

"I'm sorry I've been grumpy. I know you were trying to help me back in the cabin. And I know I . . . it feels like a mess. Me, I mean. And I just really miss Tariq. I messaged him . . ."

"Ohh, *Nate*," I mutter.

"I just . . . I think I thought maybe he'd get back with me, that there could still be hope, but when I see those posts . . . he looks so happy. And I'm . . . I don't know what I am, Jack, but happy I definitely ain't."

I turn onto my side to face him too. He chuckles. "What?" I say.

"Now it really feels like a sleepover, like when we were younger. Whispering late at night."

I smile. "Happy days."

He sighs. "Yeah. *Once.*"

"We'll get your happy back, pumpkin."

He laughs again. "You're such a dick." There's a bit more silence. "Um . . . Jack?"

"Yeah?"

"Is it possible to have a bit more duvet?"

I sigh. "How much more duvet do you need, Nate?"

"OK, it's just . . . don't laugh, but I have this thing, this . . . It probably sounds stupid, but I always imagine there's a monster in the bedroom hungry for limbs, and if any part of me is exposed and not under the duvet, the creature will eat them. So. My left arm, foot, and lower leg are all currently in peril."

"*What?*"

"You may as well know because I won't sleep otherwise."

"But this savage human-flesh-eating beast is fooled if the limbs it seeks are under a relatively thin piece of material?"

"I didn't say it was logical."

I sweep more duvet over to his side. "Ridiculous."

Nate makes a contented little noise and rolls onto his back. "Jack?"

"Yeah, I'm still here."

"I'm sorry about . . . the stuff in year nine."

I wait to see if there's any more, like some actual explanation of why he totally stopped speaking to me, but he just sighs deeply, and there clearly isn't. Still, it's better than nothing. "No worries," I mutter.

More silence. I think about Dylan. I think about the fact that Nate misses Tariq so badly and I don't miss Dylan in the same way. I've barely even thought about Dylan in that sense. I've just been annoyed, felt competitive, wanted some kind of revenge, I don't know. I thought Dylan was my everything. I *said* he was in several Instagram posts. Maybe he's not.

Nate's making little sniffing noises. Poor Nate. This whole thing has really messed him up. I don't want him to have the worst summer ever — we're sixteen, we've just finished our GCSEs, and, I know because everyone tells you, life doesn't get much better than this.

"Nate? Do you want a hug?"

He hesitates. "I'm good, thanks," he mutters finally.

* * *

I'm woken by the sound of a delivery truck reversing into a service bay somewhere under our window. It doesn't seem to bother Nate, who remains asleep, a look of blissful contentment on his face. I reach for my phone.

A text from Mum: *Hope you're not dead. Don't forget about Elliot — he's doing some talent show near godforsaken Stoke-on-Trent if you happen to be passing? Love you, blah, blah.*

Elliot. It gives me an idea. Nate and Elliot have met before, years ago, when we were ten, but they got along really well. Plus, Elliot's a laugh, which might be good for Nate, and I'm sure whatever the talent show act is he's doing will be . . . well, even if it's crap, it'll be funny, so it's win-win as far as I'm concerned.

I tap on Instagram and am instantly irritated by Dylan and Tariq's picture of them enjoying some sort of luxury breakfast in a fabulous hotel they clearly checked into after their VIP-gig-thing last night. Fresh orange juice, croissant, a plate of fresh fruit, and two steaming mugs of coffee—looks divine. Also looks fake AF since Dylan loathes coffee, but that's not the point. It's getting a lot of love. They've done that thing where they've asked a question at the end of the post: *What's your favorite breakfast?* Unbelievably, people have replied: *French toast, Muffins, Full English!*—it's so mind-numbingly banal. I mull my options. I haven't braved the breakfast buffet here yet, but I'm reasonably confident it's going to be hard to compete with them on this. But then, the camera can be *very selective* about what it sees.

I hop out of bed, have a quick shower, and pull on some clothes. Nate is asleep throughout all of this—he's clearly not going to be breakfasting with me, but maybe if the old grump gets more sleep, he'll be a bit happier.

"Farewell, my prince," I whisper to him. "Sweet dreams, my handsome, beautiful boy!"

"Piss off, Jack," Nate mutters.

I'm unclear whether he heard that or whether he's just dreaming, because either is a possibility. Nate makes a little snuffling noise and turns over.

"Tariq," he mutters. *"Puffle."*

And that settles it. Mission: Distract Nate from Obsessing About Tariq must begin in earnest.

I complete my look by wrapping a black pashmina around myself, because part of me does feel I need to recognize I too have lost a boyfriend, and I should, technically, enter a period of mourning—the black pashmina giving just the right hint of glamorous widow who's a bit sad but totally up for a new man, should one come along.

* * *

The breakfast buffet, like every breakfast buffet I've ever been to, is an absolute disgrace. The two members of staff in charge of the fiasco are run ragged, simultaneously trying to clear stacks of dirty crockery, show people to tables, and refill serving dishes. Ninety percent of the breakfast guests appear to be aggressively heterosexual men, many wearing branded polo shirts for things like elevator maintenance companies, and apparently with a very low tolerance threshold for waiting in line while a fabulous gay teenager, in a beautiful, if melancholy, pashmina (and who maybe has just a hint of eyeliner on) tries to select a fried egg that's actually still runny for his plate.

I don't want a repeat of the incident at the campsite canteen, so I fill my plate as quickly as I can: gray boiled mushrooms, an entirely superfluous tomato (gross, but a nice pop of color), some bacon that appears to have been *boiled* for some reason, and hurry back to my table to attempt a few photos. But none of them looks as good as the one Dylan and Tariq took at their luxury hotel. The lighting is all wrong, for a start, plus there's no white cotton tablecloth or heavy-looking silver cutlery to really set it off. The only option here is the close-up, but I'm not going to post a close-up of a low-quality sausage when Dylan had pics of freshly baked croissants and "preserves." I abandon my cooked breakfast due to its foulness and start hunting around the "continental selection," where I happen upon *pancakes*. Now, a stack of pancakes, with a pat of melted butter sitting on top, oozing buttery goodness down the side of the stack, and maybe a few berries on the side is *exactly* the sort of thing I need everyone to see on Insta.

Problem: the pancakes are *cold*. And for butter to melt, pleasingly and glisteningly, I need them *warm*. So I throw them in the industrial-looking toaster oven, which has a little conveyer belt to carry your items along, spitting them out the other end once toasted. While that's happening, I spoon some berries into a bowl, and then head over to the jugs of juice, because some orange, in the corner of the shot, might look vibrant and healthy too.

I do a sweep past the toaster, but the pancakes haven't emerged yet, so take my other bits back to my table.

"Morning, Jack!" It's Nate's mum, looking bright and breezy in these pink chino shorts and a rather jaunty blue-striped top. "Don't tell me my sleep-loving son is still in bed and he's left you to fend for yourself at this breakfast buffet?"

"He needs his sleep," I tell her. "I'll save him a stale croissant."

"He's in a weird mood. Is it still this Tariq business?"

I nod. "Yeah. *But* I had a thought, and I think it might help cheer him up—if you're up for a slight detour—to see my cousin Elliot perform in a talent show near Stoke-on-Trent, which I know sounds—"

"Yes!" she blurts out. "I mean, anything, some form of structure, is great. Mick is being so free and easy about this whole trip, I'm beside myself. I'm having to lie to friends and relatives, saying it's all planned and everything is wonderful—if the mums at Rose's school get wind of what's actually happening, I'll be shunned, Jack. *Shunned.* Like they did with Anne Rogers after she ditched her SUV and bought an electric bike."

I nod, even though I have no idea.

"But Nate knows Elliot and likes him?"

"They got on *so well* when we were ten and Elliot spent a few weeks of the summer at ours."

"I'll discuss it with Mick, but I'm sure we can manage it." She cocks her head to the other side of the restaurant. "Join us, you can hear Mick prattle on about how he wants to catch a fish and barbecue it on a beach, because why eat at one of Rick Stein's restaurants *like Debbie Atwood does every month with her millionaire husband* when you can drag something out of the sewage-ridden North Sea and incinerate it over a fire made with the last remaining vestiges of your hopes and dreams?"

I take a deep breath. I hope Nate's folks aren't on the rocks, relationship-wise. I don't think Nate could take that. "Sure," I say. "I just have something I need to—"

I freeze as I see smoke billowing out of the toaster, which is clearly malfunctioning for reasons completely unconnected with me. And before I can do anything else, there's this ear-shattering siren, all the breakfast guests start panicking, and even though it seems like the "fire" is controllable, everyone starts being herded out into the parking lot because of "policy" and "procedures that have to be followed" after the (unspecified) "incident at Basildon East."

As I'm shepherded out through a fire exit, I hear one of the staff members say to another, "Another prat who ignored the sign saying 'only put bread in the toaster.'"

I want to make it very clear that this is the first I've heard of the existence of such a sign, and maybe they need to think about a bigger sign or a highlighter pen, I don't know, but this is not my fault and if anyone asks, I'm going to deny all knowledge because it feels like everyone is very angry right now and I really can't be dealing with any more haters.

Let me tell you though, you have not experienced true joy until you've seen Nate blunder, confused and half-asleep, out through a fire exit wearing just his boxers and a pair of sneakers, with a duvet wrapped around his shoulders. It's a sight so messy, chaotic, and hopeless, it can't fail to warm your cynical heart.

"What the hell?" he says, as he stumbles over to me.

"Apparently some *fool* put some pancakes through the toaster."

I shrug. "Why is everyone such an idiot?" I look him up and down. "Nice outfit. *Daring*. I like how you're pushing boundaries."

Nate's parents and Rose walk over to us. "Nate Harrison!" his mum says. "Why are you standing here in your underpants?"

"Fire," Nate mutters, rubbing his hand through his bedhead hair. "You're not meant to stop to collect belongings."

"So if you'd been in the shower, you'd just be out here naked, would you? Have it all out for the world to see?"

Nate's eyes widen.

"I think he did the right thing," Nate's dad says.

"Would you rather have me naked in a parking lot or dead?" Nate asks.

His mum seriously thinks about it. "*Why* aren't you up yet anyway? It's nine a.m.!"

"Mu-um," Nate growls. He slumps down to sit on the edge of the curb, still sleepy.

"Right, well," his mum continues, "get yourself up because, change of plan. We're heading over to Stoke-on-Trent to see Jack's cousin Elliot perform in a talent show."

Nate looks up sharply. Oh, *now* he's awake! I knew this Elliot thing was a good idea.

"Since *when*?" Nate says.

His mum cocks her head slightly. "Since Jack discussed the idea with me at breakfast, because that's what people do at breakfast, they discuss things. And people who just stay in bed don't." She turns to Mr. Nate. "I assume you're 'cool' with this spontaneous and freewheeling idea?"

Mr. Nate shrugs and smiles. "Yeah? S'what it's all about, man!"

"OK, can you absolutely not use words like 'man,' Mick? It's humiliating for you." She turns back to Nate. "So, chop chop. As soon as we're allowed back in, you need to get ready."

I smile at Nate and he smiles back in this fixed, fake-looking way.

"OK?" I say.

"OK!" Nate replies.

And I know immediately there's something going on. I just don't know what.

TWENTY-TWO

NATE

It was six years ago, so chances are he won't remember, or will be as embarrassed about it as I am and won't say anything, but no sooner have we pulled up and gotten out of the bus outside this grim community center where the talent show is being held than Elliot, in all his overexcited glory, bounds up like a puppy. He's grown—of course he has—but he's still the shortest out of the three of us. His hair is blond, which I assume runs in Jack's family, but his is more choppy, chaotic, slightly haphazard, like he's just tumbled out of bed, which is a look I can totally get on board with. He's wearing a super-adorable NASA sweatshirt with jeans, and he's such a bundle of unmitigated joy that I can't keep a stupid grin from spreading over my face. And he clearly *does* remember and *isn't* embarrassed because he grins, points at me in this tableau of joy and excitement, and shouts, "TREE HOUSE!"

So, ahhh, here's the thing, and the thing is there was a thing between me and Elliot in Jack's tree house. I mean, we were ten, so as things go . . .

We kissed. We kissed each other in Jack's tree house. It wasn't . . . *We were ten.* It was super innocent, the end of a long summer when me and Elliot had become excellent friends, and I don't know exactly how it happened, but it did. It was very quick. And neither of us knew what to do about it afterward. I remember feeling like something BIG had happened. And then I quickly buried the feeling for another six years.

"That's a weird way to greet Nate," Jack says, eyes narrow with suspicion.

Elliot grins. "Nate knows what it's about!"

I laugh loudly and confidently, like Elliot's just messing around and his comment is only a bit of banter. Truth is, if Jack knows I was experimenting with kissing boys at the age of ten, he'll put two and two together and realize he wasn't the only kid questioning his sexuality at school, and that, actually, if I hadn't backed away from him, we could have faced it together. And honestly, I'm just not ready for that conversation with Jack, because *honestly*, I'm not ready to have it with myself.

Elliot goes to hug me, and then Jack, and then shakes hands with my parents. "Thanks for coming, guys!" Elliot continues. "It's really good of you. Mum says you're on some sort of wild road trip for the summer? Sounds cool. Me, I'm just doing my thing—this is my third contest actually, came third in the last one, so I'm on the up." He nods and smiles. "Did you have prom?"

"We don't talk about prom," Jack says.

Elliot nods manically, then turns to me. "How's things, Nate? It's been AGES!"

I nod. "Yeah."

"Must be weird," Dad pipes up, "when you've not seen each other since becoming men."

I squeeze my eyes shut for a moment. "Dad, can you please just *not?*"

"Ha ha, puberty!" Elliot laughs.

I'm glad he finds the whole sorry fiasco amusing.

"So I've put some free tickets for you at the door," Elliot continues, "and there's a table reserved for you at the front. I've got to go and get ready now, do my warm-ups and things, but I'll see you after, and if I win, drinks on me, I guess! Well, Mum can buy them, but I'll pay. Yabba dabba doo, right?"

"Sounds good, mate," Dad says.

"OK, so . . ." He grins at me again, then pretends to make a couple of little boxing jabs at my stomach. "Boom, boom! See you later!" And he scampers off.

"Someone's very excited," Mum says.

Jack nods. "Yeah, they were thinking about having him medicated for a while, but I don't think they ever did."

Dad rubs his hands together. "I fancy a preshow beer!"

"OK," Mum says. "So I'm driving later, then?"

"Is that OK?" Dad says.

Mum doesn't reply, just turns to us. "What do you want to drink, boys?"

"Just a Coke, please," I say.

"Aperol spritz, if they do them," Jack says. "Thank you."

Mum takes a breath, clearly about to tell Jack he can't have actual alcohol, but then sighs and says, "Oh, what the hell?"

I make to follow my parents and Rose in, but Jack tugs on my T-shirt to pull me back. "So," he says, all sly and hushed. *"Tree house."*

I shrug. "Yeah?"

"I wonder what the significance of the tree house is? I wonder why that's the first thing Elliot would say to you?"

"I guess we spent a lot of time in your tree house that summer."

I meet his eyes, unblinking.

"Lies," Jack says. "I can't wait to get to the bottom of this mystery!" He grins. "I'm going to visit the restroom. I'll see you at our VIP table in the cabaret space."

"Jack? I'm not sure it's a—"

Jack holds his hand up as he flounces off. "I know! I'm very well aware this is a shithole, thank you!"

I watch as Jack disappears into the entrance, wondering if he's guessed, or whether he somehow knows, or if I should just tell him, except, *no*, it's all too . . . everything's all too complicated. I sigh and saunter inside, and, god, yes, it is grim. There's a ramshackle bar area over to the left-hand side, a crappy stage at the front, with a glitter curtain that's seen better days, and a collection of mismatched plastic chairs around random-sized tables. There is, however, quite a sizeable crowd. Not being mean to Elliot, but maybe entertainment is thin on the ground in this neck of the woods.

"Love places like this!" Dad says, suddenly by my side with a bottle of beer.

"Really?"

He takes a swig. "This is real, no-frills entertainment, this sort of stuff. None of your autotuned fakers here." He squeezes my shoulder. *"Watch and learn!"* he says, like maybe there's any danger *I* want to go into show business, and this will somehow be an education.

He ambles over to a table near the front just as Jack reappears.

"What's the worst thing in the world?" Jack says.

"Orange juice with bits."

He blinks at me. "Worse than that."

"Polio?"

"What?" Jack screws his face up. "Can't you just avoid the extremes, Nate? Go for something in the middle?"

I shrug. "Well, I don't know, what's the worst thing in the world then?"

"OK, well, I was about to make a little lighthearted remark, but now you've mentioned 'polio' you've kind of ruined it, so." He sighs and shakes his head. "I was going to say urinals in men's toilets."

"I think there are worse things in the world, Jack. You know, that's a very *privileged* thing to say."

"Right. It was just a little observation about how awkward it is peeing next to other guys. *What's gotten into you anyway?*"

I look away from him. "Nothing."

"Are you pleased to see Elliot?"

"Buzzing," I say.

"Well, try telling your face that, Nate!" Jack hisses.

I snap my eyes back to him. Is there anything more annoying than someone telling you to cheer up all the time? It's like, get over it, this is me, I'm quite happy wallowing! I open my mouth to tell Jack precisely this, but—

"Don't you dare, Nate!" Jack says. "Don't you dare have a go at me! Elliot's fun, you like Elliot, I arranged for us to see Elliot. I let you have all the duvet you desired, to keep the malicious exposed-limb spirits at bay."

"It's not a spirit. It's a . . ." I stop myself.

"Monster, whatever it is, Nate, whatever illogical nonsense is in your messed-up head, I acquiesced to your demands. Potentially putting my own limbs in danger in the unlikely event the monster is real."

I clamp my mouth firmly shut. He's right. Annoying but true.

"So I'm not the bad guy here, Nate," Jack continues. "The bad guys are our exes, and in the last twenty minutes, they have posted a pic of themselves wearing 'his and his' hoodies with the hashtag 'gifted' in the caption. 'Hashtag gifted,' Nate! Who has gifted them this? What company is giving these morally bankrupt liars free stuff?"

I think it over for a moment. "Has it occurred to you the liars might be lying? You know, like we are too?" I actually hope they are. If they feel they have something to prove, that might mean things aren't going well for them—like, well . . . like me and Jack.

Jack breathes out through his nose. "Of course that's occurred to me. They're nothing if not sly! But that doesn't matter. It's what other people think that matters, and what they will think is that they're popular and successful and being courted by fashion companies!"

I shrug. "Well, we'll do it too, then."

"Uh-huh?" Jack nods. "And what shall we say has been 'hashtag gifted' to us, Nate?"

He stares at me, wide-eyed, waiting for an answer. "My sneakers?" I eventually suggest.

His eyes widen further. "I'm sorry?"

"My—"

"*Your sneakers?* Your skanky, muddy, battered sneakers? Who would have 'hashtag gifted' them to you? A tramp?!" He shakes his head. "Where's your mum? I really need that Aperol spritz."

And off he heads, toward the bar. When he's out of sight, I allow myself to smile, because I'd forgotten how a genuinely vexed Jack is probably one of my favorite Jacks of all.

TWENTY-THREE

JACK

They've put Elliot on last, which means they either think he's brilliant and fit to end the show, or he's the joke act that everyone will have a good laugh at. I really hope it's the former. Elliot has lost none of his wide-eyed enthusiasm, and I can't stand the thought of people laughing at him. But my fear is real, because there have been a number of *very good* acts so far, some of which could definitely take the top prize, if only because of the power of the sympathy vote. Clara Jenkins and Doris the Dancing Dog are obviously hot contenders, being as everyone (inexplicably) loves a dancing dog, although I don't see the appeal myself. Clara and Doris even have pantomime show in Worthing this year, so things are really looking exciting for them right now (in the words of the emcee). Meanwhile, a group of fifteen children have just performed a street dance act that looks like every other street dance act you've ever seen, so they also stand a chance, especially since they dedicated their performance to someone's dead aunt. *Clever tactic.*

And now it's Elliot. He comes onstage wearing a duffel coat and scarf, even though it's summer and really hot in here, and gets an instant laugh. When he gets his ukulele out, he gets another laugh, I guess because those things are automatically funny.

"This is dedicated to Carolyn," he says into the microphone. "I loved Carolyn very much, but sadly, she is no longer with us."

There's an "ahhh" of sympathy from the crowd.

"Me and Carolyn shared many good times, and everyone at school would wonder why I loved Carolyn so much, and I would tell them, 'She's the air that I breathe, she gives me life, my everything.'" He nods at the audience. "Which is true, because Carolyn was my Ventolin inhaler for my asthma, when I was ten. And this is a song I wrote, just for her . . ."

At which point, no word of a lie, he starts this song about his Ventolin inhaler, which includes the immortal chorus:

Ohhhh, when my chest is tight,
And breathing is a fight,
I grab my trusty puffer,
So I no longer suffer!
Oh, Carolyn, oh, Carolyn,

My sweet supply of Ventolin,
Generically salbutamol,
Expand my airways,
Make me well!

The audience does not know how to take him at first, and in fairness, it's weird and it's somewhat "out there"—I mean, he's in a duffel coat, singing about asthma, but from gradual nervous titters and odd chuckles at first, they actually start really enjoying it, and I have to admit, you get swept away in Elliot's sweet enthusiasm for his inhaler and the geekiness of the whole song. Plus, he wrote it himself, and while some of the scansion is an exercise in linguistic contortion, it is hilariously enjoyable.

Nate actually *whoops*.

And that is the biggest expression of delight I've seen out of him since we started this sorry trip.

I get my phone out and take a few pics. It's reasonably dark in here, and the stage lights reflect and refract nicely in the lens, and with some careful positioning, you can't really see Elliot clearly; you just get a sense of a person on a stage singing, in a dark room, with some other people in the audience watching. Perfect for my caption:

VIP tickets to a top-secret gig. Nate and I are #blessed to get to see this guy sing at such an intimate venue — definitely something ticked off the bucket list! Feels totally different live, up close and personal. Such a great day.

I smile because no sooner have I posted it than the like notifications start flashing up. Dylan and Tariq might have got Wembley, but who got the authentic, real, unplugged experience? Well, not us. But they don't know that.

Elliot gets a standing ovation when he finishes, which he looks genuinely surprised by as he takes a little bow and does a Cub Scout salute at the audience.

I glance at Nate, who's now actually *smiling* at Elliot.

So.

I'm piecing this together, but my money is on Nate *liking* Elliot. I can't be entirely sure what shenanigans went on in my tree house six years ago, but it's quite clear to me that Nate finds Elliot adorable.

So.

But that's fine, right? That's cool. Because happy Nate equals Instagrammable Nate equals higher engagement equals revenge on Dylan plus success for me as I gain followers and become some sort of influencer. So it's all good. We're all winners here. It's all . . . good.

TWENTY-FOUR

NATE

Elliot wins! Of course he does, because he's awesome! He bounds up to our table afterward like he's won the lottery, which he kind of *has* because the prize money is a whole five hundred pounds.

"Yabba dabba doo!" he howls, as he high-fives us all.

Elliot's mum, Jane, who is also at our table, makes a concerned face. "Have you had sugar, Elliot?"

"No, a bit, some," Elliot replies. "I'm OK. I'm good!"

Jane sighs. She seems like a woman on the edge. She has slightly wild hair and googly eyes, and only half pays attention to anyone else at the table because she's always watching Elliot.

Elliot sits down and Jack leans over to him. "Sensational. Triumphant. Five stars."

"Thanks, Jack!" Elliot grins.

"You were really funny, mate," my dad adds. He turns to Jane. "You've got a right one here!"

Jane rolls her eyes. "Try living with him when he's strumming that instrument almost every waking hour!"

"*Oo-er!*" Elliot grins.

Jane shakes her head. "Seriously, El, not now."

Elliot's eyes meet mine. "Congratulations," I say.

"Thanks!" He smiles.

I feel myself blush.

And then Rose pipes up, and whether it's just classic Rose or it's because it's well past her bedtime, I don't know, but she says, apropos of nothing,

"Nate and Jack are husbands."

Elliot's eyes widen. "Ohhhhh," he says. "Oh, I didn't realize. Ohh."

"Um—" I begin.

"Ohh, *yay!*" Elliot continues, smiling.

"No, you see, that's not true," I say. "We're—"

"We're definitely *not,*" Jack interrupts.

"Definitely not," I confirm.

"Oh god, are you actually?" Mum asks.

I screw my face up. "What? No, I just said—"

"Just, there's a lot of denial happening, which normally—"

"Means something that isn't a thing is actually *a thing*," Dad chimes in. "We thought Rose was winding you up before."

"*She was.*" I scowl.

"I was deadly serious," Rose says, totally deadpan.

"Jack and me are—" And I say "barely friends" at the exact same time he says "good friends," and then he just crosses his arms, sits back in his chair, and stares at me like I've thrown shit at him.

"OMG, *awkward*," Rose mutters, slurping her Coke.

I decide the best thing now is just to shut up. Thing is, I didn't mean it in a bad way—it's just that we weren't really friends at all, and now it sort of feels like we're moving toward that again, but I didn't want to presume we were full-on friends, hence the qualification of "barely," which, on reflection, I can see sounds bad. You see, this is why I really shouldn't say stuff. Some people are better just not taking part in life.

"So here's a thought!" Elliot's mum says. "The hotel Elliot and I are staying at is really quiet, it's a spa hotel, really nice, and they've got some great deals on, so why don't you guys stay the night? It's only up the road. The boys can bunk in Elliot's room, means you'll only need a room for you two and Rose."

Mum and Dad glance at each other and just as Dad opens his mouth to doubtless pour cold water on the idea, Mum's straight in with,

"If there's hot running water and some bed linen with a decent thread count, I'm in."

Dad gives her a look, which I know to be the look of *but what about the cost?*

Mum shrugs. "I don't care. I can't live like this all summer."

"Like this? Like *what*?" Dad hisses.

"*Vagabonds*," Mum says. "And I don't think it's coincidence that Karen posted pics of her last cruise on Facebook yesterday, just after I'd posted one from our damp and unsanitary campsite. *She's bragging.*"

"It wasn't damp," Dad says.

"We're doing the spa hotel," Mum insists.

So that appears to be settled.

"Sleepover!" Elliot says, looking wildly excited.

"Have you got extra beds in your room, then?" I ask Elliot.

He shakes his head, which is the reaction I was afraid he would have. "Nah, but it's a super-king-size bed. It's massive. I did an experiment and I can actually sleep across it in either direction—*that's how big it is.*" He stretches his arms out wide. "Like, even bigger than this."

"Can you really fit three boys in a bed?" I ask.

Jack snorts. "Believe me, Nate, *you can.*"

He winks at me and I ignore him hard.

"I'm going to get some air," Jack says, leaving the table.

I watch him go. He's still teasing me, which is something, but I saw the look on his face when I said we were "barely friends" and I know that I (unintentionally) hurt him because, despite the years, I *know* Jack. I owe him an apology.

"I'm Like a Bird" by Nelly Furtado starts playing over the club's speaker system. "Oh my GOOOOOD!" Elliot exclaims. "Who's dancing? I'm dancing!" And he runs into the middle of the dance floor. Rose squeals in delight too and runs up to join him, giggling and copying Elliot when he literally flaps his arms about *like a bird* on the chorus, like some overexcited pterodactyl. I cannot help smiling as I watch this boy. He's so *happy*, so *free*; he just does his thing and he doesn't care. And his joy is utterly infectious, as other people get up and copy his goofy dance, reveling in its geekiness—other kids, two middle-aged women, an older guy—all loving it. Loving this moment. Loving life.

I wish I felt like that. *Could* feel like that. And with Tariq I think I nearly was.

I down the dregs of my Coke. I want to talk to Jack. It's weird, but seeing Elliot so happy makes me want that same happiness so badly that I know I somehow have to sort my head out. Jack seems like he's dealing with it better than me—maybe I should listen to him, take a page out of his book; maybe he knows the secret. I don't know. What I *do* know is that this feeling, this wanting to talk, this sense that Jack will *get* me, well, that's a lot like what we used to have before we stopped speaking. And that means "barely friends" was pretty unforgivable. We're friends. He's my friend.

The cool evening air hits me as I push through the main exit and out into the parking lot. But there's no sign of Jack. I scooch around the cars, head around the side of the building, past a side door that has old beer kegs and drink crates stacked outside. And then farther up, in the orange glow from a streetlight, I see Jack and some other lad, in silhouette, snogging up against the wall. I watch for, like, five seconds, my stomach churning, then quickly turn and head back the way I came.

Maybe he was never that into Dylan at all. How can he be all over some other guy so quickly? I can't even think of doing that right now. And not just because of Tariq. It takes me ages to really like someone enough to even *think* about kissing them. And I'm not judging Jack, I totally respect that everyone has their own way of doing things, but it makes me wonder: Is there really any point in talking to him after all? If he's already over it maybe he never really cared anyway? Is there even a chance we can still be friends? Or have we just drifted apart too much in the last few years? And I don't know, I don't know, but I know I feel funny about seeing Jack kiss that boy, and I don't know what that feeling is, and I don't know why it's making me feel bad, but somehow it feels like a betrayal, just like it somehow felt like a betrayal when he came out in year nine, and I don't understand it and I don't like it.

TWENTY-FIVE

JACK

Connor is not what I would call a good kisser. He's quite bitey, a bit like an overenthusiastic puppy, and at the same time quite slurpy and sucky. "Slow down," I tell him. "I'm not chicken ramen."

He stops and pulls back. "Ah, sorry."

He's cute. Roughly my age. Red T-shirt and gray fleece shorts, which is a boy-next-door type of look that I really like—totally opposite to über jock Dylan, but all the better for it. He was sitting by himself when I walked outside feeling miserable and like I had to be anyplace except near Nate and Elliot as they fall in love. Nate made his feelings very clear when he said we were "barely friends," so it's stupid really, but I guess some part of me was starting to think we were getting back to how things used to be. I see how he is with Elliot though, and I realize that's not gonna happen. Our friendship is long gone. I annoy him too much. There's too much baggage. Hell, maybe I can't really forgive him for everything that's gone on.

This lad glanced up as he heard the main doors open, then looked me up and down. I'm used to that reaction with some of my outfits, but I feel this one is particularly subtle. I mean, I'm wearing chinos, for goodness' sake—skinny fit, sure, but still. And just a nice, plain T-shirt . . . with great big writing on the front that reads:

I ♥ BOYS

Mwah! Ha! Ha! Ha! Ha! Literally no one has batted an eyelid at it all night, so I was glad this boy had because what's the point if no one so much as tuts at you? And when he said,

"Having fun?"

I knew I was in with some sort of chance with him because *he* was speaking to *me*.

"No," I replied. "You?"

He shook his head. "You from 'round here? Not seen you before."

"How did you guess?"

"Your T-shirt kind of gives it away."

"Pourquoi?"

He laughed. "And the fact you just said 'pourquoi.' Both of those things could get you beaten up 'round here." He glanced at me and bit his lip. "I mean, you should have seen the fuss when I came out as bi."

He was almost smooth about it. *Almost.*

"Who are you here with?" I asked.

"My parents." He sounded glum. "My younger sister's in that dance troupe. You?"

"I'm with the guy who won," I said.

"With him, as in . . ."

I smiled. "He's my cousin."

"Oh, OK." He glanced at me again. "He's cute."

"Uh-huh."

"Runs in the family, huh?"

He blushed then and rightly so, and so did I, because *wow.*

And then our eyes met, for that second or two longer than normal that makes your heart skip a beat.

"Fancy a wander?" he said.

"Sure."

And then, after a bit of charged silence: "I'm Connor."

"And I'm Jack. Nice to meet you."

And we turned to each other, just by the wall, and started kissing. This is not love. Of course it's not. But something in me needed this, and I think something in him needed it too. It's nice. I know I won't see this lad again, and I don't even want to. I just needed to feel like someone out there might still like me.

* * *

Elliot jabbers on for the entire journey back to the hotel, which is good, because Nate is really, like, *really* silent. Not just quiet.

Silent. So something's up with him . . . again. Man, I try to do a nice thing, bring Elliot along for some of this thing, and he's still not happy.

Elliot bounds into the huge bedroom and immediately starts showing us around. "Bathroom through there—two sinks! That's 0.66 recurring of a sink each!" The fact he doesn't need to hesitate before telling us that makes me feel deeply inadequate. "Minibar," he says, pointing to a small cabinet in the main room. "I had a vodka and Coke last night—don't tell Mum!"

"Elliot, it'll show up on the bill," I tell him, but he carries on, oblivious.

"Armchairs and accent table . . ."

Pretty obvious, but great. Not entirely my style, slightly too old people's home for me; they look way too comfortable.

"Windows!"

I smirk at Nate, but he appears to be taking the tour seriously, nodding at everything Elliot's pointing out.

"The bed!" he says with a flourish. We all look at it.

It is a big bed.

"So to save awkwardness," Elliot says, "are we sleeping in our boxers, or—"

"OK, so, you're my *cousin*, Elliot," I say. "We're not gonna be naked."

"OK, but, I was going to say *or jim-jams.*" He looks at me with wide eyes and a look on his face of, *Really?*

"Oh."

"Jim-jams," Nate pipes up. "Or *loungewear*, as Jack would call it."

I nod.

"Cool, and again, to save any awkwardness, just to also say that first thing in the morning, I usually have a—"

I put my hand up. "Elliot, it's cool, I know, it's a guy thing, we probably all will have. But we don't need to talk about it."

He blinks at me. "A little sing and a dance to Britney, it's my wake-up morning routine," he says in a small voice.

I nod again. "Ah."

Nate snorts, then jumps on the bed, landing on the far right side. "I'll take this end," he says.

I wonder where Nate would prefer me. He seems off, so I reckon safest bet would be the other side, with Elliot in the middle. Plus, if Nate likes Elliot he'll probably want to be next to him anyway . . .

"You OK in the middle, Elliot?"

Elliot grins. "I'll put my *loungewear* on in the bathroom." And he nips off.

I turn to Nate. "All right?"

"Yeah. You?"

"Yeah."

His eyes flick away and then flick back to me again. "Have fun tonight?" he asks.

There's a pointedness in his tone. It puts me slightly on edge. "It was OK."

He nods. "I popped out to come and find you—I think you were with some guy."

Ohhhhh my god. Awkward. "Fast work," Nate mutters.

"Just checking I've still got it," I quip.

Nate rolls his eyes. "Not a competition, but OK."

"Who said anything about a competition?"

"Just feels like you're out to prove something," Nate says.

"Excuse me? What?"

He shrugs. "Maybe I'm wrong."

"Yeah. *You are.*" I stare at him.

He looks away. "OK. Sorry."

I stare at him. *What the actual hell?*

Elliot reappears in black shorts and a gray marl T-shirt with the NASA logo. "Wow," I say. "You really like space, huh?"

"Space is infinite," Elliot says. "Don't you ever look up there at night and think, *wow*?"

I really hope this isn't the sort of late-night chatter we're going to be having. I am way too sober if it is.

Nate and I change too and we hop into the bed, and so there the three of us are, like some wholesome fairy tale, all tucked up, in our pajamas. I have a quick check on Insta. The post from the talent show is doing well—plenty of likes and lots of comments, mainly asking who it was we saw. Ignoring them will heighten the mystery. I know how to play the game and there's more power in what's left unsaid.

Then I make the mistake of scrolling and seeing Dylan's pic— him and Tariq cuddled up together, also in some hotel bed. *You've stolen my heart and made me the happiest boy alive*, says the caption. They. Look. So. Content. And. In. Love. And all of a sudden, the snog with Connor feels cheap and pointless, and being in this stupid bed with Elliot and Nate feels ridiculous. Dylan's out there living his life, and I'm here just pretending.

* * *

It's two a.m. and we're getting no sleep, thanks to one hyperactive little ball of energy in the middle of the bed.

"So, so, so, but was there a *moment* when you realized you were gay, or did it just happen gradually?" Elliot asks. This is about his hundredth question and I really want this to end now. "Jack?"

"End of year eight," I say. I turn on my side. Discussion over.

"Nate?" Elliot blabbers on. "What about you? Like, did you know when you were ten?"

I hear Nate's sharp intake of breath.

"Strangely specific, Elliot," I say, rolling back to face them and propping myself up on my elbow. "What makes you say that?"

Elliot is silent, which is even more suspicious.

"I came out at prom," Nate says.

"Yes, but that wasn't the question," I chip in. "Elliot asked when you *knew*, and he wondered, for some reason, if you might have been ten years old?"

"Huh," Nate says.

OK, so I'm not a fool, I've managed to piece together the fact that something is going on here, and it's clearly connected to when we last all saw one another, when we were ten, and the fateful summer when we spent a lot of time in my TREE HOUSE.

"I guess, same as Jack, really," Nate continues.

"Same as me?" I say.

"Yeah?"

"So, like, around year eight or nine."

Nate hesitates. "I guess, yeah," he says.

I sigh and turn onto my side again, facing away from them. And I'm filled with the most terrible sadness, because I never knew that. I never realized. After I came out in year nine and Nate never spoke to me again, I thought it was because he felt too awkward or maybe he felt like, if he spoke to me, I would think he fancied me, or maybe he was worried if he spoke to me other people might think *he* was gay, I don't know, any number of those reasons. It didn't cross my mind that he might have been feeling the same sort of things too. And so right there, right in front of me the whole time, was the person who could have made those hateful few years better and less lonely. My best friend could have been by my side. But he wasn't.

And now I want to know other things too. I want to know: If he thought he might be gay, why didn't he speak to me? Why didn't he come around one weekend and say anything? We were *best friends.* We did everything together. He knew he could trust me. He knew I'd never make fun or spread gossip, but he said nothing. He just backed off and . . . disappeared. *He made a choice to do that!* But Elliot's here, and Nate clams up at the best of times, so I can't ask him now.

But a little later, when Elliot is gently purring in his sleep, I hear Nate whisper,

"I'm sorry."

My heart squeezes.

"Are you awake, Jack?" he whispers again.

I don't answer, just lie there. I don't know what to say.

I'm mad with him. I'm hurt.

"I was scared," Nate whispers. "I don't know if you're listening, but if you are, I was terrified. I saw all the crap you got at school after you came out, and I . . . I couldn't face it. I knew I'd get the same if I told everyone I was gay too, so I didn't. So that's why. It's not because I disapproved of you; it's because I'm a coward. I'm a coward, and I'm sorry." He chokes back a little sob. "You deserved better than me."

"It's OK, Nate."

I reach across Elliot, find his hand, and squeeze. "It's OK."

TWENTY-SIX

NATE

I'm woken by Elliot belting out "Baby One More Time" from the en suite as he showers. The boy has some lungs on him.

"It's quite the concert," Jack says from the other side of the bed, looking up from his phone. "We're very privileged to be here today, experiencing this. Would you like some hotel room tea with that vile powdered milk?"

"I can do it."

Jack slides out of bed. "Relax. I'm making some anyway."

I watch as he starts fussing around the tiny kettle and the little packets containing the tea bags. I still feel guilty about everything. The hurt in Jack's voice last night nearly killed me, but even so, I'm not sure I would have done anything differently. I don't know why other people have to make things so hard. The fallout from all the stuff at prom has only gone to prove that point, but even before that, like in year seven, at the dance, Chloe and her gang ripped me to shreds when they saw me and Jack dancing to "Embers" by Owl City—a song we had claimed as being "ours." For weeks afterward, if they saw me in the corridors, they would start to flail their arms about, legs kicking out in all directions, like they were in spasm or having a fit. I'd only been enjoying myself; I loved that song, with its message about burning brightly and not letting the fire die, even when things are tough. But the fire did die. Chloe and the others saw to that. If I'd hung out with Jack in year nine, if we'd stayed as best friends, if I'd come out too, I'd have been targeted like he was. I'm not proud of myself. He shone like a star. I was just ashes. And just when the embers were starting to glow again, I feel like this thing with Tariq has extinguished them.

Jack leans against the desk, waiting for the kettle to boil. "Dylan posted a 'felt cute, might delete later' pic this morning," he says. "*Vom.*"

I roll my eyes.

"Pouting at the camera, like that's normal first thing in the morning," he mutters. He glances at me. "You OK?"

I nod. "You?"

"Yeah." He flicks his eyes back to the kettle.

There's some clattering from the en suite, then the door flies open, and Elliot does a grand jeté into the room, wearing just a towel tied around his waist.

"Baby one more time!" he howls, performing a version of a pirouette, as the towel flies off him. Otherwise stark bollock naked, he quickly cups his hands over his crotch and fumbles for the towel.

Jack and I just stare at him.

"Shower's free," Elliot says once the towel is safely around him again. "Also, guess what?"

"I don't know, Elliot, what?" Jack says, pouring hot water into the cups.

"Guess."

Jack sighs, clearly not quite up for this yet. "The complimentary shampoo is to die for?"

Elliot grins and shakes his head. "Actually, it's not bad, but it's not that."

Jack tips some sugar into my cup.

"News of the day!" Elliot declares, clearly bored of waiting. "I've booked us all a group massage! Usually they're for bachelorette parties, but they know we're boys. It's an hour long and it's to promote relaxation and calm. My treat!" he continues. "Gonna use some of my big cash prize from last night! Have you had a massage before? I had one when we went on vacation to Lanzarote last year." He lowers his voice pointlessly. "Wear some tight boxers, that's my tip. Just in case."

I'll be honest, I'm not in love with the idea of a random stranger touching me, but it's thoughtful of Elliot and very kind of him to pay, so I do my best to smile and look grateful.

After a cup of tea, I have a shower. Except I secretly check Instagram in the bathroom, and I see a post from Tariq, and now I just feel like spending the whole day under the duvet. It's a picture of him laughing, a candid sort of shot, which genuinely looks candid, just Tariq, relaxed, utterly joyful, and the caption: *Yesterday ranks as one of my Top Five Best Days Ever.*

I already know that his number one Best Day Ever was the time he went to Disneyland, and his number two Best Day Ever was the day he *found out* he was going to Disneyland. That leaves three further Best Days Ever, and if one of those is taken up with whatever he was doing yesterday with Dylan, my question is, is one of the remaining two anything to do with me? Because, here's the thing—most of my Best Days Ever are connected with Tariq. Pretty much every single time he came to find me in the library was a Best Day—seriously, just that short interaction with him would put a smile on my face for *hours*. I would be walking on air I was so happy he spoke to me. The day I actually got together with Tariq is obviously a top Best Day Ever. Mum thought I'd taken up drugs because I was "acting out of character"—that's how happy I was. Kissing Tariq—Best Day Ever. Spending the day with Tariq in the shopping center, and even though we didn't do anything that would make anyone think we were boyfriends, just *knowing*, having that little secret? Best. Day. Ever.

But do I feature in his top five? Did I ever? Or did I once, but have now been replaced by better memories, better days, a better boy?

Anyway, all this is playing on my mind as Dad signs the massage consent forms ("Ooh, it says there may be intimate touching! I'm signing a form giving permission for my teenage

217

son to be 'intimately touched'! Go on, son, go and get 'intimately touched'!") and we are introduced to the people who will be doing our massages. Elliot is with a very kind-looking young woman called Maria, who oozes gentleness. Jack is with Javier, who is Spanish and beautiful, with devastating eyes and an aura of calm. And I'm with Olga, who is exactly like you'd imagine. Before I know it, we're all lying facedown on massage tables, boxers on (I took Elliot's advice), and towels over us from the waist down, in this candlelit room that smells of lavender and other herbs I don't know the names of, with gentle music playing—mainly the odd ripple of water, some wind, the sound of a quiet bell, some whales shagging, I don't know.

"Is this pressure OK?" Maria purrs at Elliot.

"Mmm," he replies.

"This feels all right?" Javier asks Jack.

"Huh, *yeeeeah*," Jack moans. "Ahhh, yeeeeeah . . ."

Olga whacks me hard on the back. "YOU HAVE MANY KNOTS! WE NEED MUCH PRESSURE!"

I grimace and bite into the pillow. I'm not sure what the protocol is, but I sense I'm just meant to take it. We lie in silence for a bit, the other two making occasional groans of what definitely sounds like pleasure, while Olga works away on me like a pneumatic drill, pummeling my flesh and muttering things like, "So many knots!" and, "Ach! So tight!"

Of course, Elliot can't stay quiet for long, so after about five minutes, he pipes up with, "So we can spend the day in the spa here if you boys fancy it? Jack?"

"Yes, perfect," he moans. "Oh my god, this is better than red velvet cake."

"Nate? Or do you think your folks will want to get away?"

"I mean, ARGH! AH! AH! I'm sure they'll AHHH! HA! ARGH! UG! Be happy to stick around for a—WAAAAA AHH! Christ!"

"RELAX!" commands Olga. "So TENSE! These knots!"

I release a breath. "I'll do whatever."

"We could swim for a bit," Elliot says.

"Yeah."

"And there's a sauna, steam room, and some relaxation pods . . ."

"Hm," I mutter, finding it hard to muster the enthusiasm for anything because all I can think about is, *AM I ONE OF TARIQ'S TOP FIVE DAYS?* And to a lesser extent: *Am I just one giant bruise at this point?*

"What's up, Nate?" Jack asks.

It almost makes me smile, the way Jack just *knows* something is up. He's always had this sort of sixth sense. He'd know when I was worrying about a test or upset about something. But what I'm upset about today is stupid. And I don't really want to share it. So I just say, "Nothing."

"'Cause you sound kinda sad," he continues.

I don't know what Olga does, but something pings sharply by my spine. "ARGH! I'm fine."

"Sometimes it's good to talk," Elliot adds. "If you're sad."

"I'm not sad." I take a deep breath, then exhale. "I'm—AAAARGH!—not."

"We had this guy come to our school, year eight, it was, and he did this whole speech on how it's good to talk, especially boys because apparently we're really bad at it? He said we should share our concerns, anxieties, and fears. So I told this other boy who was one of my friends that I was worried about the fact I hadn't started puberty yet, you know, I thought we could have an adult conversation about it? Anyway, he nodded and listened, and then he went and told everyone and then at lunchtime I got gaffer taped to one of the goalposts on the playing field by some bigger, very definitely pubescent boys, with a sign around my neck that read, 'I've got no pubes.' But that aside, yay for talking."

I do actually laugh at this. "I'm sorry, Elliot. It's not funny."

"Yeah, I know," he says. "It's fine."

I sigh again as Olga works her thumb under my shoulder blade. It's starting to feel nicer. There's tension releasing. "It's just Tariq," I say. And then I explain the Top Five Day thing, just blurt it all out, because if I stop to think about it too much, I'll never say it.

No one says anything.

Nothing from Jack.

Elliot — totally silent.

So now I feel stupid. This is why I don't talk. You just end up making a fool of yourself.

"At the time, did you feel it was?"

It's Javier. I twist my head to the right. Brilliant. Now the spa staff are joining in with my tragic life.

"What do you mean?" I ask.

"At the time, did you feel you might be having a best day ever?"

I sigh. "I guess. I mean, yes, from my point of view. I think, hope, maybe from his."

"Then that's all the matters," Javier says. "No one can take that away from you. Not anyone. Everything else changes, but you'll always have that."

I mull over what he's said.

"Mm, Javier, your advice is as good as your hands," Jack says. "Which, just so you know, are those of an *angel*."

"You're very kind," Javier says.

"Mmm." Jack giggles. *God*, that boy.

"He is right!" Olga suddenly barks, simultaneously kneading her hands into my upper thigh, which makes me yelp with surprise.

"Yeah, but I don't want it to change. I want to always be in his Top Five, because he'll be in mine. I don't want bloody *Dylan* to replace me."

"You cannot control the feelings of others," Maria says. "You cannot, and you should not try. That's their life. And this is yours. You need your own best days."

"I'll tell you some of my best days," Jack says.

I'm not sure I want to know. This will be about when he came out, how liberated he felt, his new mates in the LGBTQ+ club — and probably the boys he's flirted with, kissed, and what have you.

"Jack and Nate's Paranormal Investigations," he continues.

I laugh. It's a million miles from what I was expecting.

"What?" Elliot giggles. "You two were . . . ghost hunters?"

"Uh-huh!" Jack says.

"We were nine," I add, just in case Elliot thought this was, like, last year or something.

"Did you catch any?" Elliot asks.

"Well, Nate tried to exorcise the demon he was convinced resided inside Daisy McGuire."

"And Jack wanted to drive a stake through the heart of the guy at the end of my road because he thought he was a vampire," I say.

"I saw him drinking blood, Nate!"

"Nah, I still think it was more likely cranberry juice."

"Daisy McGuire's mum was *livid* we threw that bucket of holy water over her. *So ungrateful,*" Jack says.

I chuckle at the memory. "Serious, though? Those rank as some of your best days?"

"Hundred percent," Jack says, meeting my eyes across our massage tables. "That was a good summer, me and you, doing that."

I smile because, yeah, it was good, and I'd forgotten about it until Jack reminded me. We used to have fun. With him, I used to feel like nobody else mattered. We were invincible.

"What would be a best day for you, Elliot?" Jack asks.

Elliot blows out a breath. "Ohh, pretty much any day when I'm doing any of my favorite things. Watching anything set in the Marvel universe, Archie and Jughead, sleeping, cupcakes, bikes, food of any sort, Fortnite, ukulele practice, *Cats*—the *original* stage musical, *not* the weird movie—ham sandwiches, dew on the grass on an autumn morning, Pringles, and nachos with melted cheese, sour cream, salsa, and guacamole." He takes a thoughtful breath. "Even just one of those things equals a best day, really."

"So *every* day is basically your best day?" Jack says.

"Basically! Ohh! And Christmas! I love Christmas! And hens."

Well, lucky Elliot. I can't imagine feeling like that. Things started turning sour the moment I turned thirteen and only seem to have gotten worse. The only saving grace is you're not sixteen forever. Thank god for that. Imagine if you were, and you were just stuck in this permanent rut of stress, gloom, FOMO, and social media shitstorms. Unless you're Elliot.

"We need a photo!" Jack announces.

Maria does the honors, as we all crane our necks up from our massage tables. Jack's giving it staring-into-the-middle-distance eyes, Elliot's actually attempting to dab, and I was trying a smile before Olga gave me a very firm fist in my glute and made me actually howl. I'm sure it'll be an excellent photo. I tell Jack to caption it as *One of the best days ever* because despite everything with Tariq, one good thing that's happened is that I've finally started to be honest with Jack, and he doesn't hate me for it, and it feels like maybe we're reconnecting a bit. And you know what? Being friends again with Jack? Yeah, that *would* be one of the best days ever.

"You don't know how much I envy you," I tell Elliot as we settle down again.

"Hey," Elliot says. "You'll get there. It might not seem it right now, but you'll get there." His eyes meet mine. "Do you need a hug?"

Know what? Maybe I *am* ready for hugs again. Maybe I've spent too long pushing people away and drowning in my own thoughts. I smile at Elliot. "Maybe later."

"OK, maybe later." He smiles back.

TWENTY-SEVEN

JACK

"Would you like a hug?"

"Maybe later."

Which is why, after our massage session was over, I left Nate and Elliot to do their own thing and made some feeble excuse about wanting to check out the lifeguard by the pool—who, by the way, doesn't exist. They're sweet together, although I can't help feeling a little bit hurt that Nate has always point-blank refused my hugs, yet very much leaves open the prospect of future hugs from my cousin. But fine. That's the way of love and romance, and I detect that's very much what's going on here. And honestly, if it makes Nate happy, if it cheers him up, then it's all good as far as I'm concerned.

Then I'm smiling again because thinking about the paranormal investigations reminds me of all the other random stuff Nate and I used to do—not just the ghost hunters, but the secret club in the tree house and the detective agency we formed to solve low-level crimes in the area, using talcum powder to dust for fingerprints. Those were great days. Wonderful days. And I think some of my best because . . . well, they just were.

So I'm just sitting alone with my thoughts (and a virgin mojito complete with pink cocktail umbrella) by the side of the pool, on a very aesthetically pleasing rattan sofa, about to take an epic selfie, when I become aware of another person, who takes the sofa opposite. On the one hand, I hate it when people infringe on my space—especially when there's no shortage of alternative space nearby. You know, like those people who come and sit next to you on the train when there are plenty of other seats literally everywhere else—you just want to shoot them. So on the one hand, I did want to shoot this person. But on the other, they might be a hot boy, in which case, everything is forgiven and I'm going to be sweetness and light.

They are not a hot boy.

They are a girl.

But not just any girl.

My mouth drops open because can this really be true?

"Leila Bhatia?" I say out loud. My eyes widen and she looks

up from her phone. "Oh. My. Actual. Days." She looks relatively unimpressed, but I carry on because, Oh. My. Actual. Days! "I love your account, I've followed it for years, the aesthetic is—" I make the sign of a chef kissing his fingers. "And you're very witty, and I respect and thank you for your support of the LGBTQ-plus community, and I buy everything you recommend. You are without question my favorite influencer and I am very influenced by you. I love you. Actually. *Hi*."

"Hi," she says. She doesn't smile. I don't care. This is so cool. A million things are racing through my head, but they all end with ARE WE GOING TO GET A PIC TOGETHER OH YES WE ARE!

"Wow, so, here you are. Is this one of those paid promotion things? Are you doing something for the hotel?"

Leila nods. "I am."

"Cool. So, cool." I can't take my eyes off her. I can't believe it's really her. Leila Bhatia!

"Are you just going to stare at me?"

"Oh, no, sorry."

"Because it's slightly awkward."

"Yes."

"What's that you're drinking?"

"Mojito. *Virgin*. That's to say, the drink is, not—"

Leila puts her hand up to stop me. "OK—"

I don't know why I'm babbling, I just can't believe I'm sitting opposite Leila Bhatia!

"Could you order me one?"

My eyes nearly pop out. "OH MY GOD YES!" I shout.

She stares at me a moment, then blinks once. "Thank you."

I scamper off to the bar, order another mojito, and carry it back, placing it carefully in front of Leila, who is busy on her phone, probably influencing people and other important stuff. If I'm nice to her, she might like me, and if she likes me, she might help me. If I can just get a pic of her and me to post or, even better, if I can be tagged in one of her photos that *she* posts, I will be over the moon and this will totally be number-one best day ever and *take that* Dylan and Tariq, who's the victor now, baby?!

"How much do I owe you?" she says.

I shake my head.

She rolls her eyes, pulls a five-pound note out of her bag, and puts it on the table between us. I just look at it. I don't want to take it. "It's fine," I say. "You can get the next one." I clock the look of surprise in her eyes. "Not that there will necessarily be a 'next one,' I'm not saying . . ." I lick my lips. Why am I like this? I can't even think straight. "Just to be clear, I'm gay."

She looks up from sipping her drink. "And you're telling me that because?"

"Oh, I was worried I was sort of making it sound like this was a date, which . . ." *Shut up, Jack!* "Oh god, I'm sorry, I'm fanboying all over you. I'm so embarrassed, I'm so sorry." I sit back on the sofa. "I'm Jack by the way."

Now she smiles. "Hey, Jack."

"Hey."

"Sorry, I'm not normally as morose as this, but as per, crap is kicking off online." She rolls her eyes.

"Yeah?" I say.

She nods. "Call me intolerant and close-minded—which is in fact what some people are calling me—but I don't think certain influencers should make bold claims online about how drinking beetroot juice and turmeric can cure everything from diabetes to cancer without, you know, just a small shred of medical evidence."

"Ohhhh."

"It's one thing being slung some cash for saying you like some makeup that's actually relatively shit, but messing with people's health?" She whistles. "It's low. And it's wrong."

"You've spoken out. You've done the right thing."

She gives me a small smile. "Well, I think so, but apparently that just means I'm 'in the pay of big pharma' and these days every opinion must be respected, even when it's clearly bullshit, so what can you do?"

I sip my drink. My god, I had no idea this influencer thing was so complex. I just want some free clothes and to be one of the ones who get a free Virgin Atlantic flight.

"You know what this mojito needs?"

"Rum. It needs rum."

She nods solemnly.

"To be honest," I continue, "I only ordered it because all the others have tacky names—Sex on the Beach? Screaming Orgasm? I thought this was a classy joint."

She laughs. "So what's a classy boy like you doing here?"

"Well, there's a thing . . ." I say. And I tell her. I tell her it all. I keep it as brief as I can, highlights, bullet points, anything I've said that's particularly witty or clever.

"Your ex dumped you *at prom?*" she says when I've finished.

"Oh, you're back at the start? Yes. That's basically the shape of it." I drop my eyes, but when I glance up again, she's staring at me with pity.

"That's so shitty," she says. "Actually, that's just terrible behavior."

I shrug. "Well, hey, things happen."

She studies me for a moment. "Why aren't you more angry? Isn't this what this whole highlights reel is about? Revenge?"

"Maybe."

She nods. "I could get on board with that."

I laugh. It comes out a little nervous. "What do you mean?"

"Jack, you might be exactly what I've been looking for."

I'm all ears. Literally, I just want to hear everything she is about to say.

"Influencing is so much bullshit. All I'm doing is using my platform to sell people crap. But what *you* need is sweet, sweet revenge. So much worthier! And so much fun!" She grins at me, eyes sparkling. "Maybe I could help you? Maybe I could see what I could do to get you some shots he'll be envious of." She slurps the last of her mojito. "How about a festival?"

My eyes widen. "Um, *yes!*"

"I'm doing a promo for one in a couple of days. I could easily swing some extra passes for you and Nate."

This is all too fabulous. And then I remember the slight issue. "Um, I might need one or two more, you see—"

She smiles at me. "Aww, I wondered how you were getting around when you're not even old enough to buy alcohol. You're with your parents, aren't you?"

I feel my cheeks heat up a bit. "Kinda."

"Cute."

The worst word that any boy hates being described as.

"That's fine, Jack. It's a family-friendly festival, so actually a real family would be fine. I'm going to give you my number . . ." She holds her hand out for my phone and I watch, mesmerized, as she types it in.

"I won't sell it on any forums," I tell her when she hands it back to me.

She frowns. "Wow. Thanks."

"OK, but I'm just saying. You can trust me."

"Message me tomorrow for the deets," she continues, ignoring me. "And let's really show your horrible exes just what an amazing summer you're having!"

* * *

There's absolutely no point in asking his dad—it's Nate's mum who makes the decisions in this family, so it's her I must persuade. I have an angle. I just hope she goes for it.

"Afternoon!" I chirp, approaching her sun lounger by the side of the pool. She's wearing a floppy sun hat and a white linen smock, and honestly, her skin is so pale I'm worried she's going to do herself an injury sitting out in the sun like this. "Some much needed R and R I see!"

She takes her sunglasses off. "Are you boys having a nice day?"

"One word—*fabulous.*"

She laughs. "It is nice here. Where's my son and does he still have an attitude problem?"

I sit down on the edge of the lounger next to her. "This thing with Tariq hit him hard. I'm working on it." I swallow, my stomach heavy. "You know, he's been actually *laughing* with Elliot . . ."

"They still get on well, do they?"

"Oh, yes, they . . . *Really well.* You know, I was thinking, maybe Elliot could come along with us for a bit? If you guys don't mind. I think . . . Nate might really like that?"

She meets my eyes, trying to work me out. She'll have a job; I'm not sure *I* can work me out. I'm just doing a nice thing for Nate—so why do I feel kinda weird and sad about it? "Does Nate *like* him?" she says.

"Pfft. How should I know? I don't know." Really now, she should know the rules: parents don't get to ask their kid's mates about stuff like that.

She leans toward me. "Say no more," she whispers, giving me a wink.

"OK then."

"This trip is all about going with the flow, because as Mick keeps telling me, I'm lacking spontaneity!"

I seize my chance. "OK, well, that's a good motto to live your life by—"

"It really isn't."

"OK, but sometimes living in and for the moment can be a—"

"Really stupid thing to do."

"OK, but also it can be—"

"Irresponsible."

"And—"

"A recipe for waking up in one, two, or five years' time with a truckload of debt, no pension, and the only thing you have to show for it is some photos of some donkey trek in Peru."

"OK, but—"

"Oh! The stories you'll be able to tell though!" She smiles, looking wistfully into the distance.

"Exactly!"

"Which is lucky, because stories are all you will have, as you freeze to death while eating instant noodles in a damp studio apartment because you didn't bother getting a job, but at least you 'lived life.'"

"How do you fancy attending a festival?"

"Jack." She closes and opens her eyes slowly. *"No."*

My eyes widen. "OK, but festivals are fun."

"Jack," she says. "A festival? Really? Think of the germs."

"And the fun!" I say. "Just for one or two nights? See, we've been given free tickets by an Instagram influencer I met, and it's a *family* festival, which means it won't be full of people on drugs."

"They'll just be less obvious about it, but trust me, it will be."

"I think Nate might like it . . ."

She narrows her eyes. "Clever move. Now mine: only on condition you all attend, without complaint, a day that I have planned tomorrow."

I purse my lips. "What . . . what *type* of day?"

"You have to agree to it."

"Is it shopping? Can we go shopping? Is there a Zara we could hang out in for a bit?" If it was that, we could definitely do the "hashtag gifted" post I've been dying for.

"Jack, you have to agree. I'm not telling you. Live for the moment, go with the flow, remember?"

I mean, how bad could it be? This is Nate's mum we're talking about, she's hardly going to put us all in mortal danger doing something humiliating, way out of our comfort zone.

"You have a deal," I say.

TWENTY-EIGHT

NATE

Jack has literally been gone all day, so I'm guessing his pursuit of the legendary "pool boy" he mentioned went well. I was a bit sad though. After he mentioned Jack and Nate's Paranormal Investigations, I got thinking about all the other hilarious stuff we used to get up to—sure, there was the detective agency where we basically accused my next-door neighbor of brutally murdering his wife and burying her under the patio (in fact, she had gone to Scunthorpe for a week, which, in fairness, is actually worse), but also there was the two-man production of *Wicked* we mounted in Jack's sitting room and the craft shop we opened, selling homemade bookmarks and potpourri. I mean, I don't want to be stereotypical, but did *everyone* know we were gay before we did? They *were* great days, and part of me wanted to laugh with him more about all that stuff. But he went off, like Jack does, doing his thing, and, well . . .

Anyway, it's fine, I've been with Elliot all day, and *what* a day it's been. After the massage we went to the spa. We tried the sauna but my anxiety about the possibility of a door malfunction kicked in, and I started to panic about how we would be slowly cooked alive, so we had to go. Elliot was fine about it though, and because the other spa users were (a) a lot of hairy old men in Speedos and (b) a drunken bachelorette party who kept yelling at Elliot to "get yer tits out" even though Elliot doesn't have tits he can get out, we decided to leave. So we played table tennis, then we had some lunch (ham and cheese toasted sandwiches), then we had a swim, then we played giant chess, then giant Connect 4, then Elliot signed us up for a tour of local spots of supernatural interest by renowned local "ghost hunter" Dr. Edith D'eath, (*not* a made-up name, they had the gall to claim), and I had to say, "Elliot, can we not just have a sit-down?" And he was fine with that, so we had a sit-down, and now I'm here in reception, knackered, and waiting for my parents so we can get on the road again. Elliot is sitting next to me on the sofa, his leg pressed against mine (not deliberately, I think, he's just spatially unaware), as he literally talks about whatever is in his head at any given moment.

"Aren't those flowers nice on the table? I got given flowers on Valentine's Day this year, can you believe it? At school! Well, not flowers, just a single rose, I thought it must be from my mum but

235

it turned out it was this girl called Molly, I actually pricked my finger on the thorn and I thought, Oh no, maybe now I'll fall asleep for a thousand years . . . Oh, that's spinning wheels, isn't it? What even is a spinning wheel? Do people still use them? Oh, hi, Mum—"

"Elliot," she says, standing in front of us. "Nate's parents have very kindly asked if you'd like to join them for part of their road trip."

OK, that's total news to me, and I have no idea why they wouldn't ask me first, but, hey, Elliot's cool so I guess it'll be fun. Elliot is now buzzing with excitement about the idea, which is very sweet, and actually, now things are a bit easier between me and Jack, maybe we'll all start to have a better time.

"Roooooooaaaaaad triiiiiiiip!" Elliot squeals.

He wants to high-five me. I let him.

"OK, so," his mum continues, "you don't have enough underwear, so—"

"Mu-um," Elliot growls. "I can *buy* underwear. I'm a man of means now."

"Fine," she says. "Just make sure you do. I know what you boys are like, you'd happily run around in the same pair for a week if you could."

Elliot slaps his forehead. "Lies! Stereotypes!"

"Right, well, have fun, and—"

Elliot's eyes widen, waiting, I've no doubt, for the thing parents always say, even with a hint of a joke in their voice (despite meaning it), about not "doing anything they wouldn't do" which basically means have sex, take drugs, drink, or perform motorcycle stunts without a helmet through hoops of fire over hundred-foot drops. Sensibly, he doesn't even let her start. "I will! I will!" he says. "I'll be sensible. I'll call you. I won't do any of the things you're fretting about, and if I do, I won't tell you."

"Don't get a tattoo," she says.

Elliot holds his hands out, like *WTF?*

She narrows her eyes. "Or a piercing."

"Not even get my nipple pierced?" He grins.

"We've been through this, and no." She cocks her head. "OK?"

"OK."

"We good?"

"Uh-huh."

She nods at Elliot, and he nods back. Then he stands up and gives her a hug. "Love you, miss you," he says.

She pecks him on the cheek.

As she goes, he turns to me and says in a deliberately loud whisper, "Right! Let's download Grindr and lie about our age!" Then waves and gives her a thumbs-up.

"Who dis?" I say, as Jack rounds the corner and bounds up to us.

"Boys," Jack says, squeezing himself between me and Elliot on the sofa. He stretches his arms out across each of our shoulders and pulls us into him. "So, I've been busy making plans, networking, and so on. Long story short, met Leila Bhatia in the actual living flesh . . ." He waits for some reaction from me or Elliot, but obviously he gets none because I've literally no idea who that is.

"Aaand thanks to all my charms, I've bagged us VIP free tickets for a festival, so yay for me! Any questions or compliments?"

"Yes," I say. "My mum will never agree to a festival."

"Aha!" Jack says.

I briefly close my eyes. "What have you done?"

"She's agreed to it! Yay for me again! Any further questions or compliments?"

"No, Jack," I say. "My mother does not simply agree to us going to a festival. What did you say to her *exactly*?"

Jack runs his tongue along his lips. "Anything is possible when you're prepared to give and take. We have something *we* want to do; she has something *she* wants us to do."

"Oh no," I mutter. "You've made a pact with the devil."

"What's the worst it could be?" Jack smiles. "Come on! What's the worst thing it could possibly be?"

I take a deep breath. "An Outward Bound center where we're forced to do something in water with a load of other kids our age."

Jack nods, tight-lipped.

"Jack?" I say.

"OK, so it's an Outward Bound center with some other kids our age, OK, *yes*, but I'm not sure there's water involved."

"What's the center called?"

Jack chews his lip. "White Water Lakes."

"Right," I say. "Well, that's it. We're fucked." Just as I dared to imagine we might start having a good time, *this* happens, because THIS IS MY LIFE SO OF COURSE IT DOES!

"It sounded fine!" Jack protests.

"Argh! This is what she does! She's always trying to get me to do things she thinks her nightmare sister and my incredibly critical grandma would approve of! Seriously, it's always awful museums for their educational value, bloody *art galleries*, frickin' anything involving physical exertion in the outdoors because my grandma comes from a generation who think boys especially need wholesome physical pursuits else we'll just jerk ourselves off to death. You've literally just given her everything she's ever dreamed of!"

"OK, well, I was just trying to do a nice thing for us," Jack mutters.

We sit in silence for a bit until Elliot says, "Kid at my school actually died kayaking."

I take an unsteady breath.

There's a lot of huffing and banging to my right. "Don't worry, you healthy, fit boys. Just relax while your ageing parents and small sister pack all the luggage back into the bus!" It's Mum, with Dad and Rose in tow.

"I didn't know where you were. Nobody tells me anything, *as per.*"

She gives me a very pleased-with-herself smile. A smile that basically says, *Joke's on you, you're gonna be in a canoe within twenty-four hours!*

"Hear you're joining us, Elliot?" Dad says.

"Buzzing!" Elliot grins.

Rose rolls her eyes. "Just what this sausage party needs—more sausage."

"Rose!" I'm totally outraged. What the hell? "You can't say things like that! Where did you even get that from?"

Rose shrugs.

"Probably just one of those Disney Channel shows," Mum says, tapping her phone. "Why isn't Google Maps loading?"

I screw my face up. "Really, Mum? Really? I'm pretty confident that's one phrase that's never been broadcast on the Disney Channel, but only I seem bothered, so that's cool."

Jack leaps up and takes Rose's hand. "You are *hilarious* and I love that, and as a reward, I'm going to tell you a magical story during the journey. Would you like that?" Jack smiles at me maliciously.

"Yes, please, Jack," Rose says, all saccharine sweet.

"Very well," Jack says. "Once upon a time there was a handsome, charismatic, intelligent, and weirdly single prince, and a mean, grumpy, spiteful ogre. Even though the prince tried to do nice things for the ogre, he just got it slapped back in his face the whole time because the ogre was an old miser who just wallowed in gloom and was a literal killer of joy. In fact, the ogre had killed all the joy in the whole kingdom, so there was no joy left and everyone was *very* sad. But the brave prince had a plan because he knew the ogre didn't used to be so bitter—"

"Right!" I say. "So I hear we're off to the Outward Bound center?"

"That's tomorrow," Mum says. "We're staying the night at Auntie Karen's."

I stare at her as the blood drains from my face. "Oh *no*."

TWENTY-NINE

JACK

I'd assumed Nate's lack of enthusiasm about staying the night with Auntie Karen was just Nate being Nate, but within five seconds of meeting the woman, I can see she's a nightmare. I'm not sure how much older than Mrs. Nate she actually is, but she gives the impression it's at least ten years. She wears a blunt bob cut and a permanent look of disapproval. But that's not the worst of it.

"I wasn't expecting quite so many of you," she says as she ushers us all in through the massive front door of her huge farmhouse, somewhere just north of Cambridge. "I've put you boys in the barn; I'm sure you'll prefer having more space to all bunking up in one room together, and there's plenty of straw in there."

"In the barn with straw—like *animals*?" I hiss at Nate.

Nate just shrugs and gives me an *I told you so* type of look.

"Sorry, Karen," Nate's mum says. "We've somewhat multiplied."

"Hmm, positively viral," Karen replies. "In you come anyway—shoes off, boys, please! We don't need three pairs of muddy trotters running through the house."

"Oh my god," I mutter as I kick my sparkling silver sneakers off.

"It'll get worse," Nate whispers.

We're herded through to the huge kitchen at the back of the house, which is decked out in marble countertops, an Aga stove, four other ovens fitted into a unit on the wall, and even a built-in coffee machine. On one of the walls some words are painted: "Have hope. Be strong. Laugh loud. Play hard. Live in the moment. Dream BIG. Smile often," and so on. It's so inspirational it makes me want to slit my wrists. "Sit down, everyone," Karen instructs us. "I've made a stew—as I say, I wasn't expecting so many of you, but hopefully I can make it stretch."

I raise my hand. "I'm very happy to not eat. I had—"

"Well, it's made now, so we don't want to waste it, do we?" Karen snaps. She starts slopping it out into some small bowls. "A cow died to make this stew."

I look, unblinking, at Nate, who just shakes his head. At least she's serving it to us in crockery. I was half expecting to be eating from a trough on the floor. When the stew has been handed out, Nate's mum takes a small spoonful and immediately says, "Oh my goodness, this is delicious, Karen, thank you so much!"

and everyone makes little noises of agreement, and then we all eat in agonizing silence for what feels like ten minutes. And for the purposes of full disclosure, the stew is *not* delicious. The meat is tough, the stock watery and thin, and the vegetables hard. All the kitchen equipment known to man cannot help Karen cook, but then it's very clear that Karen does not see food as a pleasurable thing—it's purely functional. I can tell from the look of hard focus on her face that Karen eats only to stay alive, and if she could just take a pill instead of an actual meal, she would. Although she would still want a kitchen with five ovens.

"How are the kids?" Nate's mum asks.

"Izzy is having a gap year before university—she's building wells in Africa."

"Oh, where in Africa?" I ask.

Karen's brow furrows. *"Africa!"*

I blow out a small breath.

"Jonty's in his final year at St. Marks High—he's predicted all As for A levels and he's got a place at Oxford. I think they liked the fact he's head boy and rugby captain. He's actually down in Twickers for the week."

I glance at Nate and mouth, *Twickers?* because anyone who is called Jonty and goes to "Twickers" (rather than Twickenham) needs to be obliterated. But Nate just looks scared and shakes his head at me again.

Karen glances at Nate with an overly wide smile. "What about you, Nate?"

Nate puts his fork down.

"Sorry," Karen says. "Can you put that in your bowl, not on the table, please?"

"Sorry," Nate says, hurriedly picking the fork back up.

"So are you staying on for sixth form, or what?" Karen asks.

"Um . . . yeah."

Karen waits for more, but Nate's clammed up and I don't blame him. Karen shakes her head and turns to Nate's mum. "He doesn't talk much—is he going through a moody phase?"

"He's all right," Nate's dad says.

Now he's finally spoken, Karen has someone new to terrorize. "So, *Micky*, such a terrible shame you lost your job at the yogurt factory."

"Yeah."

Karen nods, looking very concerned. "But I suppose everyone is turning against dairy these days—what with the environment and all, and if you don't adapt, you die. We've cut down to six international fights a year and bought bamboo toothbrushes. What about you guys? I see you're trundling around the country in that clapped-out bus—is it even unleaded?"

Nate's dad goes to speak.

"Rhetorical question!" Karen says, raising her hand to stop him. "I'm just saying we all need to be mindful of our consumption these days. That's why we made a conscious decision not to fly on vacation this summer—we're taking a cruise instead. Those ships are something else, let me tell you. The food is out of this world. And the shows! West. End. Standard."

"You know that cruise ships emit three times more carbon than aircraft, right?" I smile.

Karen stares at me. She literally wants to speak to my manager, *right now.*

But it's OK. Nate's mum jumps in with an overly chirpy, "Oh, that sounds wonderful, Karen!" I don't know why she's so submissive and simpering toward her older sister, but it's really pissing me off.

"You should definitely go on a cruise—if you ever get the chance," Karen says, eyes full of tragedy that she thinks we never will because we're not as rich as her.

"Oh, I have," I say.

Karen raises her eyebrows.

Nate actually puts his head in his hands and makes a little whining noise, like a sort of . . . cry for help, I suppose. I get that he wants me to shut up, but I'm not going to sit here and allow this to happen. I don't like people making other people feel like shit.

"Hated it," I merrily continue. "It was just hundreds of obnoxious snobs with no class cooped up on a floating prison. The food wasn't high quality. There was just a lot of it—the variety hiding the fact it's actually nothing special, like an all-inclusive hotel buffet. And the musicals were crap—if I want to see a production of *Grease*—and to be perfectly honest, why would I?—I'll see the proper show with the full cast, stage hydraulics, and flying, thanks." I grin at Karen. "Oh, I'm not saying any of that will happen to you. It was just my experience. I hope you enjoy it, *Karen.*"

Karen's face looks like she's chewing a wasp, that's how much she now hates me.

And then, joy of joys, Elliot pipes up. "Yeah, my gran went on a cruise and it was a brand-new ship and everyone was super excited, until the plumbing malfunctioned and basically all the toilets—" He stops, realizing everyone is just staring at him in horror. "Anyway, it was pretty icky, puke- and poop-wise."

The mention of "poop" makes Rose giggle. "I don't want any more stew. It's horrible," she whispers to Nate's dad, way too loudly.

Karen smiles through all this and then turns to Nate again. "So, *Nate*. How's your love life? Got yourself a nice girlfriend yet?"

OK, so where *do* people get off asking this question?

My god, I want to cancel Karen so badly.

Nate shakes his head, pushing a piece of carrot around his bowl.

But Karen isn't giving up. "Really? I find that surprising, sixteen years old and no girlfriend. Jonty got together with Alice when they were fourteen, and they're still together now."

"No, I'm single," Nate mutters.

"Haven't got your eye on anyone?"

I mean, this woman really is not giving up.

"You're not a *bad*-looking lad—"

Seriously? She actually said that?

"I'm sure there's a young lady out there somewhere for you—"

Nate looks like he's about cry. I can't let this carry on. "Actually!" I say. "Nate, Elliot, and I are all single and we've all had it up to here with love and romance. We're *over it*. Nothing but

246

trouble. People only let you down in the end, and like the words of wisdom on your wall say—" I point at the wall. *"Give up. Stay angry."*

"No, that's *never* give up. *Never* stay angry," Karen says.

"Oh," I say. "That's confusing. All the words are so jumbled up and next to each other. I thought the 'never' was connected to the words below it: *Never* keep your promise."

Karen scowls at me. "That's just, Keep your promise."

"Well, I'm glad we've cleared that up." I stretch and yawn. "I'm *bushed*. Time to cozy down with the other farmyard animals, boys. Karen, is it permitted to use your bathroom, or should I just go in the middle of a field?"

Karen narrows her eyes. "It's up the stairs, first on the right."

"Awesome." I beat my fist on my chest. "Live, laugh, love, everyone!" and I head out to find the bathroom.

Helpfully, the bathroom is also decked out with words on the wall, which is good because if it weren't for the "Shower, enjoy, relax, clean, bathe, tranquility," how would I know what to do in there?

Truth is, I feel bad for Nate, and I feel bad for how I was with him earlier on this trip, at the cabin, and the Travel Inn, when I accused him of not telling people he was gay. Just because I guess I make it look easy, doesn't mean it is for him. And also, it's no one's business but his. God, what if Karen's continuing her interrogation right now? What if poor Nate's cracking under the pressure? I send him a text, just to let him know he's got this, and what better than one of the many quotes on Karen's bathroom wall:

Walk like a champion.

Moments later, Nate replies with,

I swear to god, go fuck yourself.

I chuckle, because any response but especially that sort of response means he's probably OK and there's only a small chance he's furious with me for behaving like I did in front of Karen.

I'm walking along the landing toward the stairs when I hear voices. It's Mr. and Mrs. Nate, having a hissed conversation by the door to their bedroom.

"I don't know, Mick," Mrs. Nate is saying. "She just always makes me feel so bad about myself."

"Well, don't let her!" Mr. Nate replies.

"It's always a competition!" Mrs. Nate continues. "She always has to prove how much more money they have or how their house is bigger, their kids more successful!"

"Is all this because she's going on a cruise?"

"*No*, Mick, it's not because she's going on a cruise. It's . . . well, it's bloody *everything*, isn't it?"

And then I hear the door slam and Mr. Nate sigh heavily.

When I get down to the barn, Nate has already got my sleeping bag out and set it up next to his, with Elliot on his other side. "I got your sleeping bag ready," he says to me.

A smile creeps across my face at his cute little way of being grateful. "Thanks, Nate."

He gives me a small, slightly shy smile back, then sighs and says, "I know I should have told her I was gay."

"Hey," I say. "What you do or don't tell people is entirely up to you. And I was wrong to suggest otherwise, so I'm sorry."

Nate's eyes widen.

"Also, no way would I want to come out to that utter passive-aggressive bitch—why does your mum put up with it? Literally, her sister is a monster."

"She's always been like that. Always trying to show us how much better she and her family are compared to ours."

I nod. "Trust me, no one who has to have 'laugh loud' written on their kitchen wall is ever doing any laughing, and if you're going to have 'shower' and 'bathe' written on your bathroom wall, then why not 'urinate' and 'evacuate your bowels'?"

Nate and Elliot both laugh.

"Well, it's OK. I added them," I say.

Nate turns to me, deadly serious. "Oh god, please say you didn't."

I give him a little wink. "Night, night, sleep tight, hope all the fleas and ticks in this rank barn don't bite!"

Nate scowls, pads over to the light switch, and flicks it off. I hear him stumble through the straw, back to our little camp, and get in his sleeping bag, doing a hell of a lot of huffing and puffing.

"Jack?" he says. "You didn't?"

"I'm asleep."

"Jack? I won't sleep unless you tell me. I know you didn't, but I need you to say it."

"OK then. *I didn't.*"

There's silence for a bit. I can almost hear his mind ticking over. "Argh!" Nate growls. "That makes it sound like you're just saying that now!"

Elliot and I both chuckle.

"OK, something else," Nate says. "That story you told Rose on the way here? About the prince and the ogre? Was that supposed to be about us?"

"Oh! Ho, ho!" I laugh. "*Someone* is clearly going to get a top grade in GCSE English!"

"Shut up, Jack."

"Shut yourself up!"

"I actually hate you."

"Oooooh!" Elliot coos. "Now, now, boys!"

"Nate, is it that you need a hug?" I say.

"No, I'm good, thanks," Nate replies with a real edge to his voice.

Nobody says a word, but Nate is clearly restless, and after a bit he growls, "*Jack!* All I can hear is your breathing!"

"I mean, I have to breathe."

"Well, do it less loudly! Christ! Or I swear to god, I will smother you in the night."

I sit up in my sleeping bag. "Nate, those are very harsh words. You speak of *murder* and *hate*."

"I do," he grumbles.

"But you should speak of *love*."

"Shut. Up."

"Don't make me wrestle you, Nate!" I warn him.

"Yeah, you don't want to be wrestled by Jack," Elliot tells him.

"I just want to sleep now," Nate says.

"You should never go to bed or leave a room on a cross word, Nate."

"That's pretty hard with you around."

"Uh-huh," I say. "Really. And what if . . . suppose you said such mean things, and that was the last time you saw me or I died or something, and then all you would have would be your horrible words and all the guilt."

"Whatever."

"No, but, Nate, it's true! People die all the time. Every second. In the time it's taken me to say this, multiple fatalities have occurred." I take a deep breath. "All I'm saying is, tell people you love them. Hold your loved ones tight. It may be your last chance. And for the record, *I love you, Nate.*"

"Jesus," Nate mutters.

I smile to myself. It's so glorious winding him up like this.

Nate turns over in his sleeping bag. Huffs a bit. Turns again. Huffs some more. "Grrrrgh," he growls.

I wait for it.

More huffing.

More turning.

And then, eventually, in the smallest voice imaginable, "Love you," he mutters.

Finally! This is how it used to be. Gently winding each other up. Enjoying it. Laughing. It feels good to laugh with him again.

THIRTY

NATE

"Happy Sun*gay, Gay*bies!"

I open one eye and see Jack standing in front of me dressed in bright red cut-offs, a white T-shirt, and rainbow suspenders. "Happy Sun*gay*," I croak. He's an absolute *gay vision* and I love him for it. Proud. Confident. He's him and he doesn't care. Like he didn't care about sticking it to Auntie Karen last night — just brilliant. Not sure my parents will think that, but I've been dying to say something for ages.

Elliot stirs next to me. "Morning, is there breakfast?"

"Well, *great* story," Jack says, eyes sparkling. "I went to find our generous host, Karen, in the kitchen, to ask if there was a bag of feed or some turnips I could throw down for the other boys, thinking I was making a joke, but it turns out it's much worse than that. She's made some porridge."

"I like porridge," Elliot says, rubbing the sleep from his eyes.

Jack smiles at him. "Mmm, me too, especially when it's all creamy, with a nice dollop of honey or maple syrup, right? Or some fresh berries or a splodge of jam or loads of sugar sprinkled on top that just starts to caramelize?"

"Mmm!" Elliot agrees.

"Except she's made it with water and salt, and that's it. Literally, it's like we're in *Oliver Twist*. It's *gray*. And there's a great big vat of it congealing in the kitchen."

I sigh. "We'll ask my parents if we can stop at a service station on the way to White Water Lakes—maybe we can have a cooked breakfast."

"Brunch! An excellent idea!" Jack says. "And in the meantime . . ." He pulls his hands out from behind his back. "I may have borrowed a box of Pop-Tarts from the cupboard while Karen was busy beating a small child for stealing a crumb of bread." He slings us a Pop-Tart each, like a Frisbee, but it's too early and my reflexes are too slow.

"Ow! Jack! That hit me on the cheek!"

"Buck up, buttercup, it's just a Pop-Tart!" Jack smiles.

"Well, it really hurt."

"Ohh, I think it's grazed," Elliot says, peering at my cheek.

"It's *grazed*!" I look at Jack accusingly.

"Oh, I'm sorry! How was I to know you'd have such sluggish

hand-eye coordination? I'm sure it'll heal, and in the meantime, it gives you a sort of rugged, masculine quality." He grins, waggles his eyebrows and flounces out of the barn. "Love you!" he sings.

I shake my head, then notice Jack has poked his head back around the door of the barn, waiting.

I scowl at him. I'm not going to say it back. He just hit me with a Pop-Tart!

He cocks his head. Waiting.

This is the thing with Jack: he's got this way of making me feel things . . . like guilt that if I don't say it back I'll regret it, just like I regret all the things I didn't say years ago, and the truth is, I do . . . love him, as in love like a friend, obviously, not . . . Well, anyway.

He's tapping his foot now, and even glances at an imaginary watch on his wrist.

"Love you!" I say. "OK?"

Jack nods and disappears.

I sigh, and dab a bit of Sudocrem from the bottle in my backpack on the graze because I know it's just a Pop-Tart, but it actually stings quite a bit. And then I smile because, for the first time in ages, I've woken up and my first thought wasn't about Tariq, and you know what, that feels good.

* * *

"Teamwork! Coordination! Planning"

Hunter has been standing in front of us for ten minutes now, barking away about what this horrific Outward Bound course is going to involve. When we arrived at White Water Lakes, Mum and Dad booked themselves and Rose onto a paddle boat around the boating lake, whereas me, Jack, and Elliot were booked, by my mother, onto what was terrifyingly described as a "Water Survival Course—intermediate level."

Hunter is a tall, broad man, whose opening gambit was to tell us that he "doesn't suffer fools" and "has no time for losers" because "in the water, every second counts, every person counts, so ditch your ego, ditch your rivalry, and fight to survive."

Great.

To make matters worse, the other kids on this course all know each other—they're from London and doing a program over the summer that gets them out of the city. "Is it because you've never seen grass?" Jack asked one of them.

"No, it's because we're all on probation," the other kid replied.

So. *Great.*

"Communication and cooperation will be your greatest asset," Hunter continues. "Your mission sounds simple. Believe me, it's not. Using the materials provided, each team will build a raft capable of carrying the whole team across the lake to the island in the middle. First team to get there wins the prize that awaits on the island. Glory for the winners; shame for the losers. Lads, this is not a social occasion. This is not some fancy cocktail party. This is survival. This is serious. Dig deep and power through. You!" He points at Jack. "What's your name?"

"OK, so, hi, I'm Jack, and—"

"Stop!" Hunter shouts. "I just asked your name. *Listen* to commands. *Respond* accordingly."

Jack nods.

"Jack, what key word or words are you taking from what I've told you?"

"Fancy cocktail party."

Hunter's eyes darken. "Oh. We have a *joker*."

"Glory, then? Prize! I don't know, build a boat and set sail?"

Hunter stares at him with utterly unimpressed eyes, then he turns to me. "What's that on your face?"

I blink at him. "On my . . ."

"There! On your cheek!"

"Oh, it's Sudocrem. I was . . . I got a graze."

Hunter narrows his eyes. *"A graze."*

"He was hit by a Pop-Tart," Elliot adds.

"Guilty!" Jack trills, holding his hand up.

Hunter looks as though he's about to explode with rage. "Some of you may see this as a bit of fun. A harmless way to pass the time. Let me tell you something. People die in water every year. You never know when the basic skills you'll learn today will be needed."

"This is such bullshit," Jack whispers to me.

He's not wrong. It's everything I feared it would be. But while Jack being Jack worked a treat last night, I'm not sure things will end so well here, so I'm thinking he should really just keep his head down. Jack can be as cheeky as he likes to Auntie Karen—she's not going to batter him. I'm not sure I can say the same for the other kids on this course.

"Team names!" Hunter announces. He looks at Jack.

Jack rolls his eyes. "Gay Ship Lollipop."

"Fine," Hunter says. "You lads?" He points at one group of the London boys.

"Destroyer."

"Wait—" says Jack.

"And you other lads?" Hunter says, ignoring Jack.

"Armageddon."

"We're changing our name!" Jack pipes up.

Hunter gives Jack a malicious smile. "Too late. Words have consequences—first lesson. Armageddon, you're working at the far end of the shore, Destroyer, you're here, and Gay Ship Lollipop, you're at the other end. Your fight for survival begins . . . now!"

Hunter blows a whistle and we all head over to our work areas, where we're presented with six huge, empty plastic barrels, a pile of wooden planks, oars, and various lengths of rope.

Hunter's right over with us. "Any initial plan of action, lads?"

"Lash the planks together in a crisscross formation, attach to the barrels, launch into water, paddle to the island," Jack replies.

"Think. Talk. Communicate" is Hunter's response. "Is there a better way?"

Jack blinks once. "No. That's the way."

Hunter runs his tongue over his lips. *"Talk to each other. Communicate. Teamwork."* And he heads over to the next group.

"All this just so we can go to the festival," Jack mutters as he picks up one of the planks like it's a completely foreign object. "Argh! Splinter!" he squeals, dropping it on his foot. "Argh! Why is this plank so homophobic?"

"Try sucking it out!" one of the lads from the other team shouts across, smirking.

Jack's eyes widen. "Oh my days," he says in hushed tones. "They're talking to us. Let's just get on with it, eyes down, focus."

Which is all well and good, and is certainly my preferred way of dealing with this nightmare situation, but as we start trying to lash together our planks, of course Jack can't help himself but to keep glancing up at the other boys. "That one keeps looking at me!" he hisses.

"Which one?" I ask.

"Don't look!"

"OK, but which one?"

"The one that definitely *would* if it was just you and him alone in a tent with some cider because he's curious but the next day he'll totally ignore you and you'll never speak of it again and then he'll get a girlfriend."

I look over. "Oh, yeah, *him*." The boy (worryingly athletic looking, white, sagging jogging shorts that reveal gray boxers, Adidas sweatshirt, buzz cut) starts walking over to us. "Oh my god. Act normal. Act normal."

"Why you keep looking for?" the boy says.

"Why have you come over?" Jack replies without missing a beat.

"Bro, I come over 'cause you was looking over!"

"Are you sure?" Jack says. "Or were you just attracted by my strong jawline?"

The boy glares at him.

Jack sniffs. "What have you *done* anyway? Why are you on probation?" He lowers his voice. *"Was it a brutal murder?"*

I honestly wish Jack would just shut up, but apparently he's determined to get us all beaten up.

"Hacking," the lad replies.

"What, like computers?" Jack says.

The lad nods. "Yeah. Cybercrime. Specifically, a cryptocurrency scam in my case."

Jack looks impressed. "So why did they send you here?"

"I don't know!" the lad replies, clearly as exasperated as we are. "Everyone always thinks boys need physical activity, innit?"

"Right!" I say.

"And what about your mates?" Jack continues. "Are *they* murderers?"

"Nah," the lad says. "Corey helped ram-raid an ATM using a stolen forklift."

The lad looks at our open-mouthed expressions of wonder and awe. God, he must think we're so provincial and sheltered.

"Messin' with ya!" he grins. "Why do that when a simple card skimmer does all the hard work for ya?"

Jack nods, like he knows all about that. "Mm. And so, were you all in 'juvie' together? Is that what you call it? 'Juvie'?" He runs his tongue over his lips. "Did you have to wear a special . . . uniform?"

"Jack!" I hiss. I mean, really?

The lad rolls his eyes. "It's probation, like I said. Whole point is that means you don't go to juvie."

"Oh, yes, yes, mais oui!" Jack replies.

Hunter blows his whistle. "Lads!"

The boy nods at Jack, then turns and heads back to his group.

"I think he wants me," Jack says. "Do you think he realized I might be gay?"

"Hard to say." I shrug. "You're sitting there in red cut-offs and rainbow suspenders, saying things like 'mais oui' — it'd be pretty impossible for anyone to work out."

"Is anyone going to help build this raft?" Elliot asks, looking up from where he's tying a rope around two planks. "I want to win the prize. What if it's cupcakes?"

"Knowing Hunter, I feel it's more likely to be a cold shower," Jack says, "but if there's even a chance it could be cupcakes, then I agree, we must try our best. Gay boys! Assemble!"

And we get on with the raft building with surprising speed, which is basically what happens when gay boys are thinking about buttercream icing.

We're the last to launch our raft into the lake, but only just, which makes me very happy, since my entire life has been one of not just coming last in any form of competition involving physical activity, but actually coming *badly* last, like half an hour after everyone else. Jack's on one side with a paddle, I'm on the other, and Elliot's at the back, paddling alternately either side, in an attempt to keep us on course.

Hunter blows his whistle from the shore. "Jack from Gay Ship Lollipop! Where's your life jacket?"

"It's on the raft!" Jack replies.

"Put it on! Flotation aids are mandatory!"

"The color clashes with my shorts!"

"Put it on or you'll be disqualified!"

"This is barbaric!"

"Final warning!"

Jack huffs and puffs as he struggles into his life jacket, while the boys from Destroyer start wolf-whistling him. He responds by blowing them kisses. "Oh, you *sweethearts*!" He giggles. Then his face drops as he turns to me and Elliot. "Right, let's paddle and get out of this hellhole before it turns into *Lord of the Flies*."

It's surprisingly hard work. The lake is bigger than it looked from the shore, and trying to steer in a straight line toward the island in the middle is near impossible. This is made harder still as Jack decides now is the time to recreate the iconic scene from *Titanic* for the sake of Instagram. He clambers to his feet, rocking the rickety raft to and fro as he stands at the front, arms outstretched. "Nate! You know what to do!"

"Seriously?" I say.

"Correct your course! Gay Ship Lollipop! Correct your course!" Hunter shouts from the shore.

"Nate!" Jack insists. "And, Elliot? You need to get this moment on your phone."

"Jack, we need to try to get to the island!" I tell him.

"What's more important?" he snaps. "The stupid island or Instagram?"

He's not giving up, so I also struggle to my feet, clamber up behind him, and take his outstretched arms. "I'm flying!" Jack shouts.

"Did you get it?" he shouts to Elliot.

"No, I just got your backs, turn around!" Elliot says.

We do a one-eighty shuffle and assume the position again.

"I'm flying!" Jack says.

"You're on a collision course with Armageddon!" Hunter shouts. "Gay Ship Lollipop! Take evasive action!"

I look to my right and see, to my horror, Team Armageddon frantically waving at us as we career, with speed, toward them. But before I can even open my mouth, it's too late; we plow into them, the impact knocking Jack to his knees and me straight into the water.

"Wow! Bitchy!" Jack shouts at the other team, even though it's totally not their fault.

I'm frozen, shocked, in the freezing water, but manage to grasp the side of our stricken vessel. "Help!" I rasp.

Jack glances at me and takes my hand. "I'm sorry, Nate. There simply isn't room for both of us on this floating wreckage, so you'll just have to freeze to death in the water . . ." He starts singing "My Heart Will Go On."

"Just help me!"

"I'm afraid that's what you get for booking steerage!"

"Screw you! Pull me back on!"

And it's at this point that Elliot tries to help me back on the raft, but the weight of me bearing down on the side causes a catastrophic pivot situation, the entire raft upends, and both Elliot and Jack slide into the water with me.

"Gay Ship Lollipop! You've capsized!" Hunter shouts from the shore.

"Oh my god, I didn't know that. Did you know that?" Jack says.

"Get out of the water, you bunch of *pansies!*" Hunter screams.

Oh. My. God. Even the probation kids are shocked. Everyone just freezes and stares at Hunter on the shore. And me? I don't know exactly where it comes from, but I'm not putting up with it. I'm not having Hunter say that about Jack, Elliot, or me; I've spent my whole life at secondary school just ignoring those sorts of comments, and you know what? No more. It ends. *Right here.*

"*What* did you say?" I shout.

"Don't get all snowflakey on me!" Hunter shouts back. "This is survival! There's no time for any of your whiny Generation Z stuff here!"

I openly laugh at him. "Yeah, OK, Boomer!"

Jack stares at me, completely agog. He can't believe I just said that.

I can't believe it either.

And then a wide grin spreads across Jack's face.

"Hey, *Boomer?*" the hacker lad from Armageddon shouts across to Hunter. "FYI, *mate*, we're '*pansy-fying*' our raft and will now be known as the *Bi*tanic!"

"And we're the Jolly *Roger*!" another lad from Destroyer adds, making a sudden hip thrusting motion at another boy who he promptly rams into the lake.

Hunter blows his whistle, but he's lost all his power now, as the boys from the other two rafts also jump into the lake, shouting, "BOOMER!" as they plunge in.

"Ha!" says Elliot, doing an amazing job of keeping his phone in the air so it doesn't get wet. "No one takes the piss out of our Homo Love Boats!"

"Yeah, *love boat*, baby!" Jack adds.

And maybe it's the freezing water, the adrenaline, I don't know, but Jack and Elliot, simultaneously, like they have some weird gay-boy psychic connection, start singing, to the tune of the B-52's "Love Shack," *"Love Boat! Homo Love Boat!"*

And I find myself joining in. And the other lads join in.

And Hunter is just . . . standing there. He's lost; it's over.

And I'm laughing.

And so is Jack, and so is Elliot, who is busy also snapping away on his phone.

And for the first time ever, I don't care. I'm happy, I'm drenched to the bone, soaking wet, but I'm dancing about, waist deep in water singing about our "Homo Love Boat" and it feels like we're bulletproof, invincible, we're actually unstoppable.

THIRTY-ONE

JACK

The pics Elliot took look hysterical. We're all drenched. My hair is a catastrophe. I think Nate has some algae around his neck. But our faces are pictures of unadulterated *joy*. It's weird, in the circumstances, but this is the first photo where we all genuinely look happy. No faking it. Our cheeks are ruddy, our smiles broad, you can tell the laughter is really full-on, deep, proper belly laughs. The caption I add isn't fake either:

Proper jokes today with these awesome boys. Love these guys so much.

Something else. It felt good when Nate called out Hunter's bullshit comment, 'cause usually it's just me defending myself, so to have him do that, it felt . . . it felt pretty damn great, actually. So the caption is all true—I am feeling the love.

Not feeling the love is Nate's mum after she saw the state of us, although Nate's dad thought it was hilarious.

"*Micky*, they're wet through!" she said, scowling.

"They'll live!"

"This is utterly ridiculous—you don't know what's in that lake. All sorts of diseases!"

"Then why did you book it, Mum?" Nate asked, throwing his hands in the air. I was impressed. That boy is getting more dramatic by the minute.

That shut her up. Luckily, she's driving the bus today, and since we have to get to the other side of the country, just north of Gloucester, she has a *lot* of driving to do, so we were saved from further interrogation as she navigated various highways, freeways, and country lanes on our way to—*fanfare*—THE FESTIVAL! I'm determined we're gonna have a good time. Especially since Dylan and Tariq have vague-posted something really annoying: a pic of a big question mark with the caption: *Huge announcement coming later today!* I mean, piss right off. Whatever mundane little thing it is, I am *not* going to let it play on our minds. We'll show them. I cannot wait until we start posting pics of the bands and general partying, and with everyone in a much better mood now, I reckon we're going to get some fantastic posts. I'm seeing mosh pits, everyone with their hands in the air, glitter cannons and confetti, amazing light shows and music so loud it hammers through your very soul. And then chill, time has no meaning, just us and some random dudes we meet, everyone friendly, crashing in someone's tent, it doesn't matter whose, one glorious piece of summer ecstasy.

Within minutes of our arrival at "V Machine," it becomes apparent that's not what we're going to be getting. The first clue was the tagline, under the main title on the huge banner we drove under at the entrance:

V MACHINE
THE FAMILY-FRIENDLY FESTIVAL CELEBRATING ALL THINGS VEG!

We all see it. There's silence. Probably shocked. And then Nate pipes up.

"*Veg?* As in . . . carrots?"

I swallow. "I mean, it's in, it's cool, right? No one's eating meat these days."

"*I* eat meat," Nate replies darkly.

"It's not about the food. It's about the bands," I tell him. "I'm going to message Leila Bhatia, let her know we're here."

"Why do you insist on always using her full name?" Nate mutters.

I don't answer him, since Mr. Grumpy appears to have

resurfaced. Shit, shit, shit. I really hope this isn't a gigantic mistake. I'm counting on this festival to really do the business, likes-wise. I ping Leila Bhatia a quick message, supercool, like we're equals:

Heeeeeey, Leila, we have ARRIVED at V Machine! So buzzing for this, ha ha! Let me know if you're about, would love to say hi, thanks again for this amazing chance. Jack. (We met at the hotel, I'm sure you remember, but just in case, ha ha, lol)

I sit back as the VW bus slowly snakes its way in a line, along the track toward the camping area, while Nate sits there, shaking his head and actually *muttering* to himself. Up ahead, there's a human-sized parsnip and cauliflower entertaining the passing vehicles by dancing. "Join us tonight in the *Vegscape* for veg-tastic cabaret!" they shout through our open window.

I turn to Nate. "That's just the family-friendly stuff," I whisper. "Don't worry, we'll find the real party!"

"I don't know why I didn't do this before," Nate says, tapping away on his phone. "I just assumed you knew what this thing was."

"Which I do!"

"Be sure to check out the vegetarian cooking demonstrations in the *Vegzilla* tent," Nate reads aloud.

"Go to the bit about the bands."

"And don't forget to visit our mini-festival within the festival, *VegVerse*, a celebration of poetry and art with the theme of . . . wait for it, Jack, can you guess the theme?"

"Veg?" I say in a small voice.

He tucks his phone back in his pocket. "So cool, because I bloody love zucchini."

I smile. "Do you?"

"Shut up, of course I don't."

"I like tomatoes," Elliot pipes up. "But they're technically a fruit, which is *wild*."

"OK, so, we're not here for the veg. We're here to party." My phone pings. *Thank Christ.* "And that's Leila Bhatia, so now I can introduce you and we can find the VIP stuff and get properly mashed."

"No one's getting 'mashed,'" Nate's mum says. "Not on my watch. You can have one supervised glass of cider each, and that's it."

"The only things getting 'mashed' at this veg fest are the potatoes!" Nate's dad grins, twisting his head around to look at us, mouth open like a Muppet at his fabulous joke.

We all just stare at him.

* * *

"Everyone, this is *the* Leila Bhatia," I say, waving my hands up and down the length of her body like I'm demonstrating the top prize on a TV quiz show. "Instagram influencer and very kind provider of our *free* tickets to V Machine!"

Leila gives everyone a polite smile. She's dressed in skinny jeans and knee-high leather boots. She looks so utterly sophisticated and kick-ass, especially in contrast to us boys, who, due to the water incident, are down to emergency clothes reserves. Nate's back in his gym shorts (which he claims aren't gym shorts), Elliot's in these board shorts, garishly decorated with flamingos and palm trees, and it's only I, in my skinny-fit, super-soft stretch denim shorts, with rips, in pastel pink, who is maintaining any sort of standards here.

"Really glad you could make it," Leila says. "V Machine is a great festival for people who don't really like traditional festivals, so I hope you all have an amazing time!"

I laugh. "Yes, but there's some music and stuff, right?"

"Oh, yes," Leila says.

"Yes! See?" I say.

"It's more folk bands, acoustic indie stuff, obviously none of the big acts because this is all about authenticity and being eco-friendly. It wouldn't be right to fly over a huge band and all their entourage and put them on a huge stage with all those amps and lights—think of the carbon footprint!"

"I know, right?" I look at Nate, who is just staring at me, unimpressed. "So any bands we might have heard of?"

"Jasper Phats and the Oink Oinks?" Leila says.

I run my tongue over my lips. "Amazing, we'll check him and his Oink Oinks out." I turn to make introductions. "So this is Elliot, Nate, Rose, and Nate's mum and dad."

Everyone shakes hands.

"So who exactly do you influence?" Nate's dad asks. "This is a whole new world to me. Is it something I could do?"

Nate rolls his eyes. I feel a bit sorry for Nate's dad. I know he lost his job and all, and sure, I guess he's looking for new options, but I'm not sure Instagram influencer is one he should be considering.

"I'm a lifestyle blogger," Leila tells him. "I specialize in mindfulness, retreats, meditation, that sort of thing."

I nod. "She's really good. The best. She has half a million followers."

"Wow," says Nate's dad. He looks genuinely impressed. "And you . . . make money doing this?"

"I do paid promotions for brands that I respect, yes."

Nate's dad nods. So does Nate's mum. I think his parents like Leila, but then she's the most sensible person our age they've met on this trip.

I clap my hands together to move this on because I don't think Nate can take much more of his folks embarrassing him by asking perfectly reasonable questions like normal people. "We're gaining followers on our Insta account!" I tell Leila.

"Yeah, I really admire what you guys are doing—showing your exes you don't need them! Hopefully this festival will get them nice and jealous!"

"Ha ha, *yeeeah*," I say. I glance at Leila. It would be so cool to get a photo of us with her. That would definitely get some attention, especially from Dylan, because he absolutely worships the ground she walks on.

"We'll definitely get some good posts out of this festival," I say. "Like, maybe even . . . now? Look at this backdrop." I wave my hands across the vista of tents and line of Porta Potties behind me.

Leila hoots with laughter. "Horrendous."

I swallow. "Is it?"

"So horrendous it's brilliant—let's do it!"

"Hooray!" I say, and immediately start arranging us all in the best formation—Leila in the middle, me and Nate flanking her, Elliot in front, on his knees. My proposal that we all pretend to be looking at something random and strange in the distance is accepted, and we all pose with expressions that vary between wonder, disgust, and horror, with Leila actually pointing at the pretend thing, whatever it actually is.

The photo is fabulous. It's *fabulous*. I immediately upload it, tag Leila, and caption it: *Add your own caption, we're too busy #LovingLife at V Machine!* And then I add something that makes me super happy, and it's not even a lie: *#Gifted* Yeeeeeeees! Hashtag gifted, mofos!

"Right, gotta run," Leila says. "But I'll catch up with you boys later and we'll do some shots, yeah?"

We all nod like those funny dogs you see in the back of cars sometimes, but then I turn to see Nate's mum, looking like, *No way is that gonna happen.* This concerns me. We upheld our side of the bargain; we did the stupid water thing, now it's our turn.

"What I think would be a good idea, boys," she says, "is if we all did something as a family."

Nate groans.

"Family is important, Nate!" his mum continues. "Karen's always posting pictures of her family all together, doing activities. That's what normal families do. And that's what we're going to do."

Nate takes a deep breath. "You agreed, if we did the raft building . . ."

"Well, it's just one thing," his mum replies.

Nate crosses his arms. *"What?"*

Elliot looks up from the festival brochure he's reading. "How about this? There's an interactive exhibition. *One hundred surprising ways with cucumber,*" he says, looking between us with wide eyes. "If eating them's one, what are the other ninety-nine?"

"Not that, Elliot," Nate's mum says. "It sounds silly, and I'm sorry, but I'm not putting on Facebook that I've taken a group of teenage boys to an interactive cucumber exhibition. It's simply wrong."

"Then *what?*" Nate repeats.

"There's a panel event on in the VegVerse tent actually," Nate's mum sniffs. "Family, Faith, and Fennel in the context of feminist verse novels." She clears her throat. "Sounds interesting. Shall I book us tickets?"

"I'm going to find some food," Nate says. And he stomps off.

Nate's mum shakes her head and walks over to the bus, scowling. And I know I have to do something to save this situation because otherwise Nate's going to be in a bad mood, his mum is going to trash our plans—which will result in crap pics, no likes, and bang goes any hope of my influencer career.

* * *

"Yoo-hoo! Mrs. Nate!" I sing, brandishing two compostable takeaway cups, hoping half an hour is enough time for her to have calmed down.

She looks up from where she's sitting on one of those fold-away camping chairs, reading a copy of *House & Home* magazine. "Having fun?"

"I thought you might like a—" I hold up one of the cups.

"That's thoughtful. What is it?"

"It's a dairy-free turmeric latte. I know. Sorry."

She smiles. "No, that's very kind, Jack." She takes the cup from me. "Thank you."

I nod, take a swig myself, and wince. I wish I'd found somewhere that sold normal drinks. "So," I say. "Are you having a . . . good time?"

Mrs. Nate smiles and sighs. "It's OK, Jack. You don't have to make small talk. Go and enjoy yourself. You don't want to hang around with a stick-in-the-mud like me. Go on, I'm fine."

"Aww, Mrs. Nate!" I say, pulling up the other foldaway chair and sitting down next to her. "I don't think that!"

"You're the only person who doesn't." She sips her drink. "I'm only trying to do my best for everyone."

"Well, I think you're *great*."

Mrs. Nate gives me an unimpressed look.

"Look," I say. "About Nate. About *earlier* . . ."

She shakes her head. "I'm not interested, Jack. I know he had a little heartbreak over Tariq, but that doesn't excuse his bad behavior. Sometimes in life you just have to suck it up."

"But can I say something though?"

She blinks once at me.

"You can't get mad," I add. "I'm just saying this as a . . . an outside observer."

"This'll be good."

"All it is, I know you've sometimes got a downer on Nate, and I get it because sometimes I have too, but you know, he's actually a really great person."

Mrs. Nate snorts.

"No, but it's true!" I protest. "You know, on the way to our cabin in the woods, he actually saved my life? From a gunman?"

"*What?* Oh, dear Christ, what the hell—"

I put my hand up. "It's fine. As it turns out, it was just an army exercise, but when Nate saved my life, he didn't know that."

Mrs. Nate rolls her eyes.

"He's funny," I continue. "Often unintentionally, but I'm not sure that matters. And he's sensitive. And I think that's a good quality. I think lots of people storm through life and don't give a damn about other people, but Nate isn't like that. He cares. He just sometimes doesn't know quite how to show it."

"Wow, you're a big fan of my son."

I smile because, you know what? Yeah, I *am* actually. I am a Nate fan. Sure, he annoys the hell out of me at least three-quarters of the time, but I'm still a fan. I guess there's just something about him . . .

"Jack?"

I glance back at Mrs. Nate. "Well, I . . . We were best friends for a long time."

Mrs. Nate's looking at me. She's not actually smiling, but her *eyes* are kind of smiling, if you know what I mean?

I swallow.

"I mean, that's all," I say. "That's all." I take a sip of the latte. "Turmeric's good for you, did you know that? It's anti-inflammatory."

Now she smiles. I don't know why.

"So what's this in aid of, Jack? Is this some roundabout way of getting me to agree to you three going off and doing whatever you like?"

"It's just . . . the *VegVerse tent*? Of all things!"

"Sometimes educational stuff is good!"

"Why is it?"

"Because it's what people do!"

"What people?"

"People, Jack! People like my sister and my mother!"

I hold my hands out, like, *So?!*

"They don't even know we're at a festival. I dread to think what they'd say," she mutters.

I think I see what the problem is here, but I'm nervous of slagging Karen off to her own sister. Whatever Mrs. Nate feels about her, she's not going to want me wading in with my opinion, however fabulously devastating that opinion is. So I'm going to have to go with the next best thing. "About Karen's stew," I say. "Yours is better. You cook a great casserole, Mrs. Nate."

She narrows her eyes slightly. "When did you have my stew?"

"Last time I came for dinner, which, granted, was about three

years ago. But it's top food, Mrs. Nate. *So much better than Karen's.*
However many ovens she has."

Mrs. Nate laughs.

"Also," I add, boosted by her reaction to this first Karen criticism. "I don't really like all those slogans over her walls, like, what's that about?"

She laughs again.

"Ooh! Ooh!" I mock. "*Jonty* is at *Twickers!*"

She stops laughing. "Jonty's OK," she says.

"Well, maybe, but point is, Karen made Nate feel bad when she was going on about him not having a girlfriend, and I don't think that's right." I look at her. "She shouldn't be making anyone feel bad. Just 'cause she does everything by the 'rule book' but, like, who even made up the 'rule book' and who said you have to follow it?"

Mrs. Nate sighs and looks away.

"So I got you something else actually!" I say brightly. "I booked you a one-to-one session with a yoga guru."

"I'm sorry?"

"He's going to help you connect with your chakra, among other things. My treat," I tell her, handing her the details on a piece of paper. "Since you invited me along on this thing." It's the least I can do. Mum put enough cash in my account, and I haven't even contributed for gas or anything yet.

"But . . ."

"I've booked it now. No refunds. So."

"Well, when?"

"At three." I nod. "Oh! Oh dear, that clashes with the VegVerse panel event, doesn't it?"

Mrs. Nate narrows her eyes at me. "You're unbelievable."

"It's often mentioned."

"So sly!"

"Honestly, I didn't realize when I booked it."

"Ooh, I could throttle you!"

"Namaste." I get up to leave.

"Jack?" Mrs. Nate smiles at me. "Thank you."

"My pleasure!"

"Also . . . those things you said about Nate? Maybe you should tell him that."

"Oh, no, no, no. I don't think Nate would like that. He'd be weirded out."

Mrs. Nate nods. "Well, then, maybe you could just . . . show him?"

"Show him how?"

"You know what he really loves?" Mrs. Nate says.

I nod. "The tender touch of another boy."

"Curly Wurlys."

"Curly Wurlys, right. Does he? OK."

"I'm sure you can work your magic, Jack!"

"Say no more! If it'll mean a lot to Nate, I'll find him a Curly Wurly!"

THIRTY-TWO

NATE

Of course Mum wouldn't uphold her side of the bargain. I hope Jack now understands why he should never have trusted her in the first place. If there's one thing Mum loves, it's controlling my life at every turn, carefully manipulating it in any way that might possibly meet with the approval of Auntie Karen and my grandma.

I stomp around the festival site, looking for something to eat, and that does nothing to improve my mood. I understand it's a festival of vegetables, but honestly, the lack of meat is ridiculous. I know what I'm about to say is completely unacceptable and everyone will hate me, but *I like meat*. I love it actually. I love steaks and burgers and fried chicken. I adore bacon. Right now, I would kill for some smoky barbecue ribs, succulent and dripping in a rich, sweet, and sticky sauce. But all I'm seeing is chickpea curries, "burgers" that are actually mushrooms, tofu, and I JUST WANT TO CRY because all I want to do is sink my chops into the juicy goodness that is a Quarter Pounder with cheese and bacon.

Anyway, I'm just wandering around the site at this point, and I don't know how long it's been. I'm in some . . . I'm in some sort of trance, I think because of the lack of animal protein in my body, and I'm very weak and disorientated and confused when Elliot finds me.

"What are you doing?" he asks.

I stare at him, blinking, trying to focus my eyes. "I thought I could smell hot dogs," I mutter.

"I have something you might like," Elliot grins. "Ready? TA-DA!"

And there's no way of saying this that doesn't sound like a euphemism, but it's totally not: *Elliot pulls a stick of jerky from his shorts.*

I swallow and stare at it.

"Everyone's favorite salami sausage snack!" Elliot says.

"Oh my god."

"Would you like it?"

"Where did you get it from? Actually, I don't care, *yes*! Please. Yes, I would very much like it."

Elliot glances around us furtively, clearly aware that this is contraband and could get us in trouble. He passes it to me, super casual, like it's just a carrot or celery stick or something. "Quick though!" he hisses.

I mean, of course I'm quick. No sooner have I peeled open the foil wrapping than that thing is in my mouth and I've basically swallowed it whole, immediately feeling the restorative power of dead flesh. Go ahead, *judge me.*

"Oh, yes," I groan. "Thank you, Elliot." I lick my lips. "Mmmm."

"OK, cool," Elliot says. "So there's live music on the main stage, like *right now,* and since that's the whole point of being here, do you fancy it? Or if not, there's an actual funfair at the far end of the site that looks cool, or there's a stone-painting workshop, and, huh, there's still the interactive cucumber exhibition, which, I'll be honest, *does* intrigue me, and—"

I put my hand on his shoulder to stop him. "Let's do the music tent," I say.

He nods, grins, and makes a couple of little pretend jabs at my stomach with his fists. "Yabba dabba doo!"

I smile. "Yabba dabba doo, indeed."

* * *

The area in front of the main stage is rammed, but Elliot and I manage to snake our way into a good spot in the middle. The music is nineties stuff, because that's basically the main clientele at this festival, but I don't mind because a lot of the tunes are classics. Currently, some band is doing a cover of "Movin' On Up" by Primal Scream, and it's beautifully loud, and I don't know whether it's so loud the happy tune is somehow permeating into my very soul, or whether it's the blissed-up crowd and the infectious contentment of this place, but this warmth floods my body, this *relief*, this *lightness*, and I felt it yesterday, and again now, and I think the word might be *joy*. And I realize that it doesn't matter if this festival isn't what I'd been expecting; I'm here with Jack and Elliot, and together, we'll have the best time because it's not about the where, it's about the who, the people you're with, that's what matters. I wish Jack were here because I shouldn't have been grumpy with him, and I want to hug him, celebrate just being here, being us.

Elliot's right into it, hands in the air, and then the band announce they're "changing the mood a bit" and start this beautiful version of "Perfect Day" by Lou Reed that genuinely brings a tear to my eye, and Elliot is next to me, and for the first time in a long time, stuff seems possible, and life seems happy, and maybe that's why I do it, but I touch Elliot's arm, and he turns to me, and I lean in, and he leans in, and we start kissing.

And we kiss for a fair bit of time.

Then we break off, and I glance over his shoulder, and Jack's standing there, just staring at us, mouth open, eyes wide, randomly holding ten Curly Wurlys.

THIRTY-THREE

JACK

I really don't mean to stare at Nate and Elliot kissing like some
sort of perv, but I can't tear myself away. It's like I'm . . . I'm frozen, I don't know why, but everything and everyone around me
is in slow motion and grayed out, even my heart seems to have
stopped, and I swallow as Nate meets my eyes, my stomach hard,
and I think it's best to maybe leave them alone, and I start to back
off, except I forgot Leila's right behind me and I bump into her.

"Whoa!" she shouts. "I lost you for a minute there. All right,
boys?"

She's holding a stack of burger cartons and looks well pleased
with herself.

"Hi!" Nate says, cheeks bright red.

Elliot's looking at the ground. I flick my eyes to Leila.

"Why's everyone being weird?" she asks.

We all look at her and shake our heads. "No," says Nate.

Leila nods. "Okaaaaay. OK, well, *surprise!*" She hands out the burger cartons. "I bought you all a *meat*-free burger!"

"Meat-free?" Nate frowns.

Leila nods. "MEAT . . . free."

"Right," Nate says. "So, no meat?"

Leila fixes Nate with a meaningful stare. "We're at a vegetarian festival, so this is *meat*, I repeat *meat* . . . free."

Nate looks totally confused.

"It's meat, Nate, it's fully real meat. Leila's just trying to be discreet." I sigh.

Nate's eyes light up and he's got the thing in his mouth in next to no time. I manage a small smile as everyone else tucks in, but I'm feeling less enthusiastic about mine. I'm not hungry for some reason.

"Thanks so much for the MEAT-FREE burger," Nate says between mouthfuls.

"Thank Jack," Leila replies. "His idea."

Nate raises his eyebrows.

"He told me you'd be beside yourself with the food on offer here, and I had to pop to the nearest town anyway to pick up some more shampoo, so thought I'd kill two birds with one stone."

Nate nods at me, which I suppose means "thank you."

"And this is dessert," I say, holding up the Curly Wurlys. "Hope it cheers you up a bit?" And I flick my eyes to Elliot because, actually, it seems like Nate has found something to cheer him up now, so perhaps all this wasn't necessary.

"You're amazing," Nate tells me.

"Uh-huh," I reply. I sigh and look down at the ground.

"Are you OK, Jack?" Leila asks.

I glance back up at her. "Oh . . . yeah. I'm just . . . I think maybe I'm tired, that's all. I might go back to the tent and rest for a bit." I don't know why, but I'm not really feeling any of this. I glance at Nate, and he's staring at me, burger in hand, frozen in mid-chew.

I swallow. "Nice?" I ask him.

He nods and starts chewing again.

"Good," I say. I take my phone out and get Nate, with his cheeks full like a hamster, Elliot, and Leila in the frame. I think I'll sit this one out, but it's too good not to post and you gotta maintain the illusion on social media. *Top street food tonight with the boys. #Vegetarian #caring #loveanimals* I caption it, even though some of the hashtags aren't technically accurate.

The band start playing "Changes" by David Bowie and I feel like the only way the music could be any more of a metaphor would be if the song was "Why Does It Always Rain on Me?" by Travis, except why am I feeling like this and what the hell?

Thankfully, there's no time for any further analysis of my messed-up head, because Nate suddenly says,

"WHAT THE ACTUAL HELL?"

And I follow his horrified stare across the crowds of people to where Mrs. Nate is sitting on some guy's shoulders, waving her arms in the air to this classic Bowie song, with a rainbow flag painted on her cheek and an open can of beer in her hand.

"Jack?" Nate says.

I turn back to him. "That's your mum."

"I know it's my mum, Jack. What have you done?"

I blow out a breath. "What makes you think this has anything to do with—"

"Jack!" he interrupts. "My mother does not simply sit aloft some random dude's shoulders at a festival without some kind of intervention from a third party. *What have you done?*"

"OK, so, I may have booked her a session with a yoga guru, but—"

"OK," Nate says. "Please can you do something? I don't care what, but this is . . . You've no idea. If this goes viral or something, if Auntie Karen gets to see it, she'll call social services and have me and Rose taken away, I swear to god."

"Why would it go viral?" I ask him.

"There are quite a lot of phones being waved about, to be fair," Leila says.

"See!" Nate says.

"OK! OK, I'll go and . . . I'll . . ." And I back off, not sure exactly what it is I am going to do, but kind of thankful for an excuse to leave and kind of thankful to have something else to think about. Because if you're not in the middle of it, and you're not thinking about it, then it's almost as if it's not real, not happening, and right now, that's exactly what I need. Because I'm not stupid, I know what the problem is. I just can't figure out how it's happened or what I'm supposed to do about it now.

Damn it to hell.

I like Nate.

I *like him* like him.

THIRTY-FOUR

NATE

I turn my back on the horror that is my mum off her face and accidentally lock eyes with Elliot, who immediately looks straight down at his burger and continues eating.

Great. He's feeling awkward. I've messed up.

I look at Leila, who gives me a sympathetic smile. "I bumped into your dad and little sister again," she says. "She's quite a character!"

I roll my eyes. "Oh no, what did Rose say? Why are you saying she's a 'character'?"

Leila smiles. "She's convinced you and Jack should be husbands."

"Oh."

"She's asked if I want to be a bridesmaid. Just a regular one—she's head bridesmaid, apparently."

"Right. Well. No one's being a bridesmaid, sorry to disappoint."

I press my lips firmly together and glance over to where Jack is attempting to get my delirious mother's attention by jumping up in front of her and waving his arms about. Unfortunately, he just looks like all the other revelers around her, so I'm not sure it's an effective technique.

"He's certainly a loyal friend," I hear Leila say.

I turn and see she's looking at Jack too. She flicks her eyes to mine. "I know," I smile. I look over at Jack again, who is now having some sort of shouty conversation with my mum. He's standing on tiptoes, trying to get closer to her so she can hear him, and he's looking pretty exasperated. It makes me smile. And she's right. He is loyal. He's a good friend. I'm happy to have him back.

Leila tugs at my T-shirt. "I haven't mentioned this to Jack yet because I thought it might be nice surprise for him, but there's a YouTuber party thing down in London tomorrow. I could get you guys on the guest list, if you're gonna be around?"

My eyes widen. My immediate thought is that it sounds scary and will be full of intimidating, popular types, all confident and able to make even a plain white T-shirt look good on them, but I know Jack would love it. I have no idea if Mum will agree to it, although since she appears to have been replaced with some wired festivalgoer, maybe anything's possible. "Leila, that's amazing, thank you!"

Leila smiles. "Be a surprise for him, yeah?"

"Yeah." I glance at him again and then back at Leila. "He deserves a surprise."

"OK," Leila says. "I'll message you with the info. I have to go. I'm doing a podcast with one of the organizers—catch up with you later, yeah?"

I nod and smile and she's off.

Leaving me with Elliot, who is so busy with his burger he still can't look at me. I need to say something. Maybe I need to apologize or make it clear the kiss just happened, and it won't happen again, but it's all too awkward, so instead I just start flicking through my phone, swiping away at Instagram, because even though I hate that site, it's still better than talking to Elliot right now.

I freeze when I see it.

The news is out! reads the caption on Dylan's post. A post with a picture of him and Tariq, proudly showing off the rings on their fingers. *So happy right now. Exchanged promise rings with this one today. Best day of our lives and first day of our future.*

I shiver as my blood turns to ice. There are assorted hideous hashtags, and then a whacking one thousand likes. And then the comments:

Love wins!
You guys are so cute together! Babe! Congratulations!

Love wins!

Hot!!!!

Love wins!

When I finally look up, Elliot is just staring at me. "What is it?" he says.

I pass him the phone. He reads and scrolls, then looks back up at me. "Look, you know," Elliot mutters, "they have their thing, you have yours, and—"

"What thing have I got? Huh?" I ask him, fury suddenly bubbling up inside me. "What have I got?"

Elliot looks stumped.

And I push my way through the crowd, out of there, anywhere, anywhere but here, anywhere away from people, and friends, and exes, and expectations, and hopes and dreams and anywhere except my own head and my messed-up life.

THIRTY-FIVE

JACK

No way is Mrs. Nate coming down from the shoulders of this random bloke. I can't make out exactly what she's saying to me, but her session with the yoga guru was apparently "enlightening" and "life-changing" and now here she is, "releasing herself from her shackles." She tells me to tell Nate to "take a chill pill" and then loses herself in the beat once more, hands in the air, blissed out to Bowie.

There's nothing else I can do. She must be either drunk or high, which kind of annoys me because *we're* the teenagers here, so really that should be our thing, so I push my way back to the lovebirds. When I get there, though, it's only Elliot.

"Où est le Nate?" I say.

"I think you need to check Dylan's Insta," Elliot says.

So I do, and *oh*. I'm not hurt. I'm furious. Promise rings? The thing that was my idea at prom? I don't even care about their undying and eternal love and commitment; it's just maddening that Dylan doesn't have an original or creative bone in his body, and now he's getting all this love and praise for something that I came up with and that he would never have thought of on his own.

I put my phone away. "Nate's upset?"

Elliot nods.

I nod back. Chew my lip. Screw it, I'm gonna say it. "So you kissed him, then?" I need to know what the deal is. If they're getting together, that's fine. I'm sure I'll get used to it. Maybe I don't feel that way about Nate anyway. Not really. Sometimes I'm not sure I know where horny ends and romance begins.

Elliot shoves his hands in the pockets of his shorts and kicks the ground with his sneakers.

"I mean, maybe *you* should go and see if he's OK?" I continue. "If you're a thing now?"

Elliot's eyes widen. "Oh, we're not a thing."

I nod. "Uh-huh? Just a kiss?"

"Right!"

"No such thing as 'just a kiss,' Elliot!"

"No, there is!" he protests. "There with me and Nate. We've . . ." He stops himself.

"You've kissed before? In my tree house?"

Elliot's cheeks flush red and he nods. "How did you know?"

"I mean, I'm not an idiot. It was always either going to be that or a game of Doctors and Nurses, wasn't it? God, the pair of you are insatiable! Can't keep your hands off each other!"

"Jack, that's not true. Sometimes, you just get caught up in the moment. The music . . . the atmosphere . . ."

"The smell of freshly cut plywood?"

"Look," Elliot says, "I can't explain why we kissed when we were ten, but I also can't explain my obsession with slime or why stories involving snot or peeing your pants were so damn funny, *because I was ten*. But right now, we just kissed, but I think it was kind of . . . as friends?"

Elliot tentatively glances at me, like he *knows* I'm not going to let him get away with that.

"Ha!" I laugh. A small swell of relief ripples through me, but I know better than to trust it. "Ha ha ha! Oh, *excellent*! Elliot, fine, OK, more of this later. I'm going to find Nate, and when I do, maybe I'll just stick my tongue in his mouth, since that's what all the cool kids are claiming is friendship now?"

Elliot shrugs. "Well, maybe you should," he mutters.

I stop and stare at him.

He slowly lifts his eyes to meet mine. "Oh, come on," he says. "You and Nate."

I hold my hands out. "Me and Nate, *what*?"

"Well, it's obvious," Elliot says. "You and Nate. It's absolutely destined to happen. After all, *opposites attract*!"

I glare at him. How dare he know things about me that I keep excellently hidden? "That's only true of magnetic poles, Elliot. Do

I look like a magnet?" He opens his mouth to speak but I put a finger to his lips. "The answer is that although, granted, many have described my personality as 'magnetic,' I am, in fact, *not* an actual magnet."

I turn with a flourish and disappear into the heaving crowd. And then I let myself smile. I can't help being pleased about what Elliot said. It's always good to get corroboration for your silly lustings. But what the hell is going on with Nate? Happy enough to kiss Elliot, but apparently still devastated over Tariq? There's one thing to take comfort from though, I guess: I'm kind of glad someone else's head seems to be as messed up as mine currently is.

* * *

"Knockety-knock-knock!" I say, as I poke my head into our tent.

Nate looks up from where he's sitting, knees drawn up to his chin, eyes red and puffy.

I shuffle into the tent and pop myself down next to him. "Oh dear," I say. "Tariq strikes again, huh?"

Nate shakes his head.

"Look," I continue, "the whole promise rings thing is tacky, if you really want my opinion. Admittedly, I *thought* it was romantic when I tried to give Dylan one at prom, but I'm older now, more mature and sophisticated, and I see it for what it really is."

Nate sniffs.

"It'll take time to get over Tariq, and that's OK, Nate, it's OK—"

"It's not about Tariq!" Nate splutters.

"Ohhhhh!" I say. My heart quickens. If it's not about Tariq, it can only be either Elliot or . . . well, I doubt it's me. But now I'm on edge. I should never allow hope to rear its head—that's how you get hurt. So I do what I do best and deflect by flicking open the complimentary branded fan I picked up from the vegan sausage company on my way here. "Tell Auntie Jack all about it."

"What the hell is that?" Nate says.

"It's a fan, Nate. It's very humid in here. It must be all your evaporated tears."

Nate narrows his eyes at me. "Or maybe it's because of all the extra body heat now you've come in? Did you know you produce the equivalent of a two-bar electric fire?"

I flick the fan closed again. "How *dare* you? At the very least I'm a gas-flame-effect fire, if not a Scandinavian wood-burning stove." I flick the fan back open and wave it at my face. Genuinely, it is feeling hot in here and my mouth is really dry. "Seriously, what's the matter?"

Nate looks up at me briefly, then buries his face in his knees again.

"Come on, what is it?" I continue more softly.

He's unresponsive. I tentatively shuffle a bit closer, good and slow, like you would approach a junkyard dog, and put my arm across his shoulders. He tenses. "Nate?" I murmur.

"Go away."

I sigh but stay where I am.

"Seriously, Jack. Just leave me."

I remove my arm from his shoulders, reach into my bag, and

retrieve two Curly Wurlys. I open one and hand it to him, but I have to hold it there for a good ten seconds before he relents and accepts it from me. I smile, open my own, and have a chew. "Your mum told me you liked these," I say.

"Yeah, well."

"You've got so many hidden layers, Nate!"

He glares me.

"You're like an onion!"

"*Jack.*"

"So complex and —"

"Well, you're a —"

"What am I, Nate? Oh, please pick something suggestive! An eggplant?"

"No —"

"A banana?" I fake gasp. "Or maybe something exotic? A kiwi fruit? A cantaloupe melon?"

Nate finally laughs. "You're a *nightmare.*"

"Yes, but you love me." Our eyes meet, I swallow and I look down. I've said the L-word before, jokingly, but now I can feel myself wanting some different response from Nate, and I don't like it.

"I always feel like I'm being left behind," Nate mutters.

I look back up at him.

"Everyone else seems to have their lives together; they know what they want, and they're going out there and they're getting it," he continues. "It's not Tariq and Dylan as such, like . . . I get it now, they're in love and Tariq's dumped me. I get it, and it's not that. It's just the fact they've each found someone they want to do that with, and me . . ." He sighs and looks down.

"It's not a race, Nate."

He's still looking down. "It's not just this. It's everything. It's me coming out at prom when . . ." His voice is barely a whisper. ". . . when you came out in year nine, and I wanted to as well, Jack, I wanted to, but I was scared—"

"I know, Nate, you told me that, but—"

"But it's more than that! You went ahead, and you were so bold and confident, and I wanted to come with you, but I couldn't do it, so I was just stuck, sitting in my room, while you were out there, being you, living your life, and I was so envious and so jealous. I wanted that so much, but I . . ." His head slumps down further with a huge sigh.

I stare at him. I had no idea. I move closer to him again, put my arms around him, and pull him into me. "I didn't . . . I'm sorry," I murmur.

"It's not your fault," he says into my shoulder. "It's me. I just couldn't . . . I wasn't in the same place as you. And I'm sorry too, actually, because I ended up hating you for it. I hated you, Jack, and that's just another reason I stopped talking to you. It started as fear, but then it grew into something so much more . . . *poisonous*. When I saw how much crap you were getting, I was actually glad because I saw what it could be like, and I thanked god that wasn't me. Thanked god I'd kept quiet. How horrible is that? That's what sadness does to you, I reckon. Eats you up, makes you bitter. I should have supported you. Because you were my friend."

"You *are* my friend," I tell him.

"Yeah. You *are* my friend," he says.

I gently rub his back with my hand. "You know, I just assumed you didn't want anything to do with me. I thought you maybe felt betrayed that I hadn't spoken to you about it first or that maybe you didn't want other people to see us hanging out and think you were gay too."

"It wasn't that," Nate says.

"That's why I backed off. I thought that was what you wanted."

"And I thought you backed off because you had your new LGBT friends, and they were better and more fun and sparkly than I could ever dare to be, 'cause I was too scared to be myself. But I didn't hate you, Jack. Not really. I wanted us to be friends. I kept quiet, kept my head down, and didn't speak to you out of self-preservation — first because of the bullies, and then because I was trying to convince myself I didn't want it anyway because that was the only way to keep my messed-up head together. But, really, not having you . . . I was heartbroken."

I take a deep, unsteady breath, my throat tight. "Me too. Losing you as a friend broke my heart too."

"I understand if you can't, but could you, maybe . . . forgive me?" he asks in a small voice.

"Nate, I forgive you. Like, totally, it's not even . . ." I squeeze him closer. "The people I'll never forgive are the ones who made you feel like you didn't have a choice and who robbed us of all these years when we could have been there for each other." I sigh. "Fuck me, why are we still in a situation where some people have such a goddamn problem with who other people love? It's so frickin' stupid."

Nate sniffs, pulls back from me a bit, and wipes his eyes with the palms of his hands. "Huh. Maybe this trip was a good thing after all."

I smile at him and ruffle his ridiculous bedhead hair. "I promise, I won't ever leave you behind again, Nate."

"Well, I wouldn't let you!" Nate smiles. "You're stuck with me now."

THIRTY-SIX

NATE

It's late, it's raining, but Jack, Elliot, and me are happy as can be, snuggled in our tent with blankets and hot chocolate. Having Jack back as a friend and getting all that out in the open, it feels *so good*. It feels like I don't even care so much about Tariq now because I've gained something way better. I've got Jack back. The Dream Team: reunited.

While we were queuing for the dairy-free hot chocolates, I bit the bullet. "Elliot," I said. "I'm sorry I kissed you."

Elliot chuckled. "Ahh, man, you don't have to apologize. I kissed you too!"

"*Now* it all comes out!" Jack declared.

"Jack, *hush*!" I said. "I know, but what I'm trying to say is—"

"Nate," Elliot said. "Here's the thing, OK? In that moment, you were happy, am I right? It was a nice moment. Nice atmosphere. And you felt what you felt, and what you felt was *joy*, and I think when you feel joy, I think you should always grab it with both hands and enjoy it. And that's what you were doing."

I mean, I was taken aback for a moment because Elliot is not normally calm enough to make this much sense. "OK, sure, Elliot," I said. "But I did kiss you, and maybe I should have hugged you instead?"

"Why?" said Elliot.

"Because a kiss is . . . a romantic thing?"

Elliot shrugged. "*Meh*. Sometimes it is. I don't think it always has to mean you want to totally get with the person you're kissing though. There are different types of love after all—it's not all about HUH! AH! HUH! BONKING!" He said that bit *way* too loudly. People looked. And he was doing this weird thing where he was miming riding a horse, kind of thrusting his hips, with a lasso in his hand. I'm not sure if Elliot's school had sex education.

"We're not with him," Jack tells some onlookers. "Sorry, who even are you? Can you stop following us please?"

Elliot chuckles. "It's OK, Nate. I'm really not looking for anything like that with anyone right now." He smiles. "I'm just working stuff out really."

"Huh. OK. Cool," I said.

"Good kiss though!" He winked at me. "Better than . . . THE TREE HOUSE KISS-A-THON! WAAAAH!"

"Oh my god," I mutter.

Jack raised an eyebrow. "Kiss-a-thon? Huh."

Thankfully, by this time it was our turn to order, so we all got distracted with options for gelatin-free marshmallows and chocolate flakes.

I tip my cup up so the last of the rich, velvety goo slides down into my mouth.

"Boys," Jack says, "I think today has been a great day, and I think this trip, although it started in a somewhat challenging fashion, has been excellent. And so, partly in the hope that things only get more fabulous and even better, we must give appropriate thanks."

"Who to?" I ask.

"To our rainbow-sparkled, glitter-encrusted Gay Lord, of course," Jack grins. "Legs together, eyes closed."

So we all sit there, eyes closed, while Jack does his thing.

"Our Gaylord,
Who art in the nightclub known as Heaven,
Fabulous be thy name.
Give us this day
Our daily skincare regime,
And forgive us for belting show tunes,
As we forgive those who don't appreciate the wonder of just brows-
ing around Whole Foods for the fun of it.
Lead us not into a Golden Corral,
And deliver us from Joybird,

For we can't abide an unlimited salad cart and we like our fur-niture bespoke.

In the name of Madonna, Britney, and the Lady Gaga, Beyoncé."

"Beyoncé," Elliot and I repeat.

Now, I am not a religious guy—in fact, none of us are—but at that very moment my phone pings through with a message, and it's Leila confirming she's got us on the guest list for the YouTubers party in London. I turn to Jack. "It seems your prayers have been answered!" I grin.

* * *

My mum doesn't even blink when I ask her about going to the YouTubers party, let alone raise any kind of objection. But that's not even the weirdest thing. She's wearing a *kaftan*. A white, floaty *kaftan*, she's barefoot, and she's drinking kombucha with-out making any sort of the comment about how it's just "soda for Generation Snowflake," which is literally what I heard her call it when Dad brought some home once.

I glance at Jack and Elliot to check I've understood correctly. I've asked if we can go and my mum has said, *"Yeah, that's cool."* I mean, let's not even discuss her choice of words.

"So just to confirm, Mum," I say. "It's a party, in London, with YouTubers."

"And you enjoy it, Nate!" she replies, smiling.

"There . . . could be alcohol!" I say.

"Oh, I hope so! What sort of party would it be otherwise?" She laughs. We all sort of join in.

This feels all wrong and really weird. "OK," I say. "Mum. I don't get it."

"Nate!" she says, as she packs up the last of the bags and piles them in the back of the bus. "It's time I treated you like an adult. You're sixteen! You need some freedom."

I nod. "Right. So I can—"

"Make your own choices!" she says. "Also, when we're home, I'm taking the parental lock off the internet."

"Huh," Jack whispers. "Now you can finally jerk yourself unconscious."

"Shut up!" I hiss back.

Dad appears with Rose. "Ahh! Hello, lads!" He grins. "I see you've met Mum version two point one. Seems her trip to that yoga guru has caused her to have something of an epiphany, Jack!"

"Oh . . . good?" Jack says.

"Well, it is good, Jack, yes," says Mum. "Because life is short, so we must enjoy it while we can. We must live. Breathe. Love. We must smell the roses and eat the chocolate. We should dance like no one is watching. Love without conditions. We must look at the world with a childlike wonder, seeking adventure!"

"And the yoga guru said all this, did he?" I ask.

Mum shrugs. "Well, I worked some of it out for myself. I had a moment of clarity . . . after the session when we smoked a 'special cigarette' together."

My eyes widen and I nearly choke on my own tongue.

"Because like you said, Jack," Mum continues, "who wrote the rule book anyway? And who said we have to follow it?"

"Did you say that?" I ask him.

Jack shrugs. "I mean, yes? Maybe. It sounds quite eloquent, so there's a high chance it was me."

"It definitely wasn't me," Elliot adds.

Mum strides up to Elliot and grabs fistfuls of his cheeks in her hands. *"You're an adorable little bundle of joy and you have other qualities!"* she says.

Elliot looks terrified.

"Mum, leave Elliot's face alone," I tell her. "I mean, fine. I guess this is all OK. You shouldn't do drugs, that's bad, but OK, I guess it's done now. Just don't . . . I have some pamphlets at home that school gave us . . ."

Mum guffaws and I frown. Then another horror occurs to me. I'm always seeing documentaries about people my parents' age having "moments of clarity" and what it boils down to is giving everything up and living in a run-down cottage on Dartmoor with ten chickens and no hot water. "You're not quitting your job or anything, are you?"

Mum looks at Dad, who cocks his head and mouths something at her that I can't quite make out. This is distressing. I'm all for more freedom, but I don't want to live a life where we have even less money than we already do. Literally, I'm not even saying I need the *latest* sneakers; I just need sneakers. You know, I wouldn't mind a new PlayStation. That's not gonna happen if my parents embark on being hippies and start running around the hills wearing chiffon and celebrating weird pagan holidays.

"We can talk about this more once we get back home," I say. "Nobody should make any rash decisions now."

"Nate—" Dad begins.

"NOBODY SHOULD MAKE ANY RASH DECISIONS NOW!" I repeat. "OK? OK. Let's . . . get on the road, shall we? Places to go, people to see!"

Mum rolls her eyes. "*God.* Chill out, will you, Nate? You're totally killing my vibe."

THIRTY-SEVEN

JACK

So we're back in the bus and we're heading to our next stop: London. Tariq and Dylan may well have done their oh-so-popular post about their promise rings, but our forthcoming post featuring us *at a YouTubers party* will get more likes. The post with Leila Bhatia got a lot of likes and we picked up hundreds and hundreds of new followers. That will definitely have pissed Dylan off. But now with this party, what we're saying is, *We've made it, we've arrived, we are influencers, we are basically famous, AND WE DON'T NEED RINGS FROM A DEPARTMENT STORE TO GET LIKES.*

Mrs. Nate's phone keeps pinging on the journey, and Nate, who is already massively freaked out by his mum's new persona, eventually just flips and screams, "WHAT'S HAPPENING ON YOUR PHONE?"

To which his mum shakes her head and says, "Aren't I allowed some privacy, Nate?"

And Nate replies, "You never get this many notifications!"

And so his mum reveals that her sister, the infamous Auntie Karen, posted a picture of Jonty holding a rugby ball on the field at "Twickers" this morning, to which Mrs. Nate replied in the comments with the immortal phrase: *Oh fuck right off.*

And since then, it seems all hell has broken loose, family-wise.

"Oh my *god*, Mum!" Nate says. "This is serious!"

"It really isn't, Nate," Mrs. Nate says. "Karen's a total bitch, and I fucking hate her." She glances back at Rose. "You didn't hear Mummy swear, OK?"

"OK, Mum," Rose says, without looking up from her iPad. "But just so you know, I agree with you."

* * *

The hotel is just around the corner from Leicester Square, and as if that location weren't exciting enough, this isn't just any hotel. In fact, it doesn't even say it's a hotel outside the building. There's just a huge neon letter X because THAT IS WHAT THE HOTEL IS CALLED! It's called X—oh my god, how London is that? Just by the huge neon X, there's an actual red carpet and some of those red ropes you see at film premieres, with a doorman and queue of beautiful people to the left, waiting to see if they can get in. I start taking all the photos. And some video. I'm going to do a full-on Insta story about this.

"Pretty long queue," Nate says. "Should we go to Shake Shack instead?"

"*Should we go to Shake Shack instead? Can* you hear yourself?" I shake my head at him in disbelief. I take one final pic, then walk up to the bouncer, who stares at me like I'm actual shit. "We should be on the guest list," I tell him, attempting a winning smile.

The big guy takes a deep breath. "Whose list?"

"Leila Bhatia?"

The guy runs his finger lazily down his clipboard like he really doesn't believe me. Then he stops, his finger hovering. "Names?"

"Jack Parker, Nate Harrison, and Elliot Poppet."

Elliot winces slightly, like he always does when anyone says his surname, because he's had a lifetime of people either making fun of it or declaring it the cutest surname they've ever heard.

The bouncer looks at me again, then gives a small nod.

What's that meant to mean? Do we go in? I glance at Nate and mouth, *What's going on?* Nate just shrugs and puts his hands in his pockets, all awkward.

The guy eventually unclips one of the ropes, like he's in no rush whatsoever, and cocks his head for us to walk through.

"Oh!" I say. "Great! Thank you!"

But the bouncer is too busy eyeing up a young woman in a short skirt to take any notice of us. Anyway, we're into the moody, dark lobby, where there's just a shiny black counter with two glamorous women standing behind it and a set of elevators to the left. I'm totally expecting, having passed the first quest, that we'll now be asked a complex riddle, along the lines of, "One of these elevators leads to the party, and the other leads to instant death—you may ask us one question before you make your choice, but you need to know: one of us always lies, and one of us always tells the truth!" I swallow, because this is it. I'm on the cusp of finally being where I've always wanted to be. I'm not going to need Dylan to validate my existence when we're back at school in September. I'll be in the big time all by myself. As long as we clear this final hurdle. One of the women smiles and says, "What are you looking for?"

"Um . . . the YouTubers party?" I say.

She nods and smiles. "Third floor."

"Thanks!" I say, pressing the button for the elevator. "This is all very smooth," I whisper to Nate and Elliot.

"Right?" Elliot replies. "No one seems bothered that I'm only just sixteen!"

"Pipe down!" I tell him. "Besides, all the YouTubers are young. The hotel must be cool with it. The law applies less if you're rich, everyone knows it."

There's a ping and the elevator doors open. "This is it, boys, this is the moment."

"What moment's that?" Nate frowns.

"The moment we move into the upper tier of influencer society! The moment we can say we've made it, we're here. Who needs a promise ring and some crappy trip to a tacky Spanish island when you're at one of London's top hotels with all the movers and shakers?" I get my phone out again and take a selfie of us all in the elevator. I'll caption it *Moving on up!* because that's clever and will hopefully piss Dylan off.

It's the smoothest elevator I've ever been in. How the other half move between floors!

The doors open onto some kind of nirvana.

Fabulous people are everywhere. I have literally never seen so many beautiful individuals in one place. The clothes, the hair, the *aura* they're giving off—it's electric. Billowing drapes hang down around the room, sectioning off different areas that promise more fabulousness beyond; there are massive candles inside huge glass jars on the tables and central bar area; there are people with video cameras shooting interviews, and others getting photographs taken, using proper cameras, in front of a set of giant display boards that have various brand logos on them, just like you see at the movies!

"Drinks?"

I blink at the waitress standing before us with a silver tray on which there are various glasses.

"Champagne, white and red wine, gin and tonic, or we have soft drinks at the bar too," she says.

Are we allowed this? I've no idea. I don't want to look at Nate or Elliot, in case that looks weird and gives the game away, so I just confidently take a glass of champagne. Elliot does the same. So does Nate.

"Cheers, thanks, that's awesome!" Elliot says, in a really high voice that definitely gives the game away.

The waitress smiles and weaves her way back into the crowd.

"Is this free? Do we have to pay?" Nate asks.

"Just go with the flow!" I tell him.

"Because I only have ten pounds and a five-pound bookstore gift card on me," he continues.

"Let's find Leila Bhatia," I suggest. I glance at him. "Relax."

He just scowls and does anything but. I know this isn't Nate's sort of place, but he needs to understand this will be the icing on our Instagram cake. He'll get over it. Besides, Nate is generally cross and grumpy at everything. We could be lying on the most opulent feather-soft pillows being fed peeled grapes by hot boys, and he'd still find reason to scowl.

Love you, I mouth.

He gives me daggers and I laugh.

THIRTY-EIGHT

NATE

The elevator doors open onto some kind of *hellscape*.

Terrible people are everywhere. I have literally never seen so many utter douchebags in one place. The clothes, the hair, the *aura* they're all giving off—it's nauseating. The whole space is a fire hazard, a high-risk mix of flapping material, huge candles, and eau de toilette, and frankly, I'd happily see the lot of them go up in flames, running around with massive self-importance as they make videos and get their picture taken in front of a big board that's covered in logos for some new flavored alcoholic drink called Prohibition and something else named Scrummy Emma's Woodland Mix, which I assume is granola.

Anyway, Jack appears to be in his element, and I guess he deserves to have a nice time because I think this is basically everything he's ever wanted, so I decide to do my best to look like I'm having an OK time, even though I stick out like a sore thumb in my chinos and hoodie, among this crowd who are wearing stuff you might normally see in nightmares. I mean, on the catwalks. The whole situation reminds me of one of those school parties attended by all the popular and mean kids. Everyone's really good-looking and ostensibly having a good time, but there's an unmistakable simmering tension in the room, like, you sense that no one here really likes anyone else and behind all the bravado, everyone's really insecure because of the amount of bitching going on.

"Did you hear? Tom blocked Matty on Twitter and Insta after he insulted Beth on Tumblr!" a random beautiful girl says to her friend as I pass by. It has the same ring to it as hundreds of pieces of school gossip I've ever heard. It takes an age to squeeze through the crowd, so I manage to catch the reason for this influencer outrage, and apparently it has something to do with Beth endorsing a drugstore lip balm, which, I mean, *wow*, right?

I feel completely out of place swanning around with a glass of champagne in my hand, and I don't like the taste of it at all, but Elliot downs his within seconds, so I do the same, just to show I'm willing. No sooner than our glasses are empty than another waitress appears with two bottles of champagne and refills them. I don't understand why everyone is being so nice and why no one has asked us for any money or ID, but I just awkwardly follow

Jack as he winds his way through the glamorous throng, looking for Leila, while simultaneously doing some sort of live broadcast from his phone.

Elliot tugs on my sleeve. "Why is everyone so good-looking?"

"Right?"

"Maybe we could tell Jack we'll meet him at Shake Shack?" Elliot says.

"Yeah, I fancy a Shake Shack. I *like* Shake Shack. I feel like I *belong* in Shake Shack." I sigh. "But Jack's wanted this for ages, so we should probably stay."

Elliot nods.

"And Leila's right—he has done a lot of stuff for me." I shake my head, watching Jack chatting and getting a selfie with a girl I recognize from the big boards advertising granola—yes, it's Scrummy Emma herself. "It's just . . ."

"What?" says Elliot.

"Oh, nothing. It's stupid." I take a sip of my drink and hope it will help me stop worrying that this is year nine all over again—this is Jack, finding his new friends, people who are more glittering and fabulous than me, and that he's going to leave me behind because I could never shine this brightly even if I covered myself in hairspray and set myself on fire. I can't quite work it out though because we had this chat, we got it all out in the open, and I totally believed Jack when he said it would never happen again, that we were friends, best friends, and that would never end. So my stomach feels heavy and my chest feels tight because . . . ?

Why is it not enough? Why is friends not enough for me? I don't own him. He's not mine. He's going to have other friends too. What the hell is wrong with me that I don't even want to *share*? Another waitress appears in front of us with a huge platter of amazing snacks. She looks at me and smiles, so I smile back. I glance at the tray. Is this for us? More free things?

"Mini burgers, mini fish and chips, chargrilled chili prawns, and sun-dried tomato and feta mini tarts," the waitress says.

I chew my lip. "Um, we haven't paid for any of this."

The waitress laughs, but the money thing doesn't seem to be an issue, and she just extends the platter toward us.

OK, I'm starving, so fine then. I take the whole platter from her.

She looks at me, wide-eyed. "Thank you," I say.

"Um . . . OK?" she replies.

Elliot picks a prawn on a stick from the tray. "Mmm!" he says.

Anyway, Elliot and I are standing there with this huge platter of snacks, which, frankly, is quite an inconvenient way to serve them, and the waitress just frowns and heads away again, so what's suddenly gotten into her, I don't know. It's only when Elliot and I have settled on two small soft stools with the tray balanced across our laps that I realize all the other guests are just taking one item each from the food trays, before the waiting staff take the tray to someone else, and so now I feel like a total dick who has no manners and is totally uncouth but also, WHO TOLD EVERYONE ELSE HOW IT WORKS?

THIRTY-NINE

JACK

I swear to god, I leave those boys to their own devices for barely a minute, and what happens? I've just shared some small talk with none other than Scrummy Emma of Woodland Granola fame (who loved the idea of @TheHeartbreakBoys and suggested I take some hashtag gifted granola to promote on the account—WIN!) and have spotted Leila Bhatia up ahead, standing by herself, tapping away at her phone. I turn to make sure Nate and Elliot have followed, and I see them taking AN ENTIRE PLATTER OF FOOD from one of the waitresses, like that's in any way what you actually do at these things. I actually can't even. I *cannot even*. I have no *even* left. I watch in horror as they settle down on two soft poufs with the tray balanced across their laps and they tuck in like neither of them has eaten for days. *What are they doing? Do they not understand this isn't about the food, it's about networking?*

I'm going to have to leave them to it. I take a deep breath to expel the horror and stride up to Leila Bhatia.

"Leila Bhatia!" I beam.

She glances up from her phone. "Hey, Jack." Something's wrong. She looks tired and beaten down, not her usual sparkly self, full of positivity and inspirational life quotes.

"A-mazing party!" I say. "Thank you *so much* for the invite."

"Getting some good pics for your highlights reel?"

"I mean, Dylan and Tariq are going to be *livid*. But also this isn't about them because they're basically dead to me now; this is about moving on with *my* life and being happy and successful with the things that I have. And now I'm here, I can see I have so much, so thank you again."

Leila take a deep breath and gives a wry smile. "So you know the shit has hit the fan, right?"

My eyes widen. "I did not know, no. Whose shit? Which fan?"

"Turns out someone snapped a pic of me buying those burgers and carrying them back to V Machine?"

"Ohh," I say. *"Sneaky!"*

Leila cocks her head. "Sneaky? I think you mean 'deliberate attempt to shit-stir,' Jack!"

I nod. 'Yes, that's what I meant. What happened next?"

"Posted online, went viral, lots of people calling me a hypocrite, among an assortment of other charming names."

"Vile."

"Naturally, I respond. I announce that it's not right for people to police what other people eat. That you don't know what health issues or otherwise people have faced that means they need to eat certain things."

I nod. "Excellent."

"Yes," Leila says. "And after that, most people were onside, loads of tweets of support, and lots of people saying how the person who originally called me out should mind their own business and stop causing drama."

I nod. "Fabulous. Damn right too."

Leila gives me a small grimace. "Until it materializes that the person who made the original post is in fact a fourteen-year-old, and so now I stand accused of bullying a child and sending my fans after her."

"Oh, *come on!*"

"The kid's mum got involved, saying how her daughter saw me as a role model but now I'm basically trash and pretty much a child killer in her eyes . . ."

"Ludicrous. This is all ludicrous!"

Leila nods.

"You can't let them win—"

She holds her hand up. "Don't worry. It's fine."

I smile. "You've sorted it? You've found some perfect response?"

"You'll see," Leila says. She glances over at Nate and Elliot and laughs. "They're getting their money's worth!"

I roll my eyes.

"Cute," she says. "I love how they just don't care."

"I think it's not that they don't care, as such . . . it's blissful ignorance?"

Leila laughs again. "Either way, respect." She squeezes my arm. "How you doing anyway?"

I shrug. "Good, I guess. Dylan and Tariq did a big promise rings thing on their account, which was annoying, but whatever. I think . . ." I glance over at Nate. "I think there are more important things."

"And people?"

"Huh?"

Leila smiles at me, then glances around the crowded room. "So! Who have you already met?"

"Had a chat with Scrummy Emma," I say. "How amazing to have your own granola brand in all major retailers at her age!"

Leila looks unimpressed. "Right? It's incredible when she only has millionaire parents who happen to own one of the biggest supermarket chains in the UK. *How did she do it?*"

I stare at Leila.

"It's pure talent." Leila smirks. "Pure hard work and talent." She clocks my disappointed face. "Hey, you wanna meet some other people?"

My face breaks into a wide smile. "I mean, OK!"

OMG, this is it!

Leila guides me through some of the crowd, toward a group of incredibly good-looking guys, one of whom I recognize instantly as gay YouTuber Sammy Evans, like, this guy was a total inspiration

321

to me back in year nine when I came out, and I love his videos so much, and now here he is, real, in front of me, and I'm gonna get to talk to him.

"Sammy? This is my friend Jack," Leila says, getting his attention by touching his elbow.

I clock the other two guys Sammy was talking to, and the look on their faces tells me they don't appreciate this interruption — it's a look of annoyance, but it's fleeting, and then they're back to smiling as Sammy turns to shakes hands with me.

"Hey, Jack!" he smiles. "How you doing?"

"Ha ha ha!" I say. "Yep!"

"Jack's recently set up a brilliant Instagram account," Leila explains.

Sammy nods. "Yeah? Cool, what's it about?"

"Oh," I shrug, "not much really, just—"

"Sammy!" A new guy appears next to him, slapping him on the back. "How was Paris?"

"So awesome!" Sammy grins.

I nod and smile, like that's amazing, but also, I was about to talk some more.

"You doing the Virgin Atlantic gig?" New Guy asks.

"Yeah! You?"

"Yeah! Oh my god, that's gonna be out of this world!"

I nod and smile, like that's amazing, but also, I was about to talk some more.

"Sammy! Congrats, man!" another new guy says, joining the group.

"Danny boy!" Original New Guy says, bumping fists with him. "Saw your piece for Pepsi!" Sammy says to Danny Boy. "How'd you bag that one?"

I'm just grinning manically, standing there like a total friendless hanger-on, like, no one actually knows who I am, I don't know these guys, but they all know each other, and I honestly don't quite know how to extract myself. Do I just slope off? Edge backward? And they're all so successful and doing Things with Brands whereas I'm basically . . . nothing. Luckily, just as I'm about to die of an awkwardness I've never before experienced, Leila pulls me back and guides me around to this guy in his late teens, tall and skinny, dressed in black, who she introduces as Atticus, an "Instagram Poet."

"What sort of poetry is it?" I ask.

"I don't put my work in boxes," he replies, giving me a look that lets me know he thinks I'm an uncultured lout.

Nevertheless, I persevere, because it's small talk and that's what you do. "Does it . . . rhyme?"

He stares at me. For a moment I think he might hit me.

And then he laughs in my face.

Leila is pretty quick to remove me from Atticus, and then I meet a woman called Tonks, who is in PR, lives in Chelsea, brays like a horse, and liberally scatters the most offensive swear words in sentences like confetti. Tonks has just come back from "fucking Bali" and has an amazing way of not actually listening to anything you're saying, partly because whenever anyone else speaks, she just repeats, "Yah, yah, yah, yah, yah," all the way through it.

Then there's some guy who works for Simon Cowell and clearly thinks that makes him the most important person in the room; at least five "film producers" who say they've worked on big stuff like Star Wars but when I check on IMDB afterward just seem to have made a short film two years ago; an "underground DJ" who's too cool for school and looks at everyone she meets like they're actual shit and tells me this room is full of "people with so much privilege it makes me sick," although it later transpires that she has actually just left one the UK's top private schools and is now studying at Oxford. And after I've met Indigo, who was recently "canceled" after posting about a popular band and saying people should "beg, borrow, or steal a ticket," which was interpreted as condoning theft, I'm just standing with some people, and I don't even know who they are anymore, but they're jabbering on about promos and their managers and book deals, and I suddenly feel like I don't belong here and I'm not even sorry about that. I'm . . . glad. Because I don't want this. These aren't my people. I glance over at Nate and Elliot, and Nate looks up, raises his eyebrows, and gives me this goofy grin and a little wave. And my heart is suddenly so full and I smile.

"Want to get out of here?" Leila says.

"Yeah," I say. "Yeah, I do."

FORTY

NATE

"This is *so* my happy place," Elliot says, biting into his Shack-Meister. "I feel much happier here."

I think we all do. We're sitting very contentedly around a mess of Shack burgers, cheesy fries, and shakes, and with these goofballs, there isn't a single place on earth I'd rather be.

I sneak a glance at Jack. I'm delighted he didn't want to stay at the YouTubers party, but I'm curious as to why. He catches me looking. "What?" he asks.

I shrug. "Just wondering how we ended up at Shake Shack."

"Because the other place was full of some of the worst people I've ever met in my life. Seriously, scrap everything I've ever said about wanting to be part of their world. I do not fit in their world. And they sure as hell don't fit in mine."

I smile and carry on with my burger.

"And you know," Jack continues, "now I think of it, that's true of Dylan too."

I raise my eyebrows. "Yeah?"

"*Yeah*. I forced the idea of Dylan into my life. I tried to make him fit when he really didn't." He glances at me, wipes some ketchup off his chin, licks his finger, and grins. "Ohhhh. *Deeeeeep*, huh?"

"Yeah, it's deep. *Deeeeeep*."

And I laugh, but really, I'm thinking. I'm wondering if that's true of Tariq too. I thought he fit in my life, but actually maybe he never did. Maybe he was never quite what I needed, and maybe I was never quite what he needed either. And I think that's OK. I think sometimes you only get to know that after someone's actually *in* your life. And I think sometimes you only realize that someone does fit after they're *not* in your life anymore. I glance back at Jack, and he gives me a wink, so I lob a cheesy fry at him, an action that immediately results in him throwing a plastic bottle of ketchup at me.

"Sorry! Reflex action!" Jack grins at me maliciously. "Nate, you have ketchup dripping down your face—has anyone got a napkin? Actually, scrap that, let's get a selfie, Nate's never looked this stunning. This is the exact moment!"

And with that, before I've even chance to pull a tissue out, his phone is in his hand, he's got his arm stretched out behind him, and everyone's crowding in for the pic.

"Wait!" I protest. But it's too late. It's done, and Jack's busy typing up some witty caption and uploading it.

"Hashtag ketchup face, hashtag Messy Gay," Jack says, typing. "Huh. Leila? Why can't I tag you?"

"Ah." Leila smiles. "So, yes, I have something to tell you." Leila looks between us, nodding.

"Are you pregnant?" Jack asks.

Leila screws her face up. "What? No. No, Jack, I'm not."

"Sorry," Jack says. "It's just your voice sounded quite serious. Like, literally, that's the exact tone of voice my mum used when she told me she was getting divorced from my dad—I was having flashbacks." He shivers. "Ugh. So what is it?" He suddenly looks serious. "Oh god, oh, no, it's not . . . you haven't had some bad news? You're not . . . sick?"

Leila stares at him. I put my burger down. Oh god. I really hope it's not that.

"There are so many treatments now for things," Jack says. "I'm sure it'll—"

"Jack!" Leila snaps. "I've just deleted my accounts!"

My eyes widen. I glance at Elliot, who has stopped, midchew. Jack's gawping at her. "Deleted?" he gasps. "But why?"

"You just saw why," Leila says. "You saw exactly why. You don't want to be part of that world, and I don't either."

"But you were successful," Jack starts to babble, "you were

making money, you had hundreds of thousands of followers, you were *it*, Leila, you were living the dream!"

Leila shakes her head. "I was living a nightmare. I'm sick of the fake outrage and needless drama. I'm sick of pretending it's fine to make people want more, buy more, when the world is burning and what we should all be doing is wanting *less*. I'm sick of seeing people I don't respect, with little talent, rise to the top and be role models, when the world doesn't need any more vacuous fuckwits. I don't want to look back on my life in thirty years and realize it was all pointless, and maybe for some people, they won't feel it is, but I already do feel like that, so I need to change things."

Jack just sits in stunned silence. "Yeah, you know what?" he finally says. "*Respect.* You're right." He looks at me, chewing his lip a bit. "You know, Nate, maybe it's time."

I raise an eyebrow. Time for what? What's he talking about now?

"Time to quit the whole Insta influencer idea. Time to quit the whole get one over on Dylan and Tariq thing," he continues. "'Cause it is, isn't it? It's all just . . . nonsense. And, like, maybe it's just out of my system, but I don't even feel like I *need* to anymore. Don't feel I've got anything to prove, maybe 'cause . . ." I swear he blushes slightly. "Well, it doesn't matter what the reason might be." He sniffs and carefully folds a napkin into a tight square. "You know, I didn't say, and I know you don't really look on Insta so I doubt you've seen, but they're off to Ibiza tomorrow. Flying out to live the high life on the party island, celebrating promising themselves to each other, and" — he releases a breath — "I don't even care." He looks back up at me. "I just don't, Nate."

I press my lips together and nod. He's right. I don't care either. At some point, I'm not sure when, I stopped caring about using the account to get Tariq back and just started having fun. It's like a weight has lifted, the curse has gone, and it's OK, because I feel like I've gained something way better. And maybe that's why I suggest it. Maybe it's because getting it all out and then drawing a line under it would normally be way too much of a brave thing for me to do, except now, I feel like I can go there. I don't want to carry on, start the new school year with bad feelings toward Tariq and Dylan, and all the stress of everything being left unsaid. I've left so much unsaid all these years. And what I've found over this summer is that talking helps. Talking can make it better.

"We should talk to them," I say.

Jack frowns at me. "Call them, you mean?"

I shake my head. "Face-to-face. Gotta be."

"*Brave.*"

"They're gonna be at, what, Heathrow tomorrow? Leaving for Ibiza?"

Jack's eyes widen.

"Do it," Leila says. "Go and make your peace with them. It's time."

I turn to Jack. "She's right. It's time. And you know, I feel ready."

FORTY-ONE

JACK

A brief interlude just to say that the Piccadilly Line, all the way from central London to Heathrow, during morning rush hour, with all those people, and all that luggage, for all that way, is absolute hell, and I hope Dylan and Tariq really appreciate how much hell we have been through to come and see them and wish them well on their journey. I mean, that's if we get there. Nate, Elliot, and I have been stuck at Hammersmith for what feels like years. It's the twenty-first century. *In Rhianna's London.* And this is the mess we're in.

"Nate?" I say as we get off when we finally roll into Heathrow. "Whatever happens, whatever Tariq says, or doesn't say, it's OK, and . . ." I swallow. I adore him so much, I just wish I could tell him without it sounding weird because we're friends and it doesn't feel right. "It'll be OK," I say.

I squeeze his shoulder, because even if I can't quite say it, I need him to know I'm here for him.

FORTY-TWO

NATE

We're in time. I watch Tariq turn away from the check-in desk, passport and boarding pass in hand, and then stop dead as he sees me. He's dressed in chino shorts and a white short-sleeved shirt— preppy and cute. He just stares. I give him a nod and a small wave. Like I used to when I'd see him walk into the school library.

Dylan (shorts, tank top, and flip-flops like he's already at the pool, because he's one of those types) clocks Tariq, then me, then Jack, his face a picture of fury as he storms over and whisks Jack away from the check-in queue, leaving Tariq to walk over to me.

"Hey," I say.

"Nate, what are you doing here?"

"Came to see you off?" I attempt a laugh, but I can't manage it. I wanted to make this light, fun, and easy, but I feel different to how I thought I would.

Tariq looks at me pityingly. "Nate, I —"

"Can we talk though? Just quickly?"

"I guess," Tariq says. He glances over to where Dylan looks like he's having a *very* intense conversation with Jack and then back around the check-in hall. "Should we get a coffee?"

I nod. "Great."

I sit at a small table in Costa as Tariq comes over with two cappuccinos, which have inappropriately been adorned with chocolate powder in the shape of hearts.

"So?" Tariq says, stirring three sugars into his.

I swallow. "Still like the sugar, huh?" I say.

"Nate," he says. "I really don't have long. We've gotta get through security, and —"

I nod. "I know. I'm sorry. I just wanted to say . . ." And I stop because now I'm here, sitting in front of him, everything's a tangle and I can't think where to start. He wasn't right for me? I wasn't right for him? Did I try to make him fit when he didn't? Is that my fault? Was he in the wrong? I don't know and everything sounds wrong now, so I just end up saying,

"I miss you, Tariq."

Which sounds hideously needy and isn't something I even mean.

He looks down at his coffee.

"I did think we were good together," I tell him. "I really did. I thought we were a perfect match, but I guess maybe it was only me who thought that. Because if you thought that too, I think things wouldn't have happened between you and Dylan. Is that . . . is that a fair thing to say?"

There's a pause, then Tariq looks up at me again. "Dylan was there when . . . We started talking about stuff that I . . . You know, there are things that happened that you don't know about, stuff that . . ."

"Like what?"

"Like . . ." Tariq sighs. "OK, like my parents were . . . accepting when I came out to them, but the same can't be said for the rest of my family. You know, it hurt me, the stuff that was going on, and one day, I just started talking to Dylan about it, and he—"

"You could have talked to me!" I don't mean to sound so hurt, but it's hard, hearing him say this. Hearing him say there was stuff he talked to Dylan about instead of me.

"But, Nate, you weren't out yourself. You were messed up about the whole thing. That's not your fault. I don't blame you for that. I know it's hard, but right then I needed to talk to someone who had been there, done that, you know? And that was Dylan."

My throat tightens and my heart squeezes.

"When we first got together, you were so nervous about it, so . . . skittish. And I totally get that. I really do. But all the secret stuff, all the undercover and no one must find out . . . I couldn't keep living that lie. I needed someone who made me feel like it would be OK, Nate. I needed to feel safe, and Dylan made me feel safe."

I start to cry. I can't help it. I feel like I've let him down. I never made him feel like it would be OK. Like he could be happy. Like he was safe. "I'm sorry," I mutter, wiping my eyes.

"I really liked you, Nate," he says. The fact he doesn't say "love" speaks volumes. "But I didn't really know if you liked me."

"Of course I did," I say.

"You never told me."

I stare at him, trying to remember, thinking it through.

"I didn't know what was going on in your head half the time," he says. "Keep it all to yourself, don't you? Look . . . I'm not saying any of this to justify what I did. I hurt you, and I was wrong, and I'm sorry. And you're right, we were good together. I think, maybe, we're right for each other—just in some parallel universe where we collide at a slightly different time in our lives, or where our messed-up world doesn't make life a billion times harder for gay teenagers."

I wipe my eyes on the ratty piece of tissue I've got in my pocket. Maybe Tariq's right. But then maybe . . . maybe he isn't. And maybe . . . Jack is.

"No," I say. "No, we're not right for each other, not in this world or a parallel one."

Tariq stiffens slightly.

"I probably never did tell you how I thought I felt, but . . . know what? That's me, isn't it? I don't . . . I find it hard to be that open about things, but I think you knew that, and still, you didn't ask me instead. You didn't even try to talk to me about it when that was what *I* needed. But it's OK, Tariq, because that's who I am, and if that doesn't work for you, genuinely, that's OK, because I think it's better for me to find someone who is OK with it, who is fine with me as me, rather than me as some fake version of myself I try to create just so I'm not alone. And I understand what you're saying about your family, and I can't begin to imagine how hard that must be for you, but if Dylan can help with that, then Dylan is right for you. And I'm not. We can't just see each other's highlights reel, Tariq, because the thing about a highlights reel is that it's hard work. You gotta work hard to maintain that level of fakeness. It's better to be with someone who sees the full thing, warts and all, but is happy with you anyway."

Tariq takes a deep breath. "Wow. You got deep this summer."

"I've always been deep, Tariq. You just never noticed."

"Ouch."

"You're a dick."

"I know. I'm sorry."

"Is he good in bed?"

Tariq laughs. "Shut up, Nate."

"Well, enjoy your holiday. Bet you'll get some good pics for Insta, so there's that."

"Still doing yours with Jack?"

I shrug. "Not sure there's much point. I mean, you got the big one, didn't you? You got Ibiza. Drinks on the terrace and all that jazz?"

"Not really 'jazz,' more 'ambient chill.'"

"Ohh, *funny.*"

Tariq smiles at me. "So. You and Jack?"

My eyes widen.

"Always kinda inevitable," he chuckles.

"I have no idea —"

"Oh, *come on!*"

"Literally, what are you taking about?"

"You and Jack," Tariq says. He takes in my confused expression. "I mean, that's what . . . you are, aren't you?"

"Are *what?*"

"Together!" he nearly screams. "You and Jack! You're a thing, an item, boyfriends!"

I spit out my coffee. How the hell has he gotten this idea?

"Oh," Tariq says. "Or *not,* then?"

"Correct," I say. *"Not, then."*

Tariq chews his lip a bit. "OK, it's just . . . I guess your joint Instagram feed kinda gives that impression, that's all."

"Why, because it's joint?"

"No, because of what's posted."

My eyes widen. "What's *posted?* What do you mean?"

"I mean, you see it, right?"

"No, I don't really do Instagram. I mean, I've seen bits, approved some of the pics —"

"Yeah, it's not the pics."

"Then what?"

Tariq picks up his phone and starts scrolling through our feed. "Picture of you asleep in some hotel bed, caption: *Aw! Love this boy so much — look at him! Hashtag sleeping beauty."*

"That's just Jack being Jack."

"Picture of you soaking wet for some reason —"

"Yeah, I'd fallen in a lake."

"Right, caption: *Nate got a little damp today—lent him my oversized jumper to keep warm, but this calls for hot chocolate!*" Tariq raises an eyebrow. "I mean, that certainly *sounds*—"

"Jack does this thing sometimes where he—"

"Acts like he's your boyfriend?"

"I mean, no, but it's the type of thing he—"

"Sounds caring. Sounds romantic."

"Yeah, but it's Jack, Tariq! He messes around, doesn't he? He makes me say 'I love you' whenever I leave the room."

Tariq laughs. "Am I supposed to think that's normal?"

"It's in case one of us dies!"

He stops laughing. "Wow. OK. That's . . . *yeah.*"

I sip my coffee. "Just Jack, that's all. What else? Anything else?"

Tariq purses his lips and scrolls through a bit more. "I mean, OK, he calls you 'hot' in the one with your top off . . ."

"Clearly a joke. Clearly sarcasm." I glance at the pic. "Dammit, I told him not to post that one."

"To be fair, it's not bad, Nate. You've almost got abs."

"It's just the shadows. Next."

"Ah!" Tariq says, stopping scrolling and smiling. "Yeah."

I raise my eyebrows.

He hands me the phone. It's a picture I genuinely didn't know he was taking, just me, in the tent at the festival when it was raining, taken slightly in profile, and I'm just . . . smiling. I admit, it is a nice picture, and where I'm concerned, that's no mean feat. It's an accidentally really nice photo, so fine. I've no issue with it. And the caption reads: *Love it when he smiles.* I can see why Tariq might think this was suspicious, but we're just mates, and he just doesn't understand the level of our banter.

"Tariq, this whole Instagram thing, the sole purpose was to piss off Dylan, and to a certain extent you. All the pictures, the captions, they're all carefully thought out to present a version of our summer that . . . hasn't really been how it maybe looks."

Tariq frowns. "Has your summer been bad, then?"

I open my mouth to say, *Well, yeah,* but stop because, actually, no, it hasn't been bad. It's been . . . We've laughed . . . *a lot.* We've seen places and done things. We've talked . . . We've buried differences and maybe reconnected a bit. And me, I've seen what friendship can look like, and specifically, how with Jack and Elliot, I don't need to hide or be afraid, and that with them, I feel . . . stronger. Better for having them by my side. We haven't been to a super-expensive gig or a big show, and we're not off on the vacation of a lifetime, but actually, I think what we have done, the journey we've been on, is a million times better.

A smile spreads across my face. "No, Tariq, summer has been amazing."

He nods.

"You probably need to catch your flight," I continue. "Let's go."

"OK," Tariq says. "But, Nate? I am sorry. Just to reiterate that. And also, one thing that will never change—we'll always be each other's first kiss."

"Actually, Tariq, I'm sorry, but you weren't my first kiss."

And I grin, then we walk out of the coffee shop, knowing that he's got a million questions and that I'm not gonna answer any of them.

* * *

I stroll back into the check-in hall feeling lighter and happier than I've felt in a long time, so much so that I don't even really find it that annoying when Dylan strides up to us, totally ignores me, and goes straight for Tariq, saying, "Everything OK?" like *I* might have upset *him* and that Tariq needs Dylan's protection against big bad me.

Tariq nods and smiles. "Yeah, good."

"Where's Jack?" I ask.

Dylan shrugs. "Dunno. We talked and he went off." He turns back to Tariq. "We gotta go."

"What do you mean, 'he went off'?" I ask.

Dylan grimaces in irritation. "He went off! Walked off, what else do you want me to say? I'm not his keeper!"

"Well, where was he going?"

Dylan stares at me a moment. "Er, we're at an airport so take your pick from literally hundreds of destinations! Tariq? Come on."

I blow out a breath. Dylan is such a prick. I don't know what Jack ever saw in him. Except Dylan's pretty, of course, so I guess there's that. Pretty people get away with being utter shits, and no one seems to care.

Anyway, Tariq and Dylan head off to security, and I'm left just standing in the middle of check-in, thinking I should stay there because maybe Jack's gone to the toilet or to get a drink and will be back soon. But when he doesn't show after ten minutes, I text him. And then, after another couple of minutes, I text again. And then I actually call, which is when you know it's serious.

It goes straight to voicemail.

Something's not right. I felt it wasn't right in the way Dylan told me that Jack "went off" but now I know it. I do a three-sixty turn, the airport and people swimming around me, but there's no sign of him. I call Elliot, but Elliot is getting a back rub at some walk-in massage stand and Jack isn't with him. I tell Elliot to get himself over to me, and he's there in about five minutes, but there's still no sign of Jack.

"We could ask if they can do one of those lost child announcements over the loudspeaker system," Elliot suggests.

It's a good idea, and there's a big part of me that hopes we'll rock up at the lost child center and Jack will be sitting on one of the chairs with a balloon and a lollipop, waiting for us. But he's not, and he's still not there after about five announcements made over the whole airport.

"Could he have headed back to the Airbnb?" Elliot says. "Maybe he was upset after talking to Dylan and wanted to be alone for a bit?"

It's possible. I message him and leave a voicemail saying we're heading back to the house and to meet us there and to call as soon as he picks this up. But as we sit in silence on the tube back into central London, I have this increasing nagging feeling in my stomach, and when we get back to the Airbnb and there's still no Jack, and no word from him whatsoever, I just run and find my parents because I don't know what else to do.

In the middle of me gabbling the story to my folks, a text pings through:

Gone back home. Don't worry.

I don't know what happened at the airport to have caused this, but right now, I don't even care. I just want Jack back with us and I want him to be OK.

"I've gotta go and find him," I tell Dad.

He nods. "Yeah. You do. You owe him."

"What do you mean?"

"Nothing, just go."

"No, wait, tell me what you meant by that."

Dad sighs. "Nate, everything that boy has done on this trip, he's done to try to make you happy. Going to see Elliot was his idea because he thought you'd like to see him again. Inviting Elliot along was his idea too because I think he thought you . . . *liked him* liked him."

I stare at my dad.

"And now I think he needs you."

I don't have time to process what he's said; I need to get myself together, get on a train, and get back home.

"Take my card," Mum says, handing me her Visa.

"Really?"

Mum just nods, where once she would have given me a lecture about budgeting.

"OK, thanks," I say, grabbing my wallet, phone, keys, and a backpack.

"And, Nate? Talk to him, then both of you get back on a train and get down to Plymouth," Dad says.

"Why? Shouldn't we just stay—"

"You have to get to Plymouth," Dad repeats. "That's the whole point."

"Point of what? What do you mean? What's going on?"

"Get him, and bring him to Plymouth. This trip isn't over yet. You'll see."

Dad looks at me, deep into me, like he's never looked at me before, and I swallow, a chill running through me. But I know not to argue. And I don't have time to argue anyway.

The last thing I hear as I head out of the door is Rose.

"Go get your husband, Nate!"

FORTY-THREE

JACK

Dylan's words echo through my head all the way home. *It's always all about you. It's all show—I can't ever tell what's real. Who even are you, Jack? Embarrassing. You're a caricature. You could tone it down but you insist on making yourself a target. What is it—do you just crave the attention?*

It was OK. I could take it. I kept thinking, *Nate doesn't think this, Nate likes me,* but then Dylan twisted the knife:

"I see what you're doing on Instagram, trying to make it look like you and Nate are a thing, but you're not, are you? Know how I know? He wouldn't want to be with someone like you. Nobody would. That's why I ended up doing what I did, Jack. I was going to tell you after prom just to save us all the heartache of having prom ruined, but guess what? You had to go and ruin it anyway, just so the spotlight was on you again!"

As soon as he's said it, I know he's right. I don't really care about his whole character assassination—I mean, I'm pretty used to that. But the stuff about Nate cuts me up. All this time, slowly, I've been letting myself think that maybe something could happen despite all the evidence to the contrary. Despite the fact that never once has Nate told me, or even suggested, he might feel like that. All fiction. A made-up fantasy world, with a great big fake idiot at the center of it.

But I'm still OK. I need to sort my head out, but I'm still OK. Until Dylan says the one thing that I'm not ever gonna be OK with:

"Quite a lot of us are sick of your shit, so only fair to warn you, I'm hearing whispers that a lot of us aren't gonna be part of the LGBTQ-plus society next year, like, maybe it'll just be you and Nate. He can get a taste of what it's like to be with the clown no one wants to hang out with."

No way. No way am I gonna let Nate be dragged into all the crap I have put up with. I'm not going to let him be isolated and disliked. That was exactly what he was so scared of for so long. He doesn't deserve that.

So maybe the best thing I can do for Nate is just let him be. I think, I honestly think, he will be better off without me. Because even if we're just good mates, he'll be dragged down. The others will see to that.

So I go. When I finally turn my phone back on and see Nate's frantic messages and voicemails, I send a message back, just to let him know I'm OK, even though I am far from OK, but he doesn't want to be bothered with that, and there's no one else who would care how I was feeling. So I bury it, like I've always buried it, because there never really was anyone in the first place, and I guess there maybe never will be, and I've survived this long, so I'll just carry on.

Maybe in September I'll just keep my head down, get on with school stuff, speak less, not engage. I'll do what everyone wants; I'll be the version of Jack that doesn't pull any focus, doesn't annoy everyone, just exists. Let them win. There's no prize for me anyway if *I* win, so what sort of victory would that be?

Mum's in when I get home, which is annoying because you know when you just need to be alone to wallow in gloom? She looks up from a pile of legal papers on the kitchen table. "What's happened?"

I shrug. "Nothing. I'm just back." She studies me, but I ignore her. "Is there any chocolate milk?"

"It's weird you would come back and not let me know."

I shrug and open the fridge.

"Did you fight with Nate?"

I sigh, looking through the fridge shelves. "No. We're . . . cool."

She closes a folder. "Jack? There's no chocolate milk. I wasn't expecting you back this soon."

And it's that piece of news, the complete lack of chocolate milk, which pushes me over the edge. I can feel my bottom lip start to wobble. "I need to lie down," I mutter. "Tired."

And I hurry out of the kitchen, up the stairs, and straight to my bedroom.

I can't do this. I can't be this.

I thought I was strong, but I guess, in the end, I'm not.

Eventually . . .

I sleep.

* * *

Relentless hammering at my front door wakes me up.

Jesus.

If it's another recipe box company asking if they can "speak to my mum or dad," I swear I'll ram one of their organic root vegetables where the sun don't shine.

I stumble downstairs, groggy, angry, empty, hungry, with sore eyes, open the door, and see Nate standing there, looking utterly wrecked, drenched from head to toe, with a carton of chocolate milk in his hands.

"Hey," he says.

And I'm so happy to see him, so overwhelmed he would come all this way, so full of love for him, I burst into tears.

FORTY-FOUR

NATE

You know those comedy movie chases where fruit carts suddenly push out in front of the hero and old people with walking sticks cross the road right in front of them? Well, *that* was my journey back home from London. The world must see you are in a massive rush and get a real thrill from throwing everything in your way to thwart you.

London Underground was full of tourists, clogging up the tunnels and standing on both sides of the escalators so I couldn't hurry past. A broken-down train at Acton had caused severe delays. Somewhere else, a passenger had been "taken ill." I made my train from St. Pancras with two minutes to spare, gasping and puffing into a crowded car where I was forced to sit on the floor because there were no seats. We departed slightly late, and that meant we got stuck behind some random freight train, so we limped on, only getting as far as Bedford before grinding to a total stop. Twenty minutes later, we were told the freight train had managed to derail itself, the whole line was now suspended, and we had to await a rail replacement bus service. An entire hour later and this *thing* turned up, like this double-decker relic from the Second World War, chugging along, blowing out vast plumes of noxious black smoke. I didn't even care by this point. I was just happy we were moving again as we bounced and lurched around the roundabouts of Bedford, making our way to a main road. Somewhere near Market Harborough, the bus had had enough, the engine overheated, and it refused to budge. Lots of adults with clipboards and fluorescent vests made a big show of telling everyone this was "not their fault" and they were "doing their best." It was at this point an elderly woman sitting next to me called her daughter, and lo, said daughter agreed to drive from Market Harborough to Nottingham. There were three other places available in the car, and I was prepared to offer them a kidney at this point (if the old lady needed one) but I *had* to be in that car.

There were a number of businessmen and women making a lot of noise about an important meeting, and I could see my plight might not be considered grave enough so I did the only sensible thing—I lied about my age. I made out I was fourteen, therefore implying they had to help me because I'm a real live kid, and although it kills me to admit it, they all bought it, and while that's great, I also really hope I start to get a bit of facial hair soon.

By the time I finally arrived in our suburb of Nottingham I was exhausted, hungry, cold, but I was here. I'd reached where Jack would be. I even managed to buy him some chocolate milk from the shop. But fate had decreed a water main would have burst along the main street, with torrents of water flowing down the road. All it took was one ill-timed car, driving a little fast as I passed one particularly huge puddle, and I was covered, head to toe, in muddy, sludgy, water.

And so, there I am, complete drowned rat, stinking and tired, as I hammer on Jack's door.

Jack looks wrecked too. Also *crying*.

"Oh my god, it's just chocolate milk!" I tell him.

"Shut up," he says, pulling me in through the door and slamming it shut behind. "You came."

I nod slowly. "I did. Here I am. Ta-da."

He stares at me, his eyes wet and questioning. "What the hell happened to you?"

"Well, I'm covered in shit basically. Possibly literally. Can I have a shower?"

He nods.

"And then we should . . . talk?" I suggest. Whatever it is Dylan said to him obviously hit him hard. Maybe Jack liked him more than he was letting on. Maybe he's more cut up about all this than I thought. Whatever the reason, I want to make it better. I want to be for Jack what he is for me. I want to be strong for him, so he can feel strong too.

He nods again.

"I'll need some clothes," I say. "It doesn't have to be any of your best pieces."

That makes him smile. "It'll probably just be a hoodie and joggers, is that OK?"

"I think I'll cope."

Jack has one of those amazing rainfall showers in his huge bathroom, and I could have stayed in there all day, but I'm the quickest I've ever been. I change into the soft navy-blue hoodie and gray sweatpants he's left folded up for me and pad out onto the landing, where I find Jack, in a gray onesie, beckoning me toward his bedroom. "Mum's in," he whispers, which is all the explanation anyone ever needs.

I sit next to him on his double bed, and my first thought is how incredibly grown-up it is to have a double bed, and that I really need to speak to my parents about that.

I don't have to ask—he tells me exactly what Dylan said to him, word by horribly cruel word. And I'm struck again by the thing Dad said before I left, about how Jack has done everything on this trip to try to make me happy, and now again, when Dylan suggested my life would be made hell back at school, Jack's only thought was to stop that from happening by trying to put some space between us.

"You'll be better off if you don't hang out with me, Nate. That's just the truth."

"No," I tell him. "I don't care."

"But you will," he says.

"Thing is, Jack," I say, standing up and starting to wander about his room, "if this trip has shown me anything, apart from the arse ends of various parts of the UK, it's that I never needed to be scared of what other people said or thought because when I'm with you . . ." I pause because there, on top of his chest of drawers, is a photo in a frame of me and him when we were twelve. We're grinning at the camera, arms around one another's shoulders, faces red and slightly sweaty. I trace my fingers over our faces. *We were so happy.*

"My birthday party. We'd just done Laser Quest," Jack says behind me.

I put the photo back. "Where did you find it?"

"It's always been there." Jack shrugs.

I swallow and look at him. It's always been there. Through all the years we never spoke, all the years I thought he hated me, his dull, boring, one-time friend. But he never did.

"I remember, we were a team of fearless twelve-year-olds, and we had to play against that group of, like, university students because they'd screwed the bookings up."

"We annihilated them."

"We may have been small, but we were *fierce*." I smile. "I'm ready to do that again, Jack. I'm ready to be fearless. As long as we can be fearless together. I don't give a crap what Dylan says or any of the LGBTQ plus society or anyone else. If it's just you and me against a constant shitstorm, I don't care. As long as it *is* you and me. Like before. Like it always should have been." I look at him. "Agreed?"

He doesn't look convinced. "Nate . . ."

"No, you need to agree, Jack. I'm not taking any other answer, so you either agree or —"

"Or *what*? What you gonna do?"

I chew my lip a bit. "Well, you'll leave me no option. I'll have to wrestle you. Don't make me wrestle you, Jack."

He laughs. "Look, maybe . . . maybe if I tone it down a bit, you know? Next year at school? I could . . . you know, be less . . . I could be less."

My eyes widen. "Why would you even say that?"

"Because like everyone has always told me, I make myself a target. I'm *too* gay."

I scowl at him, then glance at a very noticeable blank space on his wall. "What should be here?"

"Oh. It was a Beyoncé poster. I took it down."

"You'd better not have destroyed it."

"I'm not a monster, Nate."

"Where is it?"

He indicates his desk. "It's —"

"Put it back up," I tell him. "Right now." I glance around the rest of the room while Jack Blu-Tacks the poster back on the wall. His fairy lights aren't even on, so I immediately rectify that, the string of twinkling white lights immediately creating the vibe of classy gay teen boy this place was lacking.

"That's better," I say.

Jack sniffs. "Maybe."

"You don't have to change a thing, Jack. You're living your truth, and no one should take that away from you. Me, I don't even know what my truth is, but . . ."

He raises his eyebrows.

I swallow. "But when I'm with you, I feel like I'm . . . finding out. I feel like I'm getting to know it. I feel like I don't have to pretend. I can just be me, even if I'm grumpy sometimes, even when I'm in a bad mood, and you don't seem to mind, and I like that. Just me. No filter. Not the highlights reel, the whole thing, the whole . . . messy, chaotic, happy, sad thing I call me. And, Jack?"

His eyes widen, his mouth open a little, waiting.

"Just so you know, Jack, your truth, you with no filter, the real *you*, maybe some people like Dylan don't like it, maybe they're scared of it, maybe you shine so brightly for them they know they could never compete. But me, I like it. I love it. And I should have told you that. I should have told you that ages ago. You're epic, Jack. You're fabulous. And please don't ever stop."

He looks like he might start crying again.

"OK," I say. "OK, I'm going to hug you, is that OK?"

He vaguely nods.

"OK." I wrap my arms around him and pull him close. His onesie is super soft. It's like hugging a giant guinea pig.

He sinks his face into my shoulder.

I grab hold of him with both hands.

And I never intend to let go.

FORTY-FIVE

JACK

I was not expecting Nate to turn up here today.

I was not expecting him to say what he said.

I was not expecting to go from feeling like I'd lost everything to feeling like I'd won the lottery.

The other thing I was not expecting was the news that we were both to return to the trip tomorrow by taking a train down to Plymouth for some unspecified and vague finale to this whole thing. But OK. And then I was not expecting Nate to say that he needed to stay the night at mine because while he had keys to his place, everyone was away and he didn't want to be by himself because *ghosts*. I sense a bullshit excuse, but maybe I'm just being optimistic.

So, fine, so I offer him the guest room.

The look on that boy's face. Unmistakable disappointment. And that's when I start to let myself actually think things might be changing. That we're not going to be just friends.

"It's just," he says, kicking his sock feet about on the floor. "It's weird, isn't it, how we've basically ended up sharing a bed for almost all of this trip?"

"Uh-huh?" I say.

"And, like, will I even be able to sleep by myself anymore?" He gives me a furtive glance, then adds a "Ha ha!"

He's nervous. So am I. I can hardly believe what I'm hearing. "What . . . are you saying, Nate?"

He looks up at me and chews his lip a bit.

I swallow. "Are you saying you would prefer to sleep in my bed?"

He shrugs. "I dunno."

My eyes widen. Nate's never gonna say it, not outright. This is Nate after all. "That you would prefer it if we both were sleeping in the same bed?"

"I mean, it's just . . ."

"Uh-huh?"

"It's like a security thing, I guess . . ."

"Oh, right?"

"Like, for years, I couldn't sleep without Patrick."

"Patrick?"

"My teddy bear." He gives me a look, as if to say, *And what of it?* I nod. "OK. Sure. So I'm like a kind of security blanket to you?"

"Do we have to label it, Jack?"

"Please, not Jack, call me *Blankie.*"

"We don't have to," he says. "I was only saying."

I look at him, smiling, until he meets my eyes again and gives me a guilty-looking grin back. "What?" he mutters.

"Come on, then."

His eyes actually light up, which is adorable. We get up to my room, and I arrange the bed so he has a pillow on his side, while he strips down to his boxers before hopping in. I flick the light off and do the same.

"Jack?"

"Yeah?"

"I'm actually glad all this happened the way it did."

"Sure. Me too, I guess."

We lie in silence for a bit. "Jack?"

"Mmm?"

"Love you."

I laugh. "Love you, Nate."

FORTY-SIX

NATE

"Morning, Jack. Hi, Nate."

My eyelids flutter open. It's Jack's mum, standing by the bed and placing two mugs of tea on Jack's bedside table.

"Still take sugar, Nate?"

I clear my throat and blink away the sleep. "Um . . . yeah. Thanks." Jack's eyes are closed, apparently fast asleep, on his back next to me. I glance at his mum. "We were up late talking, so we just crashed here." Which, incidentally, is the whole truth. Nothing else happened.

"Don't tell her anything, Nate," Jack says, eyes still closed. "She's only here because she sniffs gossip."

"I was just bringing you tea," his mum says.

"A likely story!" Jack replies. "We've been at it like rabbits, if you must know."

"Jack!" I immediately blush. "He's winding you up," I tell his mum.

She shrugs. "Shame. He's almost bearable when he's getting some."

Jack sits up. "OK, very good, thank you for the tea. Don't you have some criminals to set free?"

"It's not that sort of law."

"Just FYI," Jack says, "we're heading down to Plymouth today. Don't know how long for."

His mum smiles. "So does that mean everything's sorted itself out?"

Jack flicks his eyes to her. "I guess?"

She nods. "Good. And just remember, all those fuckers at school? In ten years' time, they'll friend request you on Facebook and ask you to like their page for the new cosmetics pyramid scheme they've joined, and that's when it's official—*you won.* Because you will literally have no *idea* who they are. "

"Ahh." Jack smiles. "We already have won." And he puts his hand on top of mine under the duvet, and he's right, because whatever happens or doesn't happen next, this feeling feels a lot like winning.

* * *

When we finally arrive at Plymouth, Mum, Dad, Elliot, and Rose meet us off the train and take us to where the bus is parked.

"Announcement!" Rose tells us. "I'm married to Elliot now!"

"It's been an eventful twenty-four hours," Elliot says, looking rather browbeaten.

"Elliot's my husband now, which means he will do whatever I say!"

"That's not really how marriage should work, Rose," Dad says as we clamber in the VW bus.

"All OK, boys?" Elliot asks as Dad starts the bus and pulls out of the parking lot.

I glance at Jack and smile. He smiles back and my heart flutters, just like it did when he put his hand on top of mine under the duvet. And that's a weird new development that I'm not sure I'm quite ready to face just yet. "Yeah. All OK."

"So, Nate, we have *something to tell you* . . ."

"Oh, Mr. and Mrs. Nate!" Jack claps his hands together. "You're pregnant? Congratulations! Aw, Nate, you're gonna be a—"

"Um, no, Jack. No. That's not . . ."

"God, *no*," Mum says, looking actually sick. "No offense, kids, but I'm not doing this again."

"Although in some ways"—Dad grins into the rearview mirror—"it's sort of like our little baby!"

Mum laughs. "Yes! I suppose so!"

"Are we getting a puppy?" I mean, I live in hope.

"No, Nate, we're starting a business," Dad says. "I've been looking for something new after the layoffs, and I don't want to spend any more time doing things I'm not totally passionate about. Your mum's going to help out—"

"I'm cutting down to four days a week from next term," Mum says. "And hopefully it'll be less as the business takes off."

"Well, don't keep us waiting!" Jack says. "What's the big idea?"

Dad's eyes sparkle. "Seize the day dot com. It's basically a life experiences website—a curated selection of bucket-list items so people can easily do and see the things they've always wanted to. Not just stuff like parachute jumps—"

"Or Outward Bound centers!" Mum grins.

"But also unusual camping places, restaurants that are off the beaten track, the best woodland walks, stunning views, so, like, some of it will be free stuff, others you'll have to pay for. We'll take a commission for anything booked through the site, plus ads. A one-stop shop for living in the moment and doing the stuff you always should have done but somehow never got around to." There's a wistful look on Dad's face, just for a moment. "I think that's important," he says.

"So was this whole trip a research mission for you?" I ask.

"Nah," Dad says. "I got the idea *on* the trip. You know, a free-spirited summer is great, but sometimes things would be easier and less stressful with a little bit of"—he glances sheepishly at Mum—"structure. I guess I just got inspired—and that's exactly why you should *do* these sorts of things. Magic happens when you step out of your regular routine, out of your comfort zone." He meets my eyes in the rearview mirror. "You realize what's really important to you and what you really want."

* * *

We're nearly an hour on the road before we pull up at this small stretch of unspoiled beach, somewhere near Hope Cove. There's a large wooden beach hut and they're serving freshly grilled fish and prawns, as well as local crab, mussels, and burgers to the throng of happy laid-back customers who are chilling on the beach and enjoying the live music from the band playing next to the hut.

"Ohh, this is *niiiiice*." Jack smiles. "This was worth coming back for!"

Dad looks well pleased with himself. "We'll set ourselves up on the beach, get some food and drinks, watch the sun go down." He hands us a tenner each. "Go and grab whatever you fancy." He lowers his voice. "Do you want me to get some beers, or . . ."

"I mean, you said 'beer' but what I heard was 'a really chilled, sweet rosé,'" Jack says.

"Done!" Dad says.

Jack, Elliot, and I end up pooling our money and getting this huge platter of freshly cooked seafood: flatfish, sardines, prawns, clams, whitebait, crab, with huge wedges of sourdough and butter, and basically a bucket of crispy triple-cooked fries. We sit on the sand tucking in to it, while the band plays behind us and happy people mill about, enjoying the sea air and the last of the evening sun.

Afterward, I go and find Dad, who's standing by himself at the far end of the beach, looking out across the sea.

"Hey, Nate," he says, turning as I crunch along the sand toward him.

"Hey."

"Great spot, isn't it?"

"Yeah, it's awesome. I love it."

Dad smiles and nods. "Yeah," he says, looking back out to sea. "So. You're wondering why I made a big deal out of this."

"Kinda."

"So you remember my friend Martin?"

"Yeah, the one who . . ."

"Yeah. So, we were friends back in the day, just like you and Jack. And just like you two, we'd just finished our GCSEs and—"

"Wait, you had GCSEs?"

Dad gives me a look. "Point's this: me and Martin had all these plans long ago, for the summer," he continues. "A road trip: see places, meet people, freedom. Didn't happen that year though, 'cause Martin ended up seeing this girl and wanted to spend time with her, and I ended up getting a part-time job and quite liking the money. But we promised we'd do it the year after. Except we didn't get it together that year, and the year after, we were getting ready for university, and there were loads of goodbye parties, and we didn't want to leave all our friends. And then we were at university, and we still promised we'd do it one summer, 'cept now we had new friends, and we were doing stuff with them. And so long story short, the years rolled on and we never did do it. Started jobs, couldn't get the same vacation days, got married, had kids, and somehow there was always a reason why it couldn't happen. And then earlier this year, Martin . . . And now . . . it never will."

I put my arm around his shoulders and he smiles.

"So this place," he says. "*This* was always meant to be the end of our trip. The rest of it was always kinda flexible, just see what happens kinda thing, but we were always going to finish here."

"Why?"

"Well, look at it, Nate! It's beautiful. It's perfect. It's a little corner of unspoiled paradise." He shakes his head. "I've known about this place since I came on vacation here as a kid with your gran and grandad; I wanted to show it to Martin. And now I want to show it to you. And, Nate? I want you to realize that life can be full of things you'll never do if you're not careful. So do them."

"Even if . . ."

Dad turns back to me. "They scare you? *Yes.*"

"Like, it could mess everything up?"

"*Oh.*" Dad chuckles. "Oh, you should totally tell him."

I stuff my hands in the pockets of my shorts. "Don't know what you mean by that, so."

"If I were a betting man, I would bet he liked you back, just the same."

I can't look at him, but I hope he carries on.

"Step out of that comfort zone, Nate," Dad continues. "Magic awaits when you grab life by the horns! Ooh, maybe that's what I should call the website. By the horns dot com?"

I laugh. "Yeah, *no*, Dad."

I find a pebble on the beach, pick it up, and throw it out to sea.

It goes about two meters, doesn't even reach the water. Nowhere close.

"Shit throw," Dad says.

He picks one up himself. "Martin? If you're up there, this one's for you, buddy!"

And he hurls the stone out to sea, so fast, so far, I can't even see it.

He turns back to me. "Now, when you were smaller, you were fearless. My god, that performance you did as the Tin Man that time . . ."

I flinch slightly. "What about it?"

"Well, it was . . . it was . . ." He licks his lips. "It was *brave*, Nate. So brave! It was . . . *valiant*! That's an appropriate word. *Spirited* is another similar word a person could use to describe that . . . performance."

"Bloody hell."

"So! Similar mindset now! Be plucky! Go and . . . *pluck*!"

I cringe. And I laugh, and I smile, because, know what? That's what I'm going to do. I've been in the shadows for too long, cowering, afraid, but no more. I'm ready to go out there and live. I'm ready to go out there and be the real me.

FORTY-SEVEN

JACK

Elliot's gone off to score some dessert, so I'm sitting alone on the sand when Nate comes stomping up and flops down onto the sand next to me.

"Huh," he says.

"Nice chat with Daddy?" I ask.

He sort of nods. Then he turns to me. "Jack? Serious question, no messing around, who's your perfect guy? Like, I'm talking romantically, what type of person would you go for? Be honest."

He catches me off guard with this one. I could just tell him, of course. I could just say, *You,* and get it all out there. But what if I'm wrong? What if that would be too much, too soon? At the same time, I need to actually say it, else how will he know? I guess I can always say it and then turn it into a joke at the end, if it looks like that's what I need to do. "Well, *Nate*," I begin. "He would be . . . around my height, maybe just fractionally shorter. My sort of build. No abs, he wouldn't really work out or be bothered about hitting the gym all the time because that just wouldn't be something that was important to him. He'd have light brown hair that he would probably describe as nondescript, but that I'd describe as beautiful . . ." I glance at Nate, and he's staring back me, a small smile playing on his lips. "It would be styled pretty much the way it naturally fell, but that would be cool because the way it naturally fell would be awesome. He would be kind, but he wouldn't describe himself as kind. He would be intelligent, but in a way that wasn't measured by exams. He would beat himself up relentlessly over every little thing because he would be an overthinker who cared too much, and he would have within him so much love and so much happiness waiting to burst out." I glance at Nate. He swallows. I slowly move my hand so it's on top of his. "He would be called Nate, and I would have loved him *so much* for *so long*, I just never got around to telling him, because being honest can be hard when you've got so much to lose and when so many people see that as weakness and take advantage, being that vulnerable takes more courage than I usually feel like I've got. But I do love him. And . . ." I swallow hard.

Silence.

Just the gentle lap of the waves on the shore.

Stillness.

And then, slowly, Nate leans toward me . . .

FORTY-EIGHT

NATE

I lean into him, and then . . .

FORTY-NINE

JACK

Finally . . .

FIFTY

JACK & NATE

We kiss.

FIFTY-ONE

NATE

It's one kiss. One beautiful, slow, lingering kiss on the lips. And I'm shaking, I'm actually trembling, but it's joy pumping through my veins. It's the barely believable, spectacular realization that this isn't just happening; it's *right*. All these feelings are colliding and they're confusing and weird and, yeah, kind of terrifying, but they're also stars-in-my-eyes brilliant because this, *this* is what it really feels like. To be in love. To be with the right person. To be happy.

And then we're just staring into each other's eyes, smiling.

"What?" Jack says after a bit.

"What?"

"No, seriously, what?"

I chuckle. "I'm happy. Are you?"

"Jesus, Nate! It's only taken sixteen years!" Jack laughs. "But I'm glad. Me too."

I hear the crunch of feet on sand. "La, la, la! Just returning from picking up some dessert!" Elliot says nice and loudly, carrying a big bowl of freshly fried mini-doughnuts. "Oh, HI, GUYS! Here you are!" He looks between us and lowers his voice. "I wasn't sure whether to come back. I said to the doughnut guy, 'Do you think there'll be more kissing?' but it looked like you'd stopped, so here I am!" He nods at us. "But I can totally go if you want?"

We both laugh.

"Aw," Elliot says. "Look at you two, laughing in unison. His and his laughter! Cuuuuute!" He puts the doughnuts down and reaches into his backpack. "Also . . . TA-DA!" He pulls out two golden plastic crowns. "I was going to do this anyway, whether you got together or not, and I was obviously hoping you would, because frankly the sexual tension on this trip has been *wild* and I reckon we would all have exploded if you didn't kiss just now, but since prom was so horrible for you both, we're going to do what should have been done then." He stands up. "Please both kneel so I can crown you our prom princes!"

We do as we're told, and Elliot places a crown on each of our heads. And that's the moment the little band farther up the beach start playing "Embers" by Owl City.

I instinctively turn to Jack.

He's sheepish. "I went to ask them if they'd play it while you were chatting to your dad." So weird, seeing this side of him—almost embarrassed, slightly awkward, and he can't quite look at me. He flicks his eyes up to mine. "Our song, right?"

Right. A song that's been an unhappy memory for so long, not just because of what anyone said at that year seven dance, but because it's everything Jack and I once were, everything we lost, both in ourselves and with each other.

Well, tonight, Jack and Nate are back. Tonight, we fly. Tonight, anything is possible, and I want to drink in this feeling forever. I jump up and thrust my hand out for him to take. At first he just stares, and then, seeing I'm serious, he smiles. He takes my hand and I pull him to his feet. "Let's dance," I say.

Jack isn't holding back. He's right there, jumping up and down as soon as the chorus kicks in. I used the word "dancing," but it was always more like we were deep in the mosh pit—it's hardly choreographed. It's just . . . fun. Joyful.

Elliot doesn't need any encouragement to join in, and I sure as hell don't either. I bounce up alongside Jack and I don't care, it's our dance, our song, I can be me, we can be us, and no one else matters.

We don't need a photo of this. No amount of pixels could ever capture the true brilliance of this moment. We want to feel it, live it, every sight, sound, and taste of it; not filter it, crop it, and hope people like it. This is ours, just ours. We're burning so bright, tonight will be etched on my brain, and if I do ever forget, when I get old, it won't matter, because it's also right here, deep in my heart. And I won't ever let those flames die again. Not ever.

ACKNOWLEDGMENTS

Having Jack and Nate hop across the pond, and be published in the United States, is a dream come true. I owe enormous thanks to the team at Clarion, who have championed this book and worked so hard to get *Heartbreak Boys* into your hands today. Eleanor Hinkle, my US editor, thank you for believing in this story, and in me—it's been a pleasure working with you, and I'm so happy my book found a home with Clarion. Thanks also to Lynne Polvino and Jamie Ryu for all your help and support. The awesome cover artist is Alex Cabal—and, my goodness, I love it *so much*—thank you for perfectly capturing the boys! Thanks as well to the brilliant design team, Catherine San Juan and Stephanie Hays, for making everything look so beautiful and perfectly capturing the feel of the book in design form! Shout-outs and huge thanks to the managing editorial team, Mary Magrisso and Rebecca Springer, and the copyediting and proofreading team—Erika West, Gretchen Stelter, and Emily Andrukaitis. Finally, a big thank-you to my wonderful publicist, Mitchell Thorpe, and marketing lead, Michael D'Angelo.

None of this would have been possible without the UK team as well, so thank you to Linas Alsenas, my editor at Scholastic UK, and Jenny Glencross, who also worked editorially on this book. Thank you to everyone else at Scholastic UK, including Lauren Fortune, Pete Matthews, Harriet Dunlea, Liam Drane, and the Rights team for selling *Heartbreak Boys* around the world. Joanna Moult at Skylark Literary remains the best agent any author could wish for—thank you.

Thanks to Sarah Counsell for putting up with me, and to Mum, Jonathan, Liz, Alfie, Sue and Peter Counsell, and Tricia for all your support.

This seems like an appropriate time to thank some US authors who have always been very kind about my words—Julian Winters, Lev Rosen, Phil Stamper, and Becky Albertalli—thank you, as always. A big thank-you to all the bloggers, reviewers, librarians, teachers, and booksellers out there—especially those of you who work so hard to get LGBTQ+ books into the hands of the teenagers who need them.

Finally, thank you to you for joining Jack and Nate on their road trip. I hope you had a blast. Remember to be the real, authentic you, don't dim your light for anyone, and always burn brightly.

Simon x